my husband's child

BOOKS BY ALISON RAGSDALE

Her Last Chance
Someone Else's Child
The Child Between Us
An Impossible Choice

Dignity and Grace
The Liar and Other Stories
The Art of Remembering
A Life Unexpected
Finding Heather
The Father-Daughter Club
Tuesday's Socks

my husband's child

ALISON RAGSDALE

bookouture

Published by Bookouture in 2025

An imprint of Storyfire Ltd.
Carmelite House
50 Victoria Embankment
London EC4Y 0DZ

www.bookouture.com

The authorised representative in the EEA is Hachette Ireland
8 Castlecourt Centre
Dublin 15 D15 XTP3
Ireland
(email: info@hbgi.ie)

Copyright © Alison Ragsdale, 2025

Alison Ragsdale has asserted her right to be identified as the author of this work.

All rights reserved. No part of this publication may be reproduced, stored in any retrieval system, or transmitted, in any form or by any means, electronic, mechanical, photocopying, recording or otherwise, without the prior written permission of the publishers.

ISBN: 978-1-83525-651-0
eBook ISBN: 978-1-83525-650-3

This book is a work of fiction. Names, characters, businesses, organizations, places and events other than those clearly in the public domain, are either the product of the author's imagination or are used fictitiously. Any resemblance to actual persons, living or dead, events or locales is entirely coincidental.

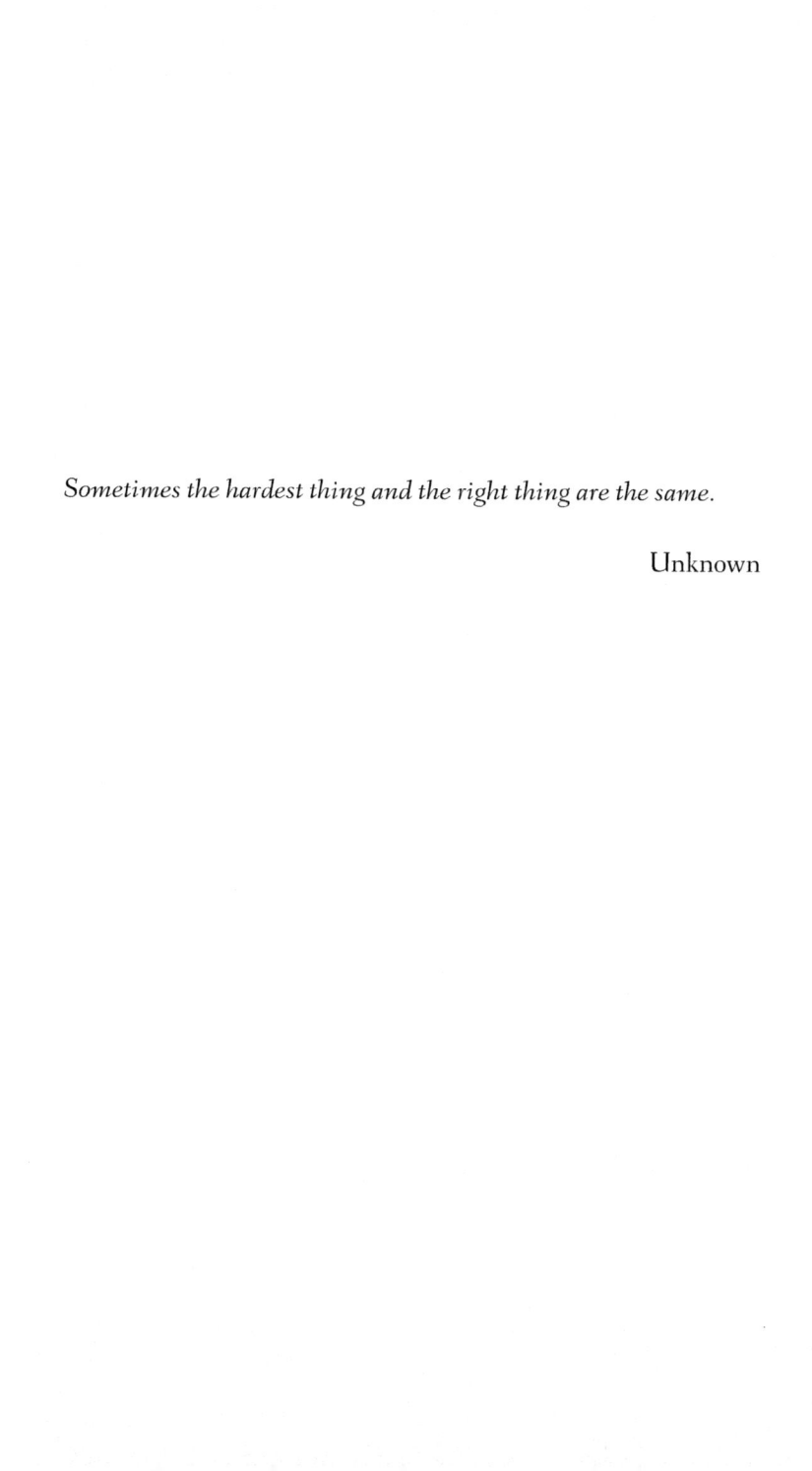

Sometimes the hardest thing and the right thing are the same.

Unknown

PROLOGUE
FEBRUARY

Cora Campbell sat bolt upright, her long dark hair clinging to her flushed cheek. Her heart was racing as, disconcerted, she was unsure whether she had dreamt the sharp peal of the doorbell, or whether it had been real.

She tapped the external processor of her cochlear implant, checking that it was working properly, and with the resultant hum, she instantly felt a sneeze coming so pressed her fingertip hard against her upper lip, as her mother had taught her to do as a child.

Across the compact living room, the fire had all but gone out while she had fallen asleep on the sofa. As she squinted at the clock on the mantel, she heard the doorbell again, but at 8.45 p.m. on a Sunday there was no one she was expecting.

The smell of woodsmoke lingering in the cooling room, she walked into the narrow hall, flipped the light on and approached the front door. Leaning in, she peered through the spyhole, but seeing only a dark, cat's-eye-shaped view of the street, illuminated by the amber street light across the way, she straightened and frowned.

Anxiety began to prickle inside her as she gripped the door

handle, and unsure why the hairs on her arms were standing to attention, she whispered to herself, 'You're being ridiculous.'

As she pulled the heavy door towards her, Cora braced herself momentarily, and then sighed with relief at the sight of the empty street at the end of her path. It likely had been some neighbourhood children messing around, playing ring-and-run, exactly as she had done while growing up here in this pretty, Victorian village on the banks of Aberdeenshire's River Dee.

Cora made to close the door when a movement pulled her eyes downwards, and she caught her breath. Her ex-husband's three-year-old daughter, Evie, stood there, her moss-green eyes wide and her long fair hair in loose spirals, clamped under a red pom-pom hat. Her little white ski jacket was zipped up to her chin and her feet were in pale pink Ugg boots. Evie's cheeks were rosy, her unicorn-emblazoned backpack was weighty on her shoulders as if it might tip her backwards.

Next to Evie, her little brother, Ross, whimpered in his stroller. The eighteen-month-old was bundled under a fluffy blanket, and Cora could see that he had on his quilted, all-in-one suit with fur around the hood, his hands in yellow mittens. Next to the stroller was a small suitcase with an old-fashioned leather luggage tag buckled to the handle.

Cora instantly looked into the darkness of the night, but there was no one else there.

Foreboding flooding her insides, she crouched down and took Evie's hand.

'Hello, little one. Where's Mummy?' She once again scanned the empty street behind the children, but all that greeted her was the stillness of the night and the scent of wood smoke from her neighbours' chimneys.

Evie held up her hand, her tiny fingers red with cold, so Cora took the child's hand in hers and began gently rubbing it between her palms.

'Mummy's gone away.'

The words speared Cora's heart as effectively as any dagger might as she took a moment to process the surreal and shocking reality that was taking shape.

Her throat aching now, Cora forced jollity into her voice. 'Let's go inside. It's too cold out here for little people.'

As she lifted Ross into her arms, a white envelope fluttered onto the ground.

Cora opened the envelope and pulled out a single sheet of paper. The note was typewritten, two lines, a handful of words that she could not believe she was seeing. She read them again, her breathing becoming shallow.

Please take care of them. They are better off with you.

PART ONE

1

APRIL – TWO MONTHS LATER

In the eight weeks that Cora had been caring for the children, everything about her peaceful, ordered life had changed.

The events that had unfolded after she'd discovered Evie and Ross on her doorstep had been surreal. For days, a maelstrom of shock, disbelief, and anger had kept her awake at night, her eyes burning as she stared at her laptop, trying every possible way she could think of to trace their mother, Holly, or their father, her ex-husband, Fraser Munro.

Cora knew that her former father-in-law, James Munro, had spoken with the police, contacted anyone he could think of that Fraser might turn to for sanctuary, even some of his old university friends, to no avail.

Cora occasionally imagined Fraser was on a sunny island somewhere, sipping icy cocktails, and painting portraits of tourists while fooling himself into believing that he was unattached to anyone or anything. As for Holly, Cora avoided thinking about her whereabouts as it only sparked anger and pain at what the children had gone through over the past two months.

Today, on a day that was unfolding like many others before

it, with Cora navigating her new existence, she sat across the kitchen table from Ross, who was eating a chocolate biscuit, his fingers now good and sticky. As she watched him licking the chocolate off the top of the biscuit and then wiping his hands on his trousers, Cora sighed, resigned to having to do yet another load of washing that afternoon.

'Not on your trousers, wee man.' She handed him a piece of kitchen paper, amused by the way he scrunched it between his palms rather than wipe his fingers on it.

Two months ago, on a perfect Sunday morning like this, Cora would have risen at dawn, eaten a quick breakfast, then packed her fishing gear and headed for the River Dee, near her home. She had learned to fly fish with her soft-spoken father, Andrew, catching salmon and sea trout. She'd sit on her fold-out chair and watch him bait their hooks. He'd got her a little bucket hat and pinned it with hooks and colourful flies, just like his own, and Cora treasured those precious mornings with her dad, the gentle calm of them now a distant memory.

Ross's face was now clownlike, with a dark, chocolate ring circling his mouth.

'You mucky pup.' She laughed at the endearing expression of mischief, deciding to let him finish before bothering to wipe his face.

'Choc-lit.' He grinned, waving his sticky fingers at her. Now twenty months old, Ross was a sunny-natured child. His white-blonde hair glistened in sunlight and his eyes, the same, distinct pale blue rimmed with black as his father's, followed Cora wherever she went, like a portrait in a gallery. He was easy, and trusting, and Cora was quickly growing to adore him.

'Yes, chocolate.' She smiled, then glanced at the broad window above the farmhouse sink, overlooking the back garden.

His sister, Evie, had finished her biscuit quickly and gone outside, the bright spring morning luring her outdoors. Now almost four, she was a quiet child, fond of reading and colouring at the coffee table in the living room, and she would often sit on a deckchair in the back garden, singing to herself as Cora worked in the planter boxes.

Though it had taken longer than it had with Ross, Cora had worked hard to develop a close bond with Evie. Cora had felt inadequate, helpless in the face of Evie's distress over the disappearance of her parents, the colossal change to her little life having rocked the child's world, but after weeks of struggling to comfort her, Cora's perseverance had paid off and, to her surprise, it had been their mutual love of nature that had provided a welcome conduit to connect them, and for Evie to begin to heal.

During the first few days of caring for the children, Cora would bundle them up against the cold March wind and, with Ross in his stroller, they'd walk the ten minutes from the house to the River Dee, then along the riverbank, the smell of damp moss and new grass coated in spring rain surrounding them. She'd take them all the way to the Dee bridge, built in 1527, its iconic golden-coloured, Elgin sandstone arches spanning the river at the spot where she and her father had often fished.

The Dee glittered in a unique way, sparks of golden light dancing across the surface, and flashes of silver drawing the eye as sea trout, or salmon, broke the surface and then slipped back below the rippling water. Spotting the fish caused great excitement in the children, Ross squealing as he pointed at the water, and Evie jumping up and down as she shouted, 'I saw one, there! Over there!'

Wanting to encourage her enthusiasm for the outdoors, Cora had taught Evie about the shrubs and flowers they passed on the riverbank, and then, back at home, about the plants in the narrow bed that ran along the drystone wall at the end of the garden.

Relieved to have found something that brought Evie joy, Cora had let her cut bunches of the silky daffodils and bright purple allium, with their pom-pom blooms, and stalks of the sturdy heathers that filled the bed. Seeing the child's interest piqued, Cora had encouraged Evie to learn about the vegetables and herbs that Cora grew in the planter boxes her father had built. She'd shown Evie how to gently turn and feed the soil, rotate the seedlings, harvest, and care for the produce as the season changed. She was always keen to get her hands into the earth and loved to point out the glistening worms that surfaced after the rain.

A little squeal drew Cora back to the moment, the sound a jarring screech that she felt vibrate in her temple, as Ross then started to bash a chocolate-smeared dinosaur figure on the table-top, his chubby hand gripping the triceratops by its tail. The happy abandon with which he was amusing himself made her smile, but the sound was amplified by her cochlear implant, turning it into something akin to dustbin lids being clanged together.

'*Easy*, sweet boy.' She reached over and gently stopped the motion. 'Not so loud. OK?'

Ross met her gaze for a few moments, the dark-rimmed eyes locked on hers, then he tipped his head to the side like a curious puppy. A tiny smile tugged at the corners of his mouth as he carefully set the dinosaur down, as if he was trying not to make a sound, the gentle, intuitive movement so touching that Cora's throat narrowed.

'Thank you,' she whispered, then kissed the tips of her fingers and blew him a kiss. 'You are such a good boy.'

Ross dipped his chin coyly, a cheeky smile taking over his face as he returned the gesture, his mouth pursed as he blew his kiss back to her from his sticky fingers.

Being a parent was undoubtedly the hardest thing Cora had ever done, and for all the unknowns, missteps, and frequent bouts of disappointment in herself at how she was coping, each smile, or hug, each touch of a small hand or air-blown kiss made her heart soar.

She had always thought that she would be a mother someday, even keeping a list of names she liked in a journal in her bottom drawer, but when her marriage to Fraser had imploded, and the subsequent, solitary years had begun slipping by, she had grown to accept that it might not happen for her.

The irony of how she had ultimately been thrown into parenthood was mind-blowing. Her ex-husband and his new wife's abandonment of their children had been appalling, and inexcusable, and Cora's own inexperience with children at the time glaring. But despite her trepidation, and her anger at both Holly and Fraser, Cora was starting to embrace her new family, even if it was borrowed, and often overwhelming.

Ross picked up the dinosaur again and slammed it onto the table, making Cora jump.

'Right, you little monkey. Let's get you cleaned up.' She rose, wiped his sticky face with a wet cloth and set him on the ground. 'Shall we go out and see what your sister's up to?' She patted his backside and followed him as he trotted to the open back door.

Outside, the April breeze was carrying the scent of the waxy rosemary that filled one corner of a planter box at the left side of the compact back garden. The smell always reminded Cora of her mother, Eliza, and the long afternoons they'd spent in the kitchen together.

Eliza Campbell, a petite redhead with turquoise eyes, a trail of freckles across the bridge of her nose, and a soft, lilting voice easy for Cora to hear, had been a keen and talented cook. She had taught Cora how to work with the ingredients that she and her father would forage for on the walk home, after a morning of fishing, and they'd use the various fleshy mushrooms, spicy watercress, and wild onions they'd found to make fragrant stews and soups, supplemented with the herbs and vegetables that Eliza grew herself.

As Cora let the memories wash over her, her heart swelled with love and longing for the kind and nurturing couple who had taken her in. The small, pebble-dash bungalow with its twin bay windows and dark slate roof, one of five that ran the length of Montague Road, was the only home Cora had ever felt she belonged in and now, looking across the sunny garden, she sighed contentedly.

The sky was bright beyond the big cherry tree that dominated the far-right corner of the space. A smattering of lacy clouds inched across the horizon as the breeze tugged at the branches, sending a sprinkling of the last, dried-up blossoms, like pale pink confetti, across the tiny lawn.

Seeing Evie on the edge of the circular patio, in the middle of the narrow patch of lawn, Cora smiled. Evie was sitting on the paving stones next to the pedestal birdbath, her head tipped to the side in concentration.

'Hi, chickadee. What are you doing?'

Evie looked up, her voice dreamy. 'The birds are singing.' She pointed behind her at the cherry tree. 'Robins.' The breeze was lifting her gilded hair from her shoulder, her cheeks glowing as she closed her moss-green eyes.

Cora's throat tightened in gratitude at the little girl's contentment, something Cora had, not so long ago, worried that she might never see again. Eventually, after weeks of upsetting scenes and sleepless nights, Evie had stopped asking when Mummy and Daddy would be coming back.

Blinking away the heartbreaking memories of cradling the child as she wept inconsolably for her parents, Cora lunged forward and caught up with Ross, who was now running at full pelt towards his sister.

'Watch out, Evie. Here comes trouble.' Cora grabbed him under his arms and swung him out in front of her, then set his feet, snug in tiny new trainers, onto the patio next to Evie. He had already outgrown much of the clothing that had been in the little suitcase, as had Evie, and Cora had enjoyed shopping for them, surprised at the lift of joy wandering around a quaint children's shop in Aberdeen had given her.

Ross tottered forwards, then plopped himself down at his sister's side as she glanced at him, a soft smile lifting the corner of her mouth.

'Listen, Rossy.' She leaned towards him and pointed at the pair of robins still sitting on a low branch of the cherry tree. 'See the birds?'

Ross's eyes followed her finger as he stuck his thumb in his mouth.

Touched by the sweet scene, and marvelling at Evie's caring nature, Cora walked to the row of planter boxes. As she absently picked some wilted leaves off a young basil plant, crushing them in her palm and breathing in their citrusy aroma, she mentally planned the menu for this coming week for James.

Thinking about her former father-in-law, the memory of arriving at his home, Locharden House, the impressive seventeenth-century manor on the family estate, to tell him about finding the children the previous night flashed through her mind.

She had been convinced that he would automatically step in. Take the children on until Holly or Fraser returned. Instead, as soon as Evie was out of earshot, pale with shock, James had pleaded with Cora to keep the children with her for a while.

Cora had been horrified. 'You're not serious?' She'd stood in the long, austere hall, the three stags' heads mounted high on the right-hand wall seeming to look on disbelieving, as she'd shifted Ross higher on her hip.

'Cora, I can't keep them here.' James had clasped the back of his neck, his cheeks florid. 'I'm an old man with health issues, too much to do, and no help.' At this, his voice had cracked, and

Cora had felt an initial rush of sympathy for him, but then, disbelieving, she'd put Ross back into his stroller.

'James, these are your grandchildren! I can't possibly care for them. I have a life, you know. Aside from being your personal chef, I have a *life*.' The peaceful existence she had carved out for herself, after she'd healed from heartbreak, had felt as if it were in serious jeopardy.

'Cora, *please*. I simply can't cope with them myself. Just keep them for a few days, then I'll sort something out.' He'd pressed his palms together as if in prayer, causing her resolve to waver.

Cora had agreed to keep the children for a few days until James could make other arrangements, but the days had turned to weeks, and now months. Both she and her former father-in-law had been unable to locate either of the children's parents, despite an exhaustive search, and as time ticked on, Cora had grown increasingly afraid that she might never get her peaceful life back.

Now, as she sniffed the crushed basil again, the only herb her ex-husband had been able to identify, an image of him floated back to her, and she sighed, recalling that the exact moment she had agreed to help him, almost seven years ago, she had had no idea that she was choosing a path that would change her life, forever. A path that had diverted her so far from her intended direction that she could hardly comprehend it.

How was it possible that the man she had divorced four years ago was still controlling her life, while remaining completely absent from it?

2

Dusting some soil from her hands, Cora crossed the lawn and sat down next to Ross, who was jabbing a twig into the space between two paving stones. Evie now lay on her back, humming softly to herself.

'You two are so sweet,' Cora said, brushing some grass from Ross's shoe. 'This is a lovely day, isn't it?'

Evie nodded, her eyes not leaving the cottony clouds creeping towards the sun.

Cora stretched her legs out in front of her, catching sight of her bare nails through the open toes of her sandals. She desperately needed a pedicure, or at least to trim and paint her nails herself, but when would she ever find the time? She wiggled her neglected toes, then laughed softly. The lot of being a mother was not one that allowed for much self-care – as she had instantly, and somewhat brutally, discovered.

As she leaned back on her hands, letting the gentle warmth of the April sunlight touch her face, she caught a trace of lavender in the air, so breathed it in. It was true that she had become an instant mother – a baptism by fire, so to speak – with no time to grow into the job, acquire the necessary skills, or stagger her inevitable mistakes. Despite her best efforts, she had days when it all felt too much, and she'd long for her old life back. Particularly, at the beginning, once the children were down for the night, she would close her bedroom door, lie on her back and stare at the ceiling, exhausted, and wondering how this had happened.

She still missed the ability to choose whatever she alone wanted to eat, wear, or watch on TV. The freedom to throw some water and an apple into a backpack and walk in the hills until her legs began to shake. But when she had those thoughts now, the joy that these children were bringing to her life softened the pangs of loss that accompanied them. This was, after all, a temporary situation, and as she breathed in the fragrant breeze and looked at Evie and Ross, content in her company, something shifted inside her.

Cora let the feeling percolate, then nodded to herself, resolving to stop counting the days since they'd come into her life, and analysing how well she was doing the job of surrogate parent, but rather to simply enjoy them, for as long as they were with her.

She glanced over at Evie, whose eyes were now closed, her mouth pulsing as she whispered the words to 'You Are My Sunshine' under her breath. Cora's heart swelled with love for the gentle little soul, as she wondered for the umpteenth time what had happened to Holly – the mouthy landlady, as Cora's mother had called her, with the big personality who had turned her back on these two innocents. As always happened when Cora thought about Holly, her mind inevitably slid back to Fraser.

She could picture the gentle, bewitching way he'd smiled the first time she had formally met him. Knowing him by reputation only, and from seeing him around the village, she'd been taken aback when he had unexpectedly come to her door and asked if she might be available to cook for his father, who had health issues, and needed a special diet.

The sparkling blue eyes with the distinct black rings seemed to drink her in. She'd taken pity on Fraser, agreeing to cook for his father for a short time, and she still remembered the nervous flutter in her stomach as Fraser had gratefully shaken her hand, the warmth of his palm sending an alarming tingle straight to her core.

'Thanks a million, Cora. Really. You're a lifesaver.'

That had been the start of her relationship with Fraser, a man she knew little about other than that he was the son of the old laird, the last surviving heir of Clan MacPhail, and something of an enigma.

Despite the peaceful scene around her, the memory of the night Fraser broke her heart three years later made her press her eyes closed. As Cora floated there momentarily, the old pain pushing up under her ribs, Ross suddenly grabbed her arm, his fingers biting into her flesh.

'Mumma!' he chimed, as Cora, her heart leaping, sucked in a breath, unsure if she had heard him correctly.

As she stared at him, she felt as if she might levitate from the stone beneath her, her heart taking flight. The mixture of shock and joy she felt at hearing this simple word was indescribable, so she reached for him and then pulled him onto her lap.

'What did you say, wee man?' She locked eyes with the little boy, hers a slightly deeper blue and lacking the distinct dark rims.

'*Mumma.*' He grinned, a fleck of chocolate still clinging to his cheek.

Cora hugged him to her chest, as, opposite her, Evie sat up and stared at the two of them, her eyes questioning and a tiny frown creasing her brow.

'Are you our mummy now?'

The simple question released a deep longing at Cora's core

that snatched her breath away. She was as close to a mother as they had right now, and while she'd wanted this, to hear this from a child of her own, Evie and Ross weren't hers, and she couldn't lie to them about that, however much she might want to.

Taking a steadying breath, she smiled at Evie. 'I'm taking care of both of you for now, sweetheart. You and Ross.'

As Evie stared, her lids flickering with the cascade of thoughts obviously filling her head, Cora let the now wriggling Ross go. What she had said was true. She would take care of these precious children that had been left so cruelly at her door, at least until their grandfather took them in, or their parents returned.

'I want *you* to be our mummy.' Evie's chin began to wobble, sending a burst of protectiveness through Cora that clutched at her heart.

Without thinking, her focus on quashing any more hurt or uncertainty in this precious child's life, Cora got up and opened her arms to Evie.

Evie stood and walked into Cora's embrace, her eyes full of tears, making Cora's chest ache.

'OK, chickadee. You're OK,' she croaked. 'Don't cry. I'll always take care of you.'

As she rocked Evie gently from side to side, Cora felt the ambiguity of what she'd said hovering like a loaded cloud above her. She shouldn't have said 'always'. Made a promise that she might not be able to keep.

Later that day, Cora strapped Ross into his car seat, a brisk southerly breeze flipping her dark hair across her mouth. Next to him, in the back of the old Volvo station wagon that James had given her to replace her tiny Fiat, soon after the night the children had appeared, Evie was nose-deep in a book about a family of musical ducks. Her favourite scarf was tied in a loose knot at her throat, the soft folds distorting the scattering of unicorns that danced over rainbows.

Every Sunday, Cora took the children to have lunch with their grandfather, and as she loaded the big bag of groceries into the boot of the car, Ross squealed what sounded like the word 'stuck'. Wincing at the harsh sound, she rushed around to the side of the car, seeing him pulling at the safety belt that was clipped across his front.

'Stuck, Mumma!'

Cora laughed, the new title sending another jolt of happiness through her as she gently moved his hands away. 'You're not stuck, silly goose. You are safe in your seat until we get to your grandpa's house.'

Evie dropped the book into her lap.

'Is Grandpa happy with us?'

Cora frowned, taken aback by the candid question. 'What do you mean, sweetheart?'

Evie blinked, then closed the book. 'Grandad is cross sometimes.' She shrugged matter-of-factly. 'Is he cross or happy with us?'

Instinct taking over, the need to comfort overwhelming, Cora reached over and squeezed Evie's hand. 'He's always happy to see you and Ross, and he loves you both very much. Don't ever worry about that, OK?'

Evie took a second, then nodded happily, as if that was all she needed to hear.

'I'm hungry.'

'Right. Let's go then.'

Relieved, Cora closed the back door and then got into the driver's seat. She glanced at Evie in the rear-view mirror, her long blonde hair caught up in a clasp behind her head and the pale pink of her corduroy jacket seeming to make her cheeks glow. The little girl was deeply intuitive, and bright for her age, and her observation of her grandfather was not completely unfounded.

It was well-known that there was enormous tension between James Munro and his son. In the village, Fraser was known primarily for his refusal to become involved in running the family estate, a crushing disappointment to his father – a typical, old-school, outdoorsy type, resilient, and with no time for fools. As a result, Fraser had spent much of his time either in the local pub, or in a little studio behind the bakery in the main street, painting atmospheric landscapes of the Cairngorms. That the closest Fraser got to embracing the land, or family estate, was to paint them, riled James beyond reason.

Despite his crusty exterior, and harshly vocal disappointment in his only son, Cora had gradually built a good relationship with the laird. He respected her love of the outdoors, especially her fishing skills, and related to her reverence and appreciation of all things nature – the polar opposite to Fraser, who appeared unable to care less about all that.

Recently, furious at whatever his son had done that had driven his new wife to abandon their children, the old laird had basically written Fraser off and made no bones about saying so often. Somewhere along the line, perhaps as Evie stood behind a half-closed door, or overheard him on the phone, she must have heard her grandfather during one of his rants, perhaps believing that his anger was directed at her, and the thought of that causing Evie anxiety, or making her feel insecure, made Cora so sad that her eyes filled.

Focusing on the road, she steered the Volvo down Montague Road, heading for the river. The ten-minute drive to Locharden House was picturesque, following the course of the River Dee as it flowed on the left of Tullich Road, and as Cora opened her window a crack, the smell of freshly cut grass seeped into the car, just as the Montague Hotel came into view. It sat right on the riverbank, a long, impressive, Victorian structure with an ornate gabled roof, and several tall chimneys reaching for the sky. The walls were a creamy white, making the dark-green window frames and front door stand out – the green also used on the wooden detail on the roof gables.

As if on cue, Evie chimed, 'There's the princess's house!'

She had named the old hotel this the first time she'd seen it, and charmed by her imagination, Cora had played along ever since.

'Yes, I wonder if she's at home today.'

Evie met her eyes in the rear-view mirror, Evie's pale-green irises full of light. 'Don't know. Probably.'

The children went quiet as the familiar road unfolded, the dense rows of pine trees on either side of the car mesmerising as they flicked past the windows. Cora let the silence fill her, rare as it was these days, and kept her eyes open for pheasants, the colourful birds often strutting straight in front of cars on this stretch of road.

As they got closer to Crathie, the tiny village where James's home was located, half a mile east of Balmoral Castle, the view opened up. The treeline receded into the distance, and as soon as they'd passed the village school – the long, white building with a tripled-peaked roof set back from the road behind a thick privet hedge – she turned left.

The fields the road now cut through formed a massive patch-work of various shades of green, undulating with the rise and fall of the land, as if slumbering giants lay beneath them, and the hedgerows that lined the road were thick with gorse, the golden blooms new and vibrant.

In the distance, the upper slopes of Lochnagar rose behind the treetops, and seeing it, Cora sighed.

Originally known for the name of the lochan at the foot of its cliffs, Lochan na Gaire, meaning little loch of the noisy sound, or Lochnagar, as it was now called, a majestic mountain of coarse red granite was considered by some to be the best

Munro in the Highlands, its beauty and spectacle unmatched. With six-hundred-foot cliff drops to the secluded lochan, Lochnagar attracted walkers and climbers from all over the world, Cora among them, until recently. As she thought wistfully about the last time she'd walked on the lower slopes, Evie's musical voice brought Cora back to earth with a bump.

'Can Grandpa play with us today?' She met Cora's eyes in the rear-view mirror. 'If he's happy?'

Cora nodded. 'I'm sure he will.' She guided the car along the road as it narrowed, tall privet hedges marking the start of James's land. 'What game do you want to play?'

Evie shrugged. 'Snap. No. Mummies and daddies.'

Cora's heart contracted at the innocent request, the child's instincts apparently telling her that despite all Cora's efforts to fill the void her parents had left behind, and while Evie might feel content with Cora, something was missing from the proper formula for a family.

3

James Munro stood at the top of the impressive front steps of Locharden House, it's stature grand enough to still make Cora pause each time she arrived. He half-filled the open front door, his Munro Ancient tartan kilt rippling in the breeze and a dark-green fleece zipped up to his chin. Duchess, his giant yellow Labrador, leaned against his leg, her tail swinging wildly behind her.

James was still what could be considered a handsome man, strong-featured, lean, and formidable at seventy-three. He had a thatch of silvery hair that he wore combed straight back from his high forehead, and his eyes were a piercing blue, ringed with black – a distinct feature that both Fraser and Ross had inherited, and something that Cora had always loved about her ex-husband.

James waved at the car as Cora navigated the small flower bed that the drive circled around in front of the house. Its centre was filled with waxy camellia bushes loaded with dusty-pink flowers, and a broad band of pristine, white anemones lined the edge, their deep-blue middles like rows of curious eyes, taking in the world.

Recalling how her former mother-in-law had adored her garden in spring and had told Cora that when the petals of an anemone close up, it means a rainstorm is approaching, Cora smiled to herself, happy that there was no such warning today.

She was hoping that the children would be able to play with Duchess in the back garden after lunch, to give her and James a chance to talk. He'd left her a voicemail saying that he had something important to discuss, and now, as she tried to guess what it might be, she pulled up near the front of the steps, the brittle crunch of the pea gravel as satisfying as it always was, under the wheels.

'*Grandpa!*' Evie waved at him, the delight in her voice touching.

Ross startled, waking from his customary nap that happened whenever he rode in the car. 'Gam-pa.' He imitated his sister as Evie popped the belt open on her car seat and waited for Cora to let her out.

'Hi, James.' Cora smiled at her ex-father-in-law as she rounded the car and opened the back door. 'Out you pop, Evie.' She held Evie's hand as she slid out of the seat.

'Hello, hello.' James walked down the steps and opened his arms to Evie, who was already running towards him. 'Oof, you are so heavy.' He hoisted her up and kissed her flushed cheek.

Duchess jumped up, her giant paws reaching above James's ribs, as Evie leaned across him and stroked the dog's head.

'Hello, Duchess.' Evie beamed. 'Good girl.'

Cora lifted Ross from his seat and set him on the ground, watching him totter towards his grandfather, then she took the bags of food out of the boot.

'What delights have you got for us today, Chef Cora?' James shifted Evie to his hip, then leaned down and took Ross's chubby hand. Duchess, sensing that she must rein in her power around Ross, padded slowly beside him, as if she were keeping him wedged safely next to his grandfather.

'I've got some lovely king scallops, fresh from Oban, and a nice bit of haddock. I thought I'd make a fisherman's pie.' Cora slammed the boot closed and walked across the drive.

The air was filled with the scent of the delicate camellias and as Cora stopped to breathe them in, savouring the fresh, lemony aroma, she heard the distinctive whistle of a song thrush coming from the row of oak trees to the left of the house. Even with the slight, robotic distortion of her cochlear implant – the three short notes, followed by a gentle trill, were musical, and held the promise of new beginnings. She could still appreciate their beauty, even though she knew that she heard them differently to most.

'Fisherman's pie sounds good, doesn't it, kiddos?' James turned and walked slowly up the broad steps, careful to let Ross take his time, Duchess following closely behind.

Cora had been James's personal chef for seven years now – three while dating and being married to his son, and four since they'd divorced. Her belief that food had the power to heal, where medicine sometimes failed, fascinated James, and he enjoyed sitting at the long kitchen table at Locharden House, talking to Cora as she prepared his meals.

Where James's keen intellect kept him impressively sharp in any conversation, his body had begun to fail him – arthritis, and the effects of years of unaddressed diabetes, continuing to take their toll.

Following the death of his beloved Rosemary, the year after Fraser and Cora were married, James's health had taken a serious turn for the worse, causing Cora to stay on for longer than she'd intended, passing up an opportunity to move to a sous-chef position at a prestigious bistro in Edinburgh. She hadn't regretted it at the time, but now, there were days when she felt her world was shrinking, her one-time career as a chef folding in on itself, and with that came a degree of sadness.

Shaking off a twinge of self-pity, Cora followed James and

the children into the house and closed the heavy door, noticing that the mail she'd set on the sideboard in the hall two days ago was still there, unopened. Frowning at this unusual behaviour, she passed the three stags' heads on the wall and nodded at each one. 'Morning, boys.'

Ahead of her, James laughed softly, without turning around. 'They've been looking forward to seeing you, too.'

Cora chuckled to herself as she hefted the shopping bags along the hall and through the formal living room, with its creamy brocade wallpaper, emerald-green curtains, and the glossy grand piano that stood in the central bay window of three, overlooking the back garden. She had always loved this room, the high, panelled ceiling that boasted a pastel mural of a hunting scene, and the three, sage-green linen sofas that formed a U-shape in front of the Regency fireplace, with its milky-marble surround. There was a sense of peace in here that Cora enjoyed, as it reminded her of her gentle-natured mother-in-law.

Rosemary had been a tall, slender blonde, with hazel eyes, long elegant fingers and a mellow, low-toned voice that Cora had found easy to hear. She and Cora had grown close, and they would often sit in this room and have coffee. They'd planned her and Fraser's wedding in this room, picked the marquee and met with the florist who had suggested they use the black-eyed anemones from the garden in Cora's bouquet.

Rosemary had been delighted. 'Oh, yes. Cora, would you like that?'

Cora had laughed, her heart full of love for the kind-hearted woman. 'Absolutely. Especially as we'll know if it's going to rain.'

Recalling the happy memory, Cora smiled softly, then crossed the back hall and walked into the airy kitchen. Duchess was in her basket next to the Aga now, licking her front paw. James had installed Ross in his high chair at the long wooden table, and Evie sat next to him, her eyes bright as she watched Cora dump the bags on the flagstone floor and begin to unload the food.

'Would you like some milk, Evie-bell?' James opened the fridge, his pet name for his granddaughter making Cora smile again.

'Uh-huh.' Evie nodded, as Cora made her eyebrows jump comically.

'Yes please, Grandpa.' Cora dipped her chin as Evie echoed, 'Yes please, Grandpa.'

Cora caught the sneaky wink that James gave Evie as he pulled the carton out of the fridge.

'Minding your Ps and Qs, eh?' He filled a glass with milk and set it in front of Evie. 'I should think so, too.'

Evie grinned up at him. 'Thank you.' She lifted the glass and took three big gulps before setting it down, a snowy moustache curling around the corners of her mouth.

'So, how are you today?' Cora watched James fill Ross's plastic cup and hand it to him before returning the milk to the fridge.

'Tickety-boo.' He nodded as he pulled a chair out and sat next to Evie. 'The sun's out, so there's not much to complain about.'

Cora tutted at the practical response. 'That's debatable. I can think of a few things.' Then, checking that the children weren't looking at her, she mouthed, 'Like where is your bloody son?'

James's mouth twisted in distaste as he nodded. 'Aye. Right enough. We do need to have a chat later.' He gestured towards the children. 'When wee ears aren't nearby.'

Curious at his newly closed expression, Cora frowned.

'Fine.' She lay the bunch of fresh thyme she'd picked from her garden on the counter, popping a tiny leaf into her mouth, the peppery tang bursting over her tongue.

'Gam-pa,' Ross chimed, drawing Cora's gaze. 'Ung-wee.'

James chuckled. 'Me too, old man. Me too.' He eyed Cora. 'So, what's new in Cora's world?'

She shook her head. 'Not much since I saw you on Friday. How was the veggie lasagne yesterday? Did you warm it in the oven like I told you to, or did you nuke it in the microwave?' She pretended to glower at him. 'Don't tell me you nuked it, or I swear...' She made a fist and widened her eyes.

'I used the oven, as instructed.' He smiled fondly at her. 'I know better than to defy the boss.'

Cora put the two brown paper packages of fish on the draining board and filled a glass with water from the brass tap. 'Smart man, right, Evie?' She sipped some water, looking over at the little girl, who was once again gulping at her milk.

'Uh-huh.' Evie nodded, putting the glass down and grinning at James. 'Be good, Grandpa.'

He laughed heartily, then wiped Ross's milky mouth with a paper napkin. 'What a state you're in, old man.' He wafted the soggy napkin and pulled a face. 'A right mess.'

Ross giggled, reaching for the napkin as James flapped it, then whipped it away before Ross could grab it.

'Oh, no you don't.'

As Cora began to assemble the ingredients for the pie, pulling things from the fridge, and the cupboards that she knew the contents of better than those in her own home, she listened to the gentle interaction between James and his grandchildren, marvelling at the patience, the compassion and affection he showered on them.

Witnessing it, even knowing everything Fraser had done to let both her and his father down, she couldn't help but feel sorry for her ex. James had never been prepared to give his son the benefit of the doubt, and the harshness of that was hard to equate against this softer version of himself that James kept solely for her and his grandchildren.

She had often been saddened at the way Fraser became cowed around his father, not defending his wish to be a painter, but rather hiding behind it while avoiding his familial responsibilities. But, over time, she had seen James's kind heart, and the way he had adored and cared for his ailing wife before she'd passed away.

Though Cora hadn't admitted it to Fraser, or even herself at the time, she had secretly begun to understand some of James's frustration with his son's wish to disassociate himself from a way of life that had existed in his family for generations.

Obviously sensing her beginning to sympathise with his father's position, Fraser had distanced himself from Cora, spending long days in his studio, and often disappearing to Aberdeen or Edinburgh for weekends. When he was home, he'd spent too much time at the pub, where, unbeknown to Cora, he'd begun to fall for the landlady, the feisty and effervescent Holly.

Drying her fingertips on a tea towel, Cora pictured her nemesis, seeing the liquid-green eyes, the long flaxen hair, and the way Holly clung to Fraser's arm whenever Cora was anywhere near him, as if she might want him back. At this, Cora let out a little huff.

The thought of him now as anything other than a casual friend she could stand to be around only to keep the peace between him and his father was unthinkable, but that aside, where the hell was he, and how could he turn his back on his children?

As she angrily dumped some potatoes into the big porcelain sink, James saying that they needed to talk felt newly intriguing.

Did he know something?

With lunch behind them, Evie and Ross had their coats on and were running about on the back lawn, kicking an old football, while Duchess darted around them in large circles. Evie's jacket flapped open, and her golden hair lifted behind her in the fresh breeze, while Ross squealed every time he kicked the ball, his excitement palpable.

Watching them through the French doors at the back of the kitchen, standing side by side, Cora and James smiled at each other, and hugged their coffee cups to their fronts.

He was a head and shoulders taller than her, almost the same height as Fraser's six feet three, and, as yet, James hadn't adopted the slight stoop of many an older man. As she sipped her coffee, Cora suppressed a smile at the thought that despite his health struggles, it was his sheer stubbornness that was fending off the signs of ageing – something she couldn't help but admire.

'It's good to see them so happy, Cora. You are a wonder with those two.' He gestured towards the garden.

'They're good kids.' Cora nodded, saddened at the reminder that they were innocent victims who had done nothing to deserve their parents walking out on them.

As she thought about Fraser, and the way Holly had taken over from James, as the louder voice in Fraser's life than his own, Cora frowned. What had he been thinking leaving his wife and children behind this way? Nothing she could imagine justified his actions, or Holly's thereafter, and the complete silence that had followed their disappearances.

As if reading her mind, James let out a sigh.

'Cora, let's have that chat, m'dear.' He put his cup in the sink and gestured towards the conservatory, a classic, Victorian, glass and wood-framed structure linking the kitchen to the back garden. 'We can see the wee ones better from in there.'

Cora nodded and followed him through the French doors and into the warm, bright room. The afternoon sun filtered through the glass-paned roof, sending shafts of golden light dancing across the polished wood floor.

'It's such a gorgeous view.' She pulled one of the wicker chairs closer to the back window, checking that she could see the children. 'It never gets old.'

Behind the expanse of the west garden, beyond the row of fir trees that delineated one edge of the property line, the slopes of Lochnagar dominated the horizon, the impressive line of the summit slicing into the clear sky. This was one of Cora's favourite views in the Cairngorms, and as she stared at the familiar vista, she felt another pang of longing for her old life. Her life pre-children, when she could take a Saturday to pack a lunch, put on her battered hiking boots and head into the hills.

Seeing her expression, James sighed again. 'Well, I'll be straight with you, Cora. You deserve nothing less.' He twisted his mouth to the left, a sure sign that he had something difficult to share.

Her stomach flip-flopping, Cora leaned forward, her elbows on her knees. 'OK... This doesn't sound good.'

He shook his head. 'No drama, just facts.' He eyed her. 'It's time we faced reality. They're not coming back.' He nodded towards the children, who were now chasing each other in a circle. 'I think we have to make more permanent plans.'

Cora gasped, her chest tightening at the matter-of-fact tone, the simple statement so far from simple that it felt colossal, its impact on her life fathomless.

4

Cora forced a whisper, her throat feeling knotted. 'What do you mean, James? Have you found something out?'

He shook his head again. 'Not a damn thing. I've done everything I can to find that pair. It makes no sense, but they've simply... disappeared.' He eyed her.

'So, what are we going to do?' Cora's pulse began to tick faster, creating a dull thumping at her temple. Deep inside, she suspected what was coming, but, surely, he wouldn't ask this of her?

He hesitated.

'I know we said it'd be temporary, Cora, but I'm too old to care for the children properly. With my Rosemary gone, I can barely keep up with the estate and managing the house.' As Cora remembered the pile of unopened mail in the hall, he drew an arc above his head, glancing at the glass ceiling above them. 'What I *can* do is continue to cover all their needs. I'm thinking I'll set up a trust for them both, for when they are older. I'll fully support the children financially, if you will only agree to keep caring for them, Cora. They love and trust you, and you are doing such a wonderful job.' He held a hand up as

Cora made to protest. 'Please, just consider this before you answer. Why not move in here with me? You can take over the top floor. Raise them here, at Locharden House, and I'll do whatever I can to help, day to day.' His shoulders tensed as he pushed a hank of silver hair from his tanned forehead.

Shock rendered Cora speechless, and time seemed to grind to a halt. The small, brass carriage clock that stood on the windowsill in front of her ticked, each second that passed sounding like a metallic snap inside Cora's head – each snap taking her further away from the safety of her former life. A hint of garlic from their lunch was hanging in the air and the acidity of the coffee she'd been drinking seemed to suck the moisture from her mouth, making her lick her lips repeatedly.

As she stared at James, she noticed that the sleeve of his tartan shirt, sticking out beneath the fleece, was frayed, and the broad wedding ring that he never took off was dented where he'd smacked it a few weeks earlier on the old tractor in one of the outbuildings. He suddenly looked older, and newly vulnerable, and the realisation tugged at Cora's heart with such strength that she shook her head against it, but before she could speak, James continued.

'I just can't do it without you, Cora... But I know it's a lot to ask.'

Utterly overwhelmed, a myriad of emotions tumbling through her at what he was asking of her, she leaned back in the chair, the woven back pressing into her spine. She couldn't believe this was happening, the magnitude and significance of his request on her and her life immeasurable. Surely, he understood that?

As she saw her safe, ordered existence begin to slip even further away, she forced her rapid breathing to slow down, and spoke as kindly, but as purposefully as she could.

'James, I've already had them for *two months*. You're asking me to give up my life and independence for... for *Fraser*. I would essentially become a sacrifice to the choices your son has made. To his mistakes. Yet *again!*' As she said it, her heart contracted. 'Not the children, of course. I don't mean them. They are the best thing he's ever done, honestly.' She looked out the window at Ross, who was now sitting on the grass, his thumb firmly in his mouth, while Evie ran in circles around him. 'It's too much, James.' She swallowed hard, tears pressing behind her eyes. 'I love them. You know I do, but...' She felt as if the walls were closing in on her, the moral and emotional arguments doing battle inside her, the whole situation surreal.

As he surveyed her face, and her insides turned somersaults, all Cora could think was, *Damn you, Fraser Munro. You have turned my life upside down, yet again.*

James stared at her for a moment longer, then, registering her tortured expression, he nodded, his eyes glistening.

'OK, Cora. I know you've done more than anyone in your position should have to. I should never have asked you.' He stood up slowly. 'I'll sort something else out.'

Seeing resignation warp his handsome features, sympathy and the compulsion to share his burden took over. 'James, I'm sorry. It was just unexpected. I meant what I said, but give me some time to think everything through.' She halted, catching a flash of hope light up his pale-blue eyes. As she gave him that hope, her control over her own life was being sucked into quicksand as she watched, helpless to stop it.

She needed to make him understand how hard this was for her. The children had come to mean so much to her, but they were not hers, something she'd consciously remind herself of whenever Ross called her Mumma, and when Evie had said she wanted Cora to be their mother. She had to protect herself from any more hurt, or loss in her life, and the longer Evie and Ross stayed with her, the harder that was becoming. The longer they were with her, the more she was beginning to believe that maybe they *could* be hers, perhaps forever, and that thought no longer terrified her as it once had, which, in itself, was frightening.

Cora watched James walk back into the kitchen, and followed him, her heart a lead weight. He went to the Aga, opened the heavy door, and slid a log in from the basket by the side of it. He looked as if he carried the weight of the world on his back, and she hesitated at the table, unsure whether she should sit or get the children ready to go.

James dragged his fingers through his wavy silver hair, then cleared his throat, the sound a metallic rattle in Cora's ear. Seeing the troubled look on his face, it was clear that he had more to say. More to ask.

'What is it?' Cora kept the frustration from her voice, and just as she was about to press him again, Evie trotted back into the kitchen.

'Can we go home now?'

At this, James met Cora's eyes as she opened her arms to the little girl and lifted her up onto her hip.

'This *is* home, Evie.' She moved a stray hair that was clinging to Evie's eyelashes.

'The other home.' Evie nestled her chin into Cora's collarbone, her breath carrying a trace of her lunch.

Feeling Evie's arms go around her neck, the tight squeeze that followed as profound as if the child was pinching Cora's heart between her fingers, Cora sighed. How could she put these children through yet another upheaval? They'd only just adjusted to being without their parents, to sharing the tiny spare room at Cora's house, eating at her pretty tiled table in the sunny kitchen, or watching cartoons on the sofa as she hoovered around them on her days off.

Deep in her heart, she knew that, despite her protests, despite what she thought she wanted for herself, her life had changed, and now, while it might be up to her what happened next, how could she possibly put herself first and still sleep at night?

Cora's best friend Aisha Pakram's mouth fell open, revealing the tiny gap between her bottom teeth. 'Are you *serious?*' She clamped her hands over her cap of crimson hair, her warm brown eyes wide.

Cora pressed her palm down in mid-air. 'Shh, they're not long asleep.' She pointed at the ceiling. 'I'm deadly serious. And, what's more, as soon as they were safely in the car, James asked me if I'd consider becoming their legal guardian, if anything should happen to him.' She lifted her wine glass from the coffee table and sat back on the sofa. 'I'm in a corner, Aisha. What the hell am I supposed to say?' She crossed her feet under her and watched as Aisha did the same, in the armchair next to the fire.

'You could say no, Cora.' She shook her head, almost imperceptibly. 'It's an enormous ask. A mammoth thing to take on.' She sipped some wine, then balanced the glass on her knee. 'It's like instant motherhood being thrust upon you, but without all the fun stuff that got you there in the first place.' She blinked, then broke into a grin as Cora tutted at her.

'Aisha, this is serious,' Cora chided, then, despite herself, laughed at her friend's expression. Aisha had the gift of making Cora laugh, of seeing the humour in the darkest of situations, and it was only part of what Cora loved about her. 'Honestly, you are such a pain.'

Aisha laughed softly, then shook the heavy red fringe from her eyes. 'I know. I'm sorry. I just can't believe that he asked you, though. It's *insane*, and, frankly, impossible.'

Cora swirled the wine in her glass, surprised that the word impossible sparked something inside her. Was it insane of James to ask this? Was he being selfish, putting this kind of pressure on her, or just practical – or, more likely, desperate? Was there another way to ensure the children got to grow up with family, in a place they knew, surrounded by familiar people who loved them?

Cora set her glass on the table and hugged a cushion to her chest. 'I told him I needed time to think about it.'

Aisha looked startled. 'You didn't say that, did you?'

'I did, because it's true.'

Aisha unfurled her legs, crossed the room, and sat next to Cora on the sofa. 'Are you seriously considering it?'

Cora felt her cheeks begin to warm. 'I think I have to. What other options are there, for the kids?'

Aisha slumped back against the cushion behind her. 'Well, he could get a full-time nanny. Have them live there, and you could visit now and then. Be the honorary auntie who brings ice cream on Sundays.'

Cora sighed. 'He asked me if I'd consider moving in with him, to Locharden House.'

Aisha's eyebrows bounced. 'Well, there are worse places to live, I'll admit, but what about this place?' She swept her hand in an arc. 'You *love* this house.'

Cora nodded. 'I know. I do love it. I can't imagine not being here.' Her throat began to knot as an image of her beloved home, with someone else's furniture in it, flooded her mind.

When the Campbells had fostered and then adopted her at eight years old, a cautious and introverted product of the child welfare system, Cora's life had changed forever. Not only was her undiagnosed hearing issue discovered, and treated, but she had a real family for the first time in her life. A bedroom that only she slept in, and a second name that she could keep, forever. Even when, twenty years later, she'd married Fraser Munro, she had kept the Campbell name, partly out of respect to her parents, but also because she couldn't bring herself to give up something that had literally transformed her life.

The Campbells had not only given her the family she craved, but a truly happy upbringing. She had loved them deeply, treasuring her life with them, and when they had passed away within the same year, just five years ago, it had left Cora heartbroken, and the new owner of the little house on Montague Road. This home meant everything that was safe and good to Cora, and she couldn't envisage ever giving that up.

Snapping her out of her reverie, Aisha's voice sounded uncharacteristically harsh in Cora's ear. 'No, Cora. I won't let you. You *always* do this! Put other people's needs before your own. But this isn't giving in on a paint colour, or where to go on holiday, this is your whole freaking *life*.' She reached over and grabbed Cora's hand. 'Please, be real about this.'

Cora felt the force behind Aisha's grip, the pressure sending prickles up her forearm.

'Believe me, I am being real. This is so real, it's mind-boggling.'

Aisha let her hand go and sat back. 'What about the nanny option? Did you suggest it?'

Cora shook her head. 'He wants them raised by family, and even a great nanny, well...' She shrugged.

'But you're *not* their family, Cora. I'm sorry, but you're not. Fraser and that useless wench Holly are, and you shouldn't be cleaning up their mess.' The humour was gone from her voice and anger had crept in. 'Fraser's a waster. Always was. And as for her, well, I'd better keep my mouth shut.' Aisha stood up and retrieved her glass from the side table next to the armchair. 'Parenthood is not something you can try out, then decide it doesn't work for you. There's no return policy on little human beings.' She glowered over the top of the glass. 'They need to grow the hell up and face the music, wherever they are.'

In the years since Fraser had left Cora and moved in with Holly, to her tiny flat above the local pub, Cora had struggled to rebuild her life. She had initially considered leaving Ballater, packing up and starting fresh somewhere, but as the reality of that had sunk in, anger had overturned her hurt. Why should she be the one to leave? This was her home, the only one she had ever known, and all her good memories were tied up in the house on Montague Road, the garden where she'd planted vegetables with her mother, and the short walk to the Dee bridge that she and her father would take as the sun rose over the silvery river. Why should she let Fraser and Holly force her to give up the only place she'd ever felt safe and happy?

Having made the decision to stay, while happy to be in her peaceful home, living in the same village as her ex-husband had been much harder than she'd imagined. As his little family grew, he and Holly having the two children in quick succession, observing that had twisted the knife in Cora's heart.

Seeing her pain, James had grown even more frustrated, telling Cora that Fraser Munro was no son of his. James's condemnation of Fraser was common knowledge in the village, and as a result, he had stayed away from the big house, the connection between father and son fraying to a single thread – Cora.

She was the only element that still connected them, but try as she might, she couldn't forgive Fraser, either. Hence, the understanding between her and the old laird had turned from one of mutual respect to genuine affection. He'd grown to love her like a daughter, and while she felt guilty about supplanting Fraser in James's heart, she also desperately needed that sense of family that she had lost since her parents had passed away, and that Fraser had also taken from her.

Cora took a gulp of wine, the earthy red soothing her aching throat.

'I know. They are disgraceful individuals. There's no excuse for what they've done, but Evie and Ross are not to blame, are they? Why should they suffer because their parents screwed up? It's not fair, Aisha. They are sweet, good children, who deserve a proper home to grow up in, with a family that truly loves them. One that's not going to toss them to the kerb at the first challenge.' She paused, then swallowed hard, as years of painful memories began to crowd in. 'God knows, Aisha, I know what that's like.'

Aisha's face softened as Cora touched the cochlear implant behind her ear, the contact sending a gentle buzz across her skull. 'I know, love. You know that better than anyone.' Aisha gave her a sad smile. 'What you went through was horrendous. I get that. But these kids have family. They have James. You didn't have that luxury. You were shoved around from place to place, for years. Neglected, deprived, hurt...' She halted as Cora's eyes clamped shut. 'These children will never have to go through what you did, Cora. I just don't think it's your responsibility to take them on, that's all I'm saying.'

Cora opened her eyes and blinked her vision clear.

'If I don't take them on, then who will? James is getting older, Aisha. He does what he can, and he's remarkable, really, but his health is beginning to fail. He tries to hide it, but I see how he struggles.' She shrugged. 'We can all say, it's not my problem, but imagine if my parents had said the same thing? What might have happened to me?' She gulped back tears. 'Where is the line drawn between whose problem it is and doing the right thing?'

Aisha looked shocked, her hand going to the back of her head again as the three, thin gold bangles she wore slipped up towards her elbow, the tinny clink sounding like static to Cora.

'I don't know, but all I'm saying is take time to think it through. All the implications to you and your life. It might feel like the right thing now, but what if you meet someone new? Or you get a fantastic job opportunity somewhere else? You can't cook for the old guy forever, Cora.' She shrugged.

The concern that was glowing behind Aisha's eyes filled Cora with a surge of love, and gratitude. 'I hear you, Aisha. I really do. And I know that everything you are saying makes sense, and comes from love, but I look at those little faces, the trust I'm finally seeing in their eyes, and I can't imagine letting them down. They deserve better than that.' She took a breath. 'I promise I won't rush into anything, but I am going to give it serious thought.' She nodded to herself. 'I owe them, and James, that much.'

Aisha's face fell slack, her two hands now locked behind her head. 'OK, Cora. I understand. You know I'll be here, and whatever you decide, I will support you. I'm just afraid that you will get lost in all this. Your life traded for another that you didn't choose.'

'But what if I do choose it, Aisha? What if those kids are more important than me being able to hike Craigendarroch, or go fly fishing whenever I want?' She considered what she'd just said, and a decision began to solidify. 'I always wanted to be a mother. What if this is my only chance?' She paused, seeing Aisha's frown deepen. 'I love you for caring so much, but please don't worry. Whatever I decide to do, you'll be the second – or maybe the fourth – to know.' She gave a half-smile as Aisha rolled her eyes theatrically.

'Thanks for that.' She pursed her lips, then gave in to a smile. 'You are the stubbornest person I know, Cora Campbell. The stubbornest, kindest, most compassionate, selfless, pain in my arse that I've ever met.'

Cora smiled at her friend, the decision that was forming in her heart feeling gargantuan and more daunting the more real it became.

Cora closed the door behind Aisha and circled the room, switching off the lights. Their conversation had inevitably returned to Fraser and Holly, and how they had both disappeared so completely and without trace.

As she climbed the stairs, her body suddenly heavy, and ready for a hot shower, she mentally reran her conversation with James, the way she'd left it an open question as to whether she'd take the children on permanently. It was the best she could do at the time, and now, having spoken with Aisha, it felt too big to think about anymore. What she needed was sleep, and tomorrow, with a fresh perspective, she'd find her way to a decision.

Half an hour later, snuggled up under her duvet, her unread book butterflied over her stomach, Cora was aware of her phone vibrating on the bedside table. As she lifted it up, she saw the words Unknown Caller glowing in the semi-dark of the bedroom. On the point of ignoring the call, she checked the time: 10.22 p.m. was far later than anyone she knew would phone her, plus their number would be visible, so it had to be a spam call. One of those, *have you thought about replacing your windows?* calls.

But as she squinted at the screen, something inside her stirred, an insistent voice creeping into her head. *What if it isn't a crank call? What if, after all this time, it is Holly, or Fraser?*

5

Cora sat up and swiped the screen, her heart thumping under her T-shirt.

'Hello?' She held the phone to her good ear and waited. There was a strange, mechanical sound in the background, like metal grating on metal. She couldn't make it out, so waited a second, then said, 'Holly, is that you?'

Silence greeted her, then what sounded like a sigh before the line went dead.

Her pulse racing, Cora set the phone down and stared at it, wondering how she'd ever sleep now. She threw off the covers and swung her legs out, her feet seeking her slippers, as the phone's screen lit up again on the side table. Grabbing it up, she saw a text had come in. Her hands shaking, she pressed the icon, and the message appeared: *How are they?*

Gasping, Cora tapped as fast as her fingers would work: *Holly, is that you? Where are you?*

As a line of dots pulsed on the screen, indicating that whomever it was was typing, Cora held her breath. Counting the seconds, she stood up, gripping the phone and pacing at the end of her bed. After a few moments, the dots stopped, then four words appeared: *I am sorry, Cora.*

Shaking her head, she searched for the number in her incoming calls, but it had been blocked. Her momentary hope shifting to anger, Cora hissed, 'You selfish, cowardly bitch. It's not *me* you need to apologise to.' She tossed the phone onto the bed, clenched her fists, and headed for the stairs.

The kitchen was chilly, a trace of the fresh tomato bruschetta she'd made for Aisha lingering in the air, as Cora crossed the room and opened the fridge. The door creaked, the old hinges needing some WD-40 – another thing that was on her list to do that had been forgotten.

She scanned the contents, not sure what she wanted. It was after 10 p.m. and, ordinarily, she wouldn't be looking to eat at this time, but there was a void inside her that needed to be filled.

Spotting a block of Orkney Cheddar, she grabbed it, then some celery sticks she'd cut up and put in a container for Evie. Closing the fridge door, she put the items on the countertop and pulled out a small bamboo chopping board. Her mother had given it to her when she'd come back from culinary school in London. The initials CM that Eliza had had burned into the handle had darkened over the years to a deep amber colour. Each time Cora washed it and set it to dry on the draining board, it served as a reminder of her parents' pride in her choice of career.

With her love of cooking and baking with her mother, and her skill as a forager, and fly fisher, it had been no surprise to the Campbells when Cora had chosen a career in food. They'd been thrilled for her when she'd been accepted onto a three-year course at the Culinary Institute in London, but they had been even more delighted when, after graduating, she'd come home to work at the Ballater Inn.

When Cora had moved back, she had happily lived with the Campbells again as she worked her way up to sous-chef, over five years, then an opportunity had come up to move to The Rookery, a Michelin-starred restaurant at the edge of the town on the Braemar Road. The chef, Eddie Gilchrist, had once been the chef at Balmoral and there was a rumour that, under his watch, one of the Royals had chipped their tooth on a piece of oyster shell that had mistakenly been left in the bouillabaisse. Mortified, Eddie had resigned the next morning, joining The Rookery within the month.

He'd been a tyrant in the kitchen. A giant fellow with a belly that matched his booming voice as he shouted his instructions at the team. His huge hands had seemed like shovels until he picked up a single stalk of fresh watercress, or dressed a glistening piece of salmon, working with precision, and care, much like a surgeon wielding a scalpel. Rather than fear him, Cora had worshipped him and the way he manipulated flavours. She had excelled under his tutelage, honing her skills for three years, until Eddie had left for Paris to start a new venture. Cora had been unable to raise enough money to take it over, so, sadly, the restaurant had closed.

She had been heartbroken, unsure what to do next, when, one morning, Fraser Munro had knocked on the door. He'd heard about The Rookery closing and asked her to help his father. And the rest, as Cora would now say, was history.

The memory bringing another twinge of regret at what might have been for her culinary career, Cora got herself a glass of water and took her plate of food into the living room. The lamp was on next to the sofa, so she dragged the tartan blanket over her knees and lifted the laptop from the coffee table. As she bit into a piece of cheese, the dry smokiness of the Cheddar instantly sucking the moisture from her mouth, Cora tapped out Fraser's name on the keyboard.

As always happened, his name came up on a few sites, the most prominent being listed as a member of the rugby team at his boarding school in Aberdeen, seventeen years earlier, when he was sixteen. They had won the Scottish Rugby Schools' Cup that year, and Fraser had given up playing directly afterwards. James had apparently been incensed at the decision, but Fraser had told his father that quitting while you were at the top was a sensible thing to do.

As Cora looked at the old team photo, the youthful, angular jaws, the mops of hair, uneven socks and well-worn rugby boots, Fraser's face pulled her eye. He looked happy. His cheeks were flushed, his young chest already broad, and his hands firmly on his hips, a stance that spoke of pride in his achievement.

Cora took another piece of Cheddar and bit off some celery, enjoying the fresh, crisp contrast to the creaminess of the cheese. As she chewed, staring at Fraser's face, the mess of blonde hair and the shining eyes, she tried to recall if she'd seen him look that happy when they'd been together.

She remembered that there had been a quiet sadness to him, a quality that she believed had drawn her to him in the beginning. Coming from the background she had, broken people were not new to her, and Cora had grown up with a belief that if she wanted, she could help them, if not herself.

As she gulped down some water, her throat began to tighten. If, when she'd begun to get involved with him, she had known how deeply troubled Fraser was, a man trapped in a life he loathed, with a father he couldn't relate to, and a mother whom he adored and who was terminally ill, she wondered – not for the first time – if she would have let him into her heart so profoundly. Would his demons have proved too much, even for her, if he'd been honest with her from the start? Would she have made a different decision that day he'd first asked her to dinner? Would she have so easily fallen for his self-effacing humour, the way his eyes held hers so intensely when she was talking, as if there was no one else in the room, and no other sound he would rather hear than her voice? Or would the depth of his sadness have scared her away?

As ever, Cora didn't have the answer. All she knew was that she *had* let him in, and he had destroyed her heart. Whatever else happened now, she would never let him, or his actions, hurt her again. She would keep the wall she had surrounded herself with, where he was concerned, firmly in place, and, more than that, she'd even protect his children from the damage he could cause, if necessary.

A couple of hours later, Cora woke with a start, the covers over her face. She instantly touched her cochlear implant and strained to hear whatever it was that had woken her. A soft cry from the children's room propelled her out of bed, and ignoring her slippers, she darted into the hall.

The compact bedroom that had once been Cora's room was dark, save for the night light that she always left on now. The tiny glass starfish glowed reassuringly in its usual place near the skirting board, as she let her eyes adjust to the semi-darkness.

The low-profile bunk beds were against the left-hand wall, the broad safety rail on the top bunk making it hard to see Evie's full form. But as Cora stepped in closer, she could see the little girl's delicate profile, her features smooth, at rest, and her hair fanned out over the pillow.

On the bottom bunk, also behind a sturdy safety rail, Ross lay with his eyes wide open. He had pushed the Peter Rabbit quilt off, and his pyjamaed legs were pointing straight upwards, his chubby toes splayed out as if he were trying to grasp the air with them. His top was snug around his torso, and he held his balding furry elephant, Elly, close to his face.

'Hello, you,' Cora whispered, placing her palm on his little chest. 'Were you dreaming?' She eased his legs back down and replaced the quilt, tucking it in along his sides.

Ross looked at her, his pale eyes seeming to drink her in, then he smiled. A curly-lipped smile that tugged directly at Cora's heart. 'Mumma. Kiss Elly.' He held Elly out to her, then hiccupped, something he often did after he had been crying, or had eaten too quickly.

As the word Mumma once again sent a spark of happiness through Cora, she took Elly and smoothed the threadbare ears, and planted a kiss on one of them, then handed the toy back to Ross.

'Sounds like you've got the hicky-thumps.'

Ross grinned, his tongue pressed between his pearly teeth, many of whose troublesome emergence Cora had comforted him through. He hiccupped again, making her laugh softly as she touched his silky hair, spun gold that, even in the dim light, seemed to glow.

'Turn on your side, sweet boy.' She gently rolled him towards her, tightly bunching the quilt behind him. 'Now, close your eyes.'

Ross slipped his thumb into his mouth and blinked several times, silky lashes fringing his dark-rimmed blue eyes. 'Sing Michael,' he whispered around his thumb, his mouth widening as he smiled again.

'OK.' Cora nodded. 'Close your eyes then.' She waited until he obeyed, then she sang softly. 'There was a man named Michael Finnegan. He had whiskers on his chin-egan.' She halted as Ross reached for her hand, as if making sure she couldn't sneak away. Cora felt his fingers close around hers, the contact sending the joy of being needed spiralling through her, as if a chain of roses were blooming inside her, each one more perfect than the rest.

Taking a moment to centre herself, she gently touched his dimpled cheek with her free hand before whispering, 'The wind came out and blew them in again.' She paused again, seeing Ross's eyelids relax, a sure sign that sleep had won out, then she sang, almost inaudibly, 'Poor old Michael Finnegan, begin-again.'

Leaning in, Cora kissed Ross's forehead, then, when she was sure he was asleep, backed out of the room. She stopped in the doorway, reluctant to leave the cosy space she had created for the children.

The room was full of things she and James had cobbled together for them at short notice, several of which Cora had believed would be going with the children when they moved in with their grandfather.

A set of matching chests of drawers were tucked under the eaves, with a big red toy box nestled in between them. Two beanbag chairs, Evie's covered in unicorns and Ross's with penguins, sat either side of a rug littered with ladybirds sitting on toadstools. On the wall by the door was a large whiteboard, with pieces of Evie's colouring and Ross's scribbled crayon drawings held up with giant magnets that looked like frogs.

The old, double-doored oak wardrobe that had once been Cora's mother's spanned the corner opposite the bunk beds, and a wooden mobile hung below the overhead light, three layers of birds spiralling downwards, each brightly coloured, with hinged wings that moved when you touched the frame. Cora was proud of the room, and that the children had quickly grown comfortable in it, as if it had been theirs all along, despite the few personal belongings they'd arrived with.

As she backed out into the hall, wondering for the umpteenth time what their bedroom above the pub had looked like, her mind went back to the mysterious text she'd just received.

I am sorry, Cora

The words seemed newly hollow as she took another moment to soak in the gentle picture of innocent sleep. How could anyone – any half-decent parent – leave these sweet babies behind, letting their lives become disjointed and uncertain?

Cora breathed through another pulse of anger as she crossed the hall and went back to bed. As she buried herself under the covers, knowing that she wouldn't sleep now, her decision about the children loomed large – a monster in the cupboard that she couldn't soothe away with a song.

She had put herself in their shoes, and in doing so, the answer had been clear. But what if Cora had made an impulsive choice that she might regret?

6

As April drew to a close, the following Saturday was the first market day of the year, and Cora had been looking forward to it.

Ballater farmers' market offered fresh fish, local beef and cheeses, vegetables, jams and chutneys, a healthy selection of gins, and even plants. The stallholders were mostly familiar faces, good-hearted farmers, local growers, and craftspeople that Cora enjoyed chatting with as she selected her produce.

Held on the fourth Saturday of every month, from April to November, on the Glenmuick Church green, it was a place where the village gathered to support the local suppliers and to exchange news and gossip.

The striking church, designed by renowned architect J. Russell Mackenzie, dated back to 1874 and its towering steeple dominated the central square of the village. A listed building, it not only drew visitors from around the world, but was still open for services. In the church grounds, the impressive war memorial stood, and the Queen Elizabeth Diamond Jubilee Cairn and gardens.

To create the cairn, sixty stones had been carefully selected from the surrounding hills, with the permission of all the relevant landowners, James among them. It was a point of pride for him that two of the stones had come from his estate, at the foot of mighty Lochnagar, and Cora had listened numerous times as he recounted the events of the unveiling in 2012, when the village had celebrated Her Majesty's sixty years on the throne.

Aisha loved the farmers' market too, and usually met Cora at the butcher's stall, at 10 a.m. sharp, seeking her advice on the best cuts to buy for herself and her mother, Priyanka. Priyanka tragically had both dementia and multiple sclerosis and had been confined to a wheelchair for two years, ever since she'd moved into a small, assisted-living community on the outskirts of the village. Aisha would leave her job as a tasting guide at the Royal Lochnagar Distillery around 4 p.m. each day and visit Priyanka before heading home.

Cora often cooked extra portions of meals that were good for Priyanka's conditions, dishes filled with fresh vegetables, oats, rice, quinoa, nuts and seeds, and fish, especially the local salmon, which was rich in omega-3 fatty acids and vitamin D.

Today, Cora had the children ready early, as she needed to drop by Locharden House on the way to the market.

James had been patient since their conversation the previous weekend, not pressing her for her decision about keeping the children long term, but when she'd seen him the afternoon before, he'd seemed agitated. Rather than sitting in his usual spot at the kitchen table, either chatting to her or reading the paper while she cooked, he'd stayed out in the long, Victorian greenhouse at the side of the house, puttering with the orchids he grew with great success. Cora had felt his absence and when she'd gone out to check on him, he'd been pleasant but reserved, talking only about the weather, and pointedly not meeting her eye. If she hadn't known better, she'd have assumed he was avoiding something, but it was she who'd been procrastinating talking about the children.

Cora had thought about little else since her talk with Aisha, and as the days had slipped by, Cora had wondered at her destiny taking such an unexpected U-turn. Could this challenging and often stressful life be the only path she could follow now? As she'd lain awake each night, sometimes into the wee hours of the morning, wrestling with her conscience, the trajectory of her thoughts had gathered speed and the decision that had formed, while overwhelming, finally felt right.

For Cora, buried beneath all her positivity, there had always been a young girl who'd felt rejected. The child who had been moved around from foster home to residential home, and back again. That sense of being the cuckoo in the nest, of needing to change herself in order to be accepted, had left its fingerprints on her heart. Only after the Campbells had convinced her that she was everything they wanted just as she was had Cora begun to believe that she was enough. Ever since, she had lived with the desire to change someone's life the way her parents had changed hers, and when she looked at Evie and Ross, she knew what she must do. All that remained was to tell James her decision.

Ross was strapped into his car seat, his eyelids heavy. Evie sat next to him in her seat, her feet kicking out, bumping the back of the driver's seat every few seconds. Sighing, Cora secured her seat belt and reached behind her, tapping Evie's knee.

'Can you stop that, sweetheart?'

Evie stopped momentarily, then kicked the chair one more time, delivering a final thump to Cora's lower back. 'I'm bored. When are we going to Grandpa's?' she huffed.

Cora sought her eyes in the rear-view mirror. 'Right now. He's waiting for us.'

Evie blinked several times, then tipped her head to the side.

'Is he coming to the market?'

Cora moved the car slowly into the lane, her eyes on a neighbour's rainbow-coloured Mini coming towards her. 'Not today, but he's got a lot of orchids for Mr Taggart to sell, so we're going to pick them up.'

Evie considered what Cora had said, then nodded. 'They are pretty.'

'Yes, they are.' Cora smiled at her in the mirror, picturing the delicate ivory blooms with crimson centres that James favoured.

The market's regular flower vendor from Aberdeen had gladly agreed to let James put his orchids on the stall, and James enjoyed talking to the ruddy-faced giant, a former Royal Marine who'd found his way into the world of flowers as a means to manage his PTSD.

Cora had never been told his first name, so she'd just smile and say, 'Hello, Mr Taggart,' as James and he waxed lyrical about the sorry state of the world, and the changes they'd seen in their lifetimes, all the while sneaking nips of Glenlivet whisky from a monogrammed hip flask that Rosemary had given James on their fortieth wedding anniversary.

Cora halted the car at the end of Montague Road, in front of Aisha's old house, amused that while Ross had already fallen asleep, Evie was humming the Michael Finnegan song that they always sang in the car. Cora smiled, grateful that these sweet rituals she had started, out of pure instinct rather than study, had proved effective in relaxing the children, letting them lean into her way of parenting.

From the moment she and James had realised that Fraser and Holly were not coming back, Cora had wisely decided to do things her way. She wasn't party to the details of how her ex and his wife had dealt with the day-to-day operations of family life, so Cora had decided that she might as well make her own rules, and as she watched Evie in the mirror, the little girl picking up a piece of soggy biscuit that Ross had dropped and popping it into the container Cora kept in the back for rubbish, she couldn't help but feel proud. Proud of Evie's resilience, and gentle caretaking of her younger brother, but also her willingness to let Cora in, to trust again, and allow her to guide her in the only way Cora knew how. With patience, and understanding, and a dash of humour, that brought out the best in the thoughtful child.

As if reading Cora's mind, Evie clamped her hand over her mouth and giggled.

'What is it?' Cora indicated and turned left into Hamilton Road, heading out of the village.

Evie was still giggling, her face pinking up behind her palm.

'Evie, what's so funny?' Cora kept her eyes on the road, despite the temptation to look over her shoulder.

Evie dropped her hand and met Cora's eyes in the mirror. 'I popped a smelly bubble!'

At this, Cora gasped, then pressed her lips together, trying to suppress the laughter that instantly tickled the back of her throat. It was a term that Aisha had used a few weeks earlier, when she'd been talking about her little niece in Stirling, who had broken wind in the bath. Evie had overheard and, since that afternoon, had repeated the term a couple of times, usually out of context. This time, however, she'd got it right.

'Evie Munro.' Cora feigned shock, as Evie squirmed, her nose puckering.

'Just wind.' She flapped her hand, a mischievous smile lighting up her eyes.

Cora's face twitched as she tried not to grin. 'Well, I should think so – a young lady of your age.' She wiggled her eyebrows, glancing over her shoulder at Evie, who was smiling broadly. 'If you want to be a princess, and have lunch at Balmoral one day, we can't be having that happen, now, can we?'

Evie shook her head.

'Do the King and Queen pop smelly bubbles?'

Cora was unable to stop herself, a burst of laughter making

her stomach knot. 'Oh, Evie. I have no idea. But it's not very polite to say that, OK?'

Evie dipped her torso from side to side, flipping her hair over alternating shoulders, her eyes glittering. 'Auntie Aisha says it.'

'Yes, I know. And Auntie Aisha is naughty sometimes. So, let's agree to keep that for when we're alone at home, all right, chickadee?'

'All right.' Evie sat up straight and turned to Ross, who was now snoring softly. 'We're not going to say pop smelly bubbles, Rossy. It's *rude*,' she whispered.

Cora swiped at her watery eyes, then tutted. 'That's enough, missy.' She forced herself to sound as if she meant business. 'Don't let Grandpa hear you saying that, either.'

At this, Evie looked up, her smile wavering. 'Will it make him... cross?'

Cora's insides lurched at the sight of the questioning green eyes, the ease with which Evie could pivot from happy and cheeky back to insecure. 'No, it won't. It's just not the way we speak to him, sweetheart.'

Evie nodded, lifted Elly from the seat next to her and tucked it in beside Ross's leg, then turned to look out the window.

Cora was suddenly overcome, wanting to pull the car over, jump out, rush around and take Evie in her arms. Reassure her that no one was going to be cross with her, or abandon her, ever again. Instead, Cora went with distraction.

'Do you think the lady with the puppies will be at the market?'

Evie snapped her head back around, her eyes wide. 'I hope so.'

'I think we've still got some treats in the glove compartment, so if there are any pups today, you can give them a couple.' Cora recalled seeing Evie melt at the three Collie puppies that a breeder from Inverness, who sometimes turned up at the market, had been selling at the local vet's surgery a few months back.

They'd taken Duchess in for her annual check-up to help James out, and the child had sat next to the pen and talked to the little fluff-balls, naming them all, and laughing as they tumbled over each other, nipping at their siblings.

'They won't be the same ones of course, as they'll be grown up now.' Cora pulled up at the traffic light, spotting Angela Dunn, Evie's kindergarten teacher, waiting at the bus stop. 'Oh, look. There's Miss Dunn.' Cora waved at the young woman, a slender brunette with deep-set blue eyes, almost too big for her face. She waved back at Cora, and then waved at Evie, who was patting the window and grinning.

Angela had been a tremendous help to Cora when it had come time for Evie to go to school. Evie had been tearful, clinging to Cora's leg in the corridor outside the classroom, and as Cora had battled tears herself, Angela had stepped in, calm, warm and reassuring. Evie had gradually let go of Cora and followed Angela into the colourful classroom, the young teacher pointing out the paintings on the walls, the long bookcase under the window, and the low tables each with four bright red chairs, as Cora had slipped away and had a good cry alone in the car.

As was often the case in a village, Angela knew about Holly and Fraser, and the whole messy situation, and she had taken Cora aside at the school gate one afternoon to offer her support.

'I think what you're doing is *amazing*, Cora. Whatever I can do to help, I will. On this end.'

'Thanks, Angela.' Cora had smiled at the young woman. 'Gin is always helpful, and of course some babysitting, now and then...' She'd waited for the gin comment to hit home, then Angela had laughed.

'Right, understood. Not sure I can help with the gin, but I'll put the word out for a babysitter. We often get the children's older siblings looking for a way to make some pocket money, so I'll let you know.'

'Great.' Cora had watched Evie trotting towards her across the playground, her long ponytail swishing behind her, the notion that the child was running towards *her* still sometimes hard to process.

Snapping Cora back to the moment, Ross woke up and yawned. 'Elly.' He tugged the elephant out from beside his thigh and snuggled the grey bundle into his chin.

His eyes were glued to his sister, as was often the case, as Evie began kicking the back of Cora's seat again. Sighing, she accelerated, the road narrowing as she left the village behind and headed west towards the foot of Lochnagar, and Locharden House.

The twin doors to the house were firmly closed when Cora pulled up in front of the little circular bed filled with flowers. She'd thought James might be waiting for her outside, as usually happened when he was expecting her, so, puzzled, she ran up the steps and banged the big brass knocker.

After a few moments, not hearing any movement from inside, she tried again, a wisp of worry snaking through her. Just as she was about to try the handle, she heard Duchess bark and the lock clunk. Relieved, Cora turned and waved at the children, who were both watching her from the back seat of the Volvo.

When she turned back to the now open door, she caught her breath. James was leaning against the door frame, a tea towel held up to his left eye. There was blood on the collar of his tartan shirt and his hands were shaking.

'Oh, James. What's happened?' She stepped forwards, making to touch the tea towel, sympathy, and the wish to protect this stubborn old man she had grown to love, swirling inside her.

'No, no I'm fine,' he snapped, as he ducked away from her

hand. 'Don't make a fuss now.' His voice sounded raspy to her. 'You'll scare the children.' He inched backwards into the long hallway, then met her eyes, seeing the concern there. 'No real damage done, lass.' This time, he spoke more gently.

'Let me see.' Cora once again moved towards him, and when he made to move away again, she said more firmly, 'James?'

Recognising her tone, the one that indicated that she wouldn't back down, he sighed and lowered the towel. There was a nasty gash above his eye, about half an inch long. Blood had coagulated in his bushy eyebrow and his forehead was a dark red, where a lump was forming.

Her throat thickening with concern, Cora winced. 'How on earth did that happen?'

She glanced back at the car, where Evie was talking to Ross, gesticulating wildly as she spoke to her brother. Cora guessed that she was telling him one of her made-up stories, with dragons, and horses, and heroines called Susan – the name of Evie's favourite doll. Relieved that they were amusing themselves, Cora turned her focus to James, who was now walking away from her, his gait somewhat unsteady.

Using the key to remotely lock the car, Cora quickly followed him along the hall and into the kitchen. He stood at the sink, one of the doors to the cabinet above it standing open, and the old tin canister that held his favourite lapsang souchong tea leaves lay on its side on the floor.

As she got closer, Cora could see tea leaves scattered all over the countertop, in the sink, and on the floor at his feet. Putting two and two together, she picked up the canister and set it on the counter. 'Was this the culprit?' She gently closed the cabinet door as he wet the tea towel, wrung it out and replaced it over his wound.

'Aye. The bugger!' He flinched as the towel made contact with his cut. 'I dropped the tea caddy, bent down to get it and forgot the door was open. So, when I stood up...' He nodded at the cupboard. 'Stupid, really.'

Cora eased him away from the sink and guided him to a chair at the table. 'Sit here for a bit. I'll go and get the kids, then we'll clean you up.'

'No.' His voice was sharp, making her wince. 'I don't want them seeing me like this.' He frowned under the towel, his piercing blue eyes locking on hers.

'I can't leave them in the car, James. And that needs a proper looking at.' She nodded at his eye, his gruffness not smarting as it used to. He didn't scare her as he had when she'd first met him, his sheathed kindness seeping out over time, and the deep affection she had for him now reinforcing her wish to help him.

'Just get me some gauze, and plasters from upstairs, and I'll sort it myself.' He carefully lowered the towel, checking it for fresh blood. 'There, see? It's stopping.' He held the towel out to her, a small line of fresh blood, dark against the pale pink of the wet cotton.

'You might need stitches, though.' Cora stood next to him, her hands on her hips, an image of Fraser suddenly flickering behind her eyes.

When they'd lived together, he had habitually banged into things in the house, knocked his knees against the coffee table, or stubbed his toe on the stairs, laughing as he cited the family clumsiness gene. After he'd moved out, she'd sometimes seen him in the village, with the odd plaster on his nose, or wearing sunglasses on a cloudy day, and one time with an impressive black eye, and she'd tut as she crossed the road, glad that she didn't have to run about after him, playing nurse, anymore.

'Honestly, you Munros are like bulls in a china shop.' She widened her eyes at him. 'Like father like son.'

James's eyebrows pulled together. 'Aye, well I beg to differ, there.' He shook his head. 'Anyway, I think it's stopped now.'

Cora leaned in and looked at the cut. Now that the excess blood was gone, she could see that it wasn't as deep as she had first thought. It was more of a nasty scrape, the edge of the door having shoved the skin back, the torn tissue forming a fleshy concertina above his eye.

'Hmm. It doesn't look too bad.' She chewed on her bottom lip. 'I'll get you some antiseptic cream and a plaster. Just sit tight.'

James nodded, folding the bloody tea towel into a square. 'Thanks. Don't tell the children, Cora. Please.'

She smiled at him momentarily, the slightly defeated hunch of his shoulders sending a rush of pity and affection through her. He was a remarkable man, a strong man, who had endured a deal of loss in his life, and if she could help him preserve his dignity, in front of his grandchildren, she would gladly do that.

'OK, don't worry. Your secret is safe with me.'

A few minutes later, she put the first-aid kit away and began sweeping up the loose tea leaves from the floor.

'Leave it.' James took the brush from her hand. 'I am quite capable of cleaning up after myself.' His eyes were heavily hooded, and the customary smile he sported whenever she was around was nowhere to be seen.

'All right, you grumpy old bugger.' She sighed, a new certainty that it wasn't only the children who needed her now flooding through her. 'Do you want me to take the orchids to the market, like we planned?' She glanced at her watch, immediately worried that she'd been in the house for over ten minutes.

'No, never mind. I didn't box them up because of this mishap.' He pointed at his eye. 'I'll phone Dougie, and he can take them to Aberdeen. Sell them at the market there, next weekend.'

Relieved, and surprised that the formidable Mr Taggart had such a friendly and unintimidating first name, Cora nodded. 'Right. Well, if you're sure you're OK, I'd better get going.' She jabbed her thumb over her shoulder. 'Time, tide and Evie and Ross wait for no man – for long, anyway.'

James stood up, tugged his shirt down at the back and managed a smile. 'Off you go. Kiss them for me and tell them I'll see them tomorrow for lunch.'

She spun her keys around her forefinger, watching as he gingerly touched the plaster above his eye. Conflicted about leaving, but wanting to get back to the children, Cora moved in and gave him a gentle hug, catching the scent of the Imperial Leather soap he favoured.

While he stood up straight, his shoulders pulled back, and his grip firm around her back, his torso felt newly fragile inside her arms. Worry for her ex-father-in-law swelling in her heart, she stepped back from him and took in his expression. He looked vulnerable, presumably mildly shaken by what had happened to his head, and yet there was something more in his expression. There was what looked like fear there, and it was deeply disturbing to see. This kind of little mishap was another indication of the stress he was under, the distractedness she'd noticed in him more regularly, recently.

Wanting desperately to take away at least one worry that he carried, to offer him something positive to hold onto, and to make him feel less alone, Cora took a moment, then said softly, 'So, I was going to tell you tomorrow, but I've made a decision about what you asked me.'

He closed his eyes, as if afraid of what was coming next. Seeing his reaction, Cora felt surer, and more resolved about her future than she had in months.

7

James's eyes widened and he blinked repeatedly, as if he couldn't focus.

'Are you *absolutely* sure, Cora? Because after I asked you, I realised what I was *really* asking of you. It's a huge responsibility.' His voice was ragged, his obvious relief shredding it.

'I know. I've thought it through, and I am quite sure, James.' She nodded.

He grabbed her hand and, surprisingly, kissed the back of it. 'You are one in a million, Cora. Fraser didn't deserve you, and neither do I. I don't have words to tell you how much this means to me.' His eyes were full as he released her hand.

Her throat clogging with emotion, Cora shook her head. 'Oh, come on now. We are family. It's what we do.'

He pulled a greying handkerchief from his pocket and wiped his nose.

'Well, we can talk about the details more tomorrow, but for now, thank you. From the bottom of my heart. You will not be alone, Cora. I will be here and will do everything I can to help. You have my word.'

'I know. We make a good team, James. We can do this.' She

stepped forward and put her arms around his neck, feeling him relax into her embrace. 'Now, I have to go before that pair figure out a way to drive home without me.' She laughed and he joined in, his relief now palpable as, with their arms linked, they walked back to the front door.

The next day when Sunday lunch was over, the children were in the small TV room off the living room at Locharden House with Duchess. The rain had been relentless all morning, so Cora had put a jigsaw puzzle and some colouring supplies into the bag before they'd left the house.

Ross was lying on the floor with Duchess at his side, an episode of *Thomas the Tank Engine* playing on the TV. He was running a little blue train across his tummy, back and forth, making choo-choo noises, while Evie drew a picture at the lacquered Regency table under the window. It was cracked open sightly, letting the smell of spring rain, and the fragrant lilac bushes that had bloomed early this year, float in on the gentle breeze.

Cora had been popping in to check on the children every few minutes, while she cleared up after lunch, and this time, as she approached the table, her heart caught in her throat.

Evie was concentrating on her colouring, her head bent over the paper, and her shoulders hunched with intent as she busily used a yellow crayon.

Looking over her shoulder, Cora spoke softly. 'That is lovely, Evie.' She smiled as the little girl glanced up at her, then back to her drawing.

'It's us.' Evie nodded, using the crayon as a pointer.

The picture was of a garden, with tall trees at the back and bright green grass in front. A large orange-coloured ball with mouse-like ears sat in the front corner, presumably Duchess, and in the centre of the paper, four figures stood, side by side.

On the left was a tall, brown-haired figure with long, dark-blue legs and big blue eyes dominating a circular head. It wore a green top, much like the one Cora had on today, and the smile was so big, the mouth extended beyond the sides of the face. Next to that was a small figure in a red suit, another round head, hairless, but also with giant blue eyes –clearly Ross. Then a slightly taller figure, wearing a red dress, with long yellow hair, this time with green eyes. It was obviously Evie, again the smile larger than the face could contain. At the right side of the group was an extremely tall, stick man, with what was clearly a kilt on, the crossed lines of colour doing a very passable job of looking like tartan, and the long socks and big brown shoes, very like James's customary Arran socks and brown brogues. This figure also had a mop of grey hair and was holding the hand of the yellow-haired figure, and smiling his own, oversized smile.

Cora took a moment to blink her vision clear, then crouched down next to Evie.

'So, who's this?'

Evie shoved the hair away from her cheek and put the crayon down. She tapped the tall figure on the left. 'That's you, and that's Rossy. Then me, and Grandpa. And that's Duchess.' She nodded to herself. 'It's our family.' She looked at Cora, her eyes full of light, and utterly without guile.

Cora's heart contracted at the simplicity of the statement. The truth of the words sinking deeper into her core as she blinked away the tears that were pressing in behind her eyes.

'It's beautiful, Evie. You are so good at drawing. It really looks like us.' For a split second, she felt sad for Fraser, that he could be relegated from Evie's picture of family so quickly, and yet, the child was showing the world as she saw it. The truth of her existence, and for that, Cora wasn't sad. She was grateful.

. . .

Cora had put another *Thomas the Tank Engine* episode on and left the children lying on the narrow sofa, both dozy and mesmerised.

James had made coffee and was waiting for her in the conservatory, his back to the garden and a look of excited anticipation on his face.

'Here you go.' He handed her a mug, then gestured towards the French doors. 'Now the rain's stopped, shall we take a turn?'

Cora glanced over her shoulder, the toot of the train whistle coming from the TV making her smile. 'They're transfixed by Thomas, so we're OK for a few minutes.'

'We'll stay close to the house, don't worry.' He gave her a kind smile, then held the door open for her to go ahead of him into the garden.

Outside, the earthy smell of wet soil transported Cora back to her childhood, the days before the Campbells had come into her life.

She had been seven, and in a foster home in Balerno, the couple she'd lived with a pair of bus drivers for the town. Their little terraced house had backed up to a decommissioned playground, with a broken slide, two swing sets with no seats, and a creaky merry-go-round. The locals had begun using it as an unofficial dog park, letting their dogs run loose in the overgrown bushes and digging holes in the remains of the grass around the edges of the space.

After it had rained, Cora had been able to smell the mulch and soil the dogs had churned up, as she'd played in the couple's garden, the tiny, gravelled space with a lopsided shed in one corner a welcome escape from the oppressive atmosphere inside the house.

The man, John, had been moody and quiet most of the time, spending hours watching television, his socked feet crossed on an old leather stool. Cora had quickly learned to stay out of the room, especially when he was watching football, the way he'd jump up from the armchair and shout at the screen, his face turning an odd shade of purple, terrifying her.

Her hearing was already impaired by that stage, a result of a thump to the side of her head from an older child in a residential home, followed by an undiagnosed middle ear infection in the same ear, the combination having a devastating effect, but in the case of that particular foster home, her hearing loss had almost been a blessing.

The woman, Stella, had been kinder, a bossy, chain smoker who had tried to make Cora feel welcome, even getting her some gently used toys from the local charity shop, but when Cora had heard them talking late one night, when she'd come downstairs for some water, it had been Stella who'd said, 'We've got to keep her for a few more months, John. We need the new washing machine. I'm saving as much of the allowance as I can, but we've still got a bit to go.'

Even at seven, Cora had got the message loud and clear. She was a means to an end, that was all, and that end wasn't completing a family, as she had hoped.

James's cough tugged her back to the present. Taking a deep breath, she sipped some coffee and walked beside him, their feet crunching on the gravel path behind the house. The sky was brightening, and a layer of wispy clouds filtered the sunlight, casting a lacy pattern across the damp lawn.

On the horizon was the familiar sight of Lochnagar, taking up its place in the broad granite tableau of the Cairngorms. The impressive mountain range was dotted with snow-topped peaks, and north-facing corries – the horseshoe-shaped valleys that had been formed through ice erosion, or by glaciers – all countered by sweeping uplands, most with steep-sided glens etched into them, creating a picture-perfect backdrop to her village that was nothing short of breathtaking.

Over the twenty-three years she had lived in Ballater, it had become *her* village, and knowing that what was left of her family, albeit out with any genetic connection, was based here for the foreseeable future made Cora grateful every day. The reminder of how fortunate she was, and how much she'd grown to love this mismatched little crew, was the perfect segue into what she wanted to tell James.

As they turned the corner, walking along the side of the house, heading towards the driveway, Cora took a breath, then dived in.

'So, I'll keep the children with me, James, but I've decided not to move in with you here.' She nodded at the house. 'It's a wonderful place, and somewhere they love coming to, but for me to make it work, I want to stay in my own house.' She paused, letting the information she'd given him sink in.

Beside her, he slowed his pace, then stopped walking, turning to face her.

'I understand, Cora. I can't pretend I wasn't hopeful that you'd move into this old pile of bricks, but I do understand.' He smiled; his eyes filled with affection. 'I'm not going to press the point, m'dear, but if you ever change your mind, just say the word.' He emptied the remains of his coffee onto the grass behind him and turned back towards the garden.

'I will, and thanks for understanding.' She followed him, relief at his gentle acceptance of her condition making her feel lighter. 'I feel I can cope with the day-to-day better in my own territory, so to speak.'

'If you're sure.' He nodded as they turned the corner and walked into the back garden.

Cora had one more thing to say, so she touched his arm, making him come to a stop.

'James, I think it would be wise to start the guardianship application, too, just in the event that anything should happen...' Her voice trailed away, the implication not something she wanted to voice. 'You know what I'm saying.'

He eyed her, then sighed. 'I do, and I agree with you one

hundred per cent. I'll talk to Dennis Burns tomorrow and get him on it. I'll get him to phone you so you can talk directly.'

'That's fine.' She nodded.

'It could take a month or two to put it together. From what I've researched, you'll need to apply to the family court for guardianship and then there's an assessment and approval period. I suspect they'll want to grill you a bit, and me of course, then they'll come to your house. See you there, and the environment the children will be living in.' James looked anxious. 'Is that OK?'

Cora linked her arm through his and steered him back through the French doors.

'Of course. I'd expect nothing less.' She hugged his arm tightly. 'Just make sure not to pop your clogs any time soon, though. I need you around for a long time yet.'

He snorted, patted her hand. 'I'll do my best.'

'And I'll do mine, to give them all the love, and care... the life they deserve.' The last words caught in her throat with the realisation that there was no going back now.

PART TWO

8

DECEMBER – EIGHT MONTHS LATER

Having dropped Evie at school, and taken Ross with her to see Aisha, who had a day off from the distillery, Cora sat in the sunny living room of her friend's flat above the bank on Bridge Street.

It was cosy, and full of light, and Aisha's furniture was an eclectic mixture of things she'd bought while travelling in the Middle East and Asia some years ago, alongside pieces she had picked up at estate sales in the area.

Aisha had an eye for design that was distinct, and often unusual, but when she put everything together in her little Georgian home, it all fit together like a perfect jigsaw puzzle, creating an effect that was mesmerising.

Cora liked coming to Aisha's place. Not only was it in the centre of the village, surrounded by shops, cafés, and two popular pubs, but it was a ten-minute walk from Cora's house on Montague Road.

It was a pretty route that Cora enjoyed, wandering along Hawthorne Lane, with its row of sandstone terraced bungalows, several with window boxes packed with colourful flowers in spring and summer.

At the end of the lane, as she turned onto Bridge Street, Glenmuick Church green sat across the junction, and each time she saw the striking steeple, Cora thought of the Christmas service the Campbells would take her to every year. With Christmas just three weeks away, she had decided to take the children this year, for the first time, and the thought of carrying on her own family traditions with them brought with it a quiet kind of joy that Cora couldn't quite explain.

She had arrived at Aisha's around 11 a.m., so she had made them an early lunch – toast with melted cheese for Ross, and for herself and Cora, gigantic veggie omelettes. Cora enjoyed having someone cooking for her for a change and had devoured the food as Aisha chatted about her boss, the manager of the distillery, whom she fancied, but didn't want to admit it.

As Cora listened to Aisha tell the familiar tale about the awkward silences in the staffroom, the fizz of unacknowledged chemistry, and the way Bruce Allen looked at her whenever she caught him staring, Cora suddenly missed that feeling. The sense of wanting someone in your life, to be part of a pair, rather than a lone wolf. The last time she'd felt it was with Fraser, and having been so badly burned by him, who knew if or when she'd ever feel that again. While it made her sad, it wasn't enough to force her back into the dating world, and now, with the children in her life, it wasn't as easy as it might once have been.

As she considered whether, unwittingly, they had provided a useful screen for her to hide behind, Cora frowned. But she had too many other things to think about at the moment, so, shaking off the thought, she focused on Aisha, who was still chatting as they cleared their dishes and made coffee.

With the kitchen tidy, they took their steaming mugs and settled themselves in the living room. The December sky was clear and bright, and a few tiny fingers of frost still clung to the outside of the glass on the bay window overlooking the street.

Ross, now almost two and a half, lay on his stomach on the

rug in front of Aisha's gas fire. He had lined his trains up, one behind the other, and as an episode of his favourite *Thomas the Tank Engine* played on the TV above the fireplace, he whispered to himself, naming the engines, and making soft whistling noises as he moved the trains around on the carpet.

Aisha and Cora sat either end of the dark-green sofa, as Cora watched Ross fondly. He missed Evie when she was at school these days, but Cora had promised him a special treat that afternoon when they went to pick his sister up. Cora was going to take them to Mackay's, a local institution of a store where she did much of her shopping for groceries. Aside from general provisions, the shop, with its two display windows and glossy green wood-panelled door, held an impressive range of artisan cheeses, and baked goods, not to mention a large selection of whiskies, wines, and over seventy-five types of gin.

While Cora loved to cook, she wasn't keen on baking or making desserts, so taking the children to Mackay's was a highlight for them. They loved to press their noses up against the long, L-shaped glass display cabinet and choose a special treat. Cora knew that Evie, whose fourth birthday was coming up in a few days, would choose a strawberry tart, and Ross a chocolate éclair.

Harry Mackay, the third generation of Mackay to run the business, was a barrel-chested man with the ruddy complexion of someone who spent a lot of time outdoors. He was well over six feet tall and had a head of thick red hair which fluffed out over his ears. His booming voice sounded like rusty nails being pulled from a plank, to Cora, but over the years, he had become very considerate of her, speaking more softly whenever she came into the shop. He could have been intimidating to those who didn't know him, but he was a gentle giant with a heart of gold, and was always pleased to see the children, whenever Cora took them with her.

She had asked Harry to order a special cake for Evie, with a unicorn on the top, and popping in today would give Cora the chance to settle up with him, and make sure he had things in hand in time for the party Cora had planned that weekend.

As Ross rolled onto his side and pushed a red engine across the carpet, still whispering to himself, Cora crossed her legs underneath herself.

'You're coming on Saturday, right?' She eyed Aisha, who was picking at the arm of the sofa with her thumbnail.

'Are you joking? With all those kids?' Aisha rolled her eyes, then grinned at Cora's shocked expression. 'I wouldn't miss it. Especially if I get another nose around Locharden House.' She laughed softly. 'And there will be a bouncy castle, right?'

Cora chuckled. 'Yes, Aisha. There will be a bouncy castle. And we've only invited Evie's kindergarten class, which is the grand total of eleven kids. Even you can manage that, I think.'

Aisha held her cup under her nose and widened her eyes. 'Yes, but that's eleven *four-year-olds*. That's like having seventy-seven annoying adults, all in the same room.'

Cora frowned, unsure where Aisha was going with this.

'You know, eleven times seven. Like in dog years?' Aisha shrugged.

'Oh, for God's sake. You're such a wimp!' Cora extended a leg and nudged Aisha's thigh with her foot. 'They're children, not velociraptors, and I'll be there to protect you.'

'You'd better. We're not all seasoned parents, you know.' She smiled kindly at Cora.

'I'm still learning, Aisha. But it's much more fulfilling than I thought it'd be. I mean, yes, don't get me wrong, I miss certain things.' She lowered her voice to a whisper. 'There are times when I want to lock up the house for a month and hike up Kilimanjaro, or just sleep in on a Sunday. Get out to the river on my own, at dawn, to fish, take in the silence and beauty, like I used to.' She paused, a flash of nostalgia making her eyebrows lift. 'But, honestly, I wouldn't trade them for anything.' She looked over at Ross, who now lay on his back with both legs pointing at the ceiling, a train in each hand and his white-blonde head twisted to the left so that he could see the TV. 'I mean, how could you resist that gorgeousness?'

Aisha nodded, putting her empty cup next to Cora's. 'I know, love. But cards on the table?' She held Cora's gaze, the familiar phrase Aisha used when she had something hard to say making Cora sit up straighter.

'Always.'

'I worry for you. I worry that you've made them your whole life, and then what if something happens to mess with that? Where will it leave *you*?' She hesitated. 'What if those useless arseholes come back one day, and want the rug rats back?'

Cora's stomach contracted, the words punching the breath from her. It wasn't that she didn't think about that happening. In fact, she'd had several nightmares about it recently. It was more that she had buried the possibility under the daily routine of caring for the children. Not letting the monster out of the cupboard, rather than opening the door and confronting it. But even as she tried to put the possibility of losing the children out of her mind, she could not ignore the fact that, should either of their parents come back, it might be in Evie and Ross's best interest to go back to them. Their well-being her priority, she knew that she would have to be strong enough to put her own needs aside, if it came to it, and the thought was gut-wrenching.

'I get it, Aisha. Believe me, I do. But after James's fall, and the guardianship being put in place, I worry about it a little less.' She let the words float around them, feeling guilty at not being totally truthful with her friend about her fears. 'I can't live under a cloud, so I choose to believe that it's all going to be OK.' She shrugged. 'How else can I keep looking forward?'

James had fallen in the bathroom and broken his hip, in July. It had come as a shock, and yet, Cora had realised that she'd almost been waiting for something – the catalyst that would make formalising the legality of her situation, as the children's guardian, even more important.

The guardianship process had taken almost four months to complete, but signing the official documentation in Dennis Burns's office in Ballater had taken less than ten minutes. Three signatures on three sets of papers and Cora's life had changed forever.

Everything had been witnessed and notarised by Dennis's assistant, and aside from the original document that was lodged with the solicitor, one copy was in James's safe, in the wine cellar under the kitchen, and the other in Cora's new safety deposit box at the bank. Knowing it was there was a comfort to Cora, and when she went to the bank in town, she'd occasionally get her box and take the brown envelope out, read the documents and then replace them, as if reading it again made it more real, seeing the words, over and over, giving them more weight.

James was now coping well with just one walking stick, and had a lovely caregiver called Queenie, who went in every day, except for weekends, when Cora took the children over to see him. He had initially resisted the help until Cora had laid down the law, saying that she couldn't be cook and carer to him, as well as managing the children. He had reluctantly agreed to meet Queenie, and now, nearly five months since his fall, she had become part of the furniture, often sitting with them both, while Cora cooked in the big airy kitchen.

Queenie was in her mid-sixties. A former nurse who, after leaving full-time ICU nursing, had gone into the care industry as a means to stay connected to people in the community, and to make herself useful, as she put it. She was a head taller than Cora's five feet five, and had long, strawberry-blonde hair that she wore in a high ponytail, tangerine wisps framing her round face. Kindness radiated from her hazel eyes, and she had a wicked sense of humour, which of course appealed to James.

Having her at Locharden House had taken a weight off

Cora's shoulders that she hadn't known was there. Namely, the worry that James was struggling more, physically, and with no one else living with him, he was by default becoming more of her responsibility. But now, his healing was going well, and even though he could have done with fewer visits per week, James had made no noises about reducing Queenie's hours, so Cora was keeping quiet, too.

Next to Cora, Aisha was tapping her cup with her fingernails, the tinkling sound tugging Cora back to the moment.

'Sorry, I was miles away...'

Aisha nodded. 'No problem.'

Cora smiled at her friend, then set her mug on the coffee table.

'So, back to the party. Everything kicks off at noon, but if you could come a bit earlier, I'd really appreciate some help getting all the food out.'

'Sure. Can I bring a friend?' Aisha's eyes were wide.

'Um, of course. Who?' Cora's eyebrows jumped as she tried to imagine who Aisha would want to bring to a children's birthday party.

'A certain distillery manager.' Aisha blushed, not something Cora had often witnessed.

'Are you serious?' Cora twisted to face her friend, her mouth gaping. 'Finally.'

'Got to start somewhere, and he's a nosy bugger. When he knows it's at Locharden, he'll definitely want to come.' Aisha gave a little snort. 'Help a girl out?'

Cora laughed, Aisha's pleading expression comical. 'Of course he can come, you nutter. It's about time I met this mythical creature of yours.'

Aisha tipped her head to the side, in question. 'Mythical?'

Cora nodded, unfolding her legs, and standing up. 'Yes, as in, a really good guy. A kind man, with a decent job, who likes you to the point of being slightly awkward around you. Who respects and admires you, as well as wants to rip your clothes off. You know? A unicorn.'

The friends laughed heartily together and, filled with lightness for all the good in her life, Cora walked to the window.

Down on Bridge Street, she could see the bakery opposite, almost smelling the warm farmhouse loaves and rolls that they made fresh each day, except Sundays. Next to it was the chemist, full of life's necessaries, plus some little cosmetic luxuries, and both shops had a steady flow of people filtering in and out, as always.

To the left of the chemist was the Ballater Gift Store. Another double-bay-fronted shop, filled with local and Scottish souvenirs – everything from snow globes with miniature models of Balmoral Castle inside them, to pots of jam, and Highland honey. The back wall was packed with woollen scarves in all imaginable clan tartans, and there were several rotating displays of stationery and postcards. It was an Aladdin's cave that served the annual influx of tourists to the village, and the elderly woman who ran it, Callie Dean, was a fixture in Ballater, her large Labrador, Sage, that slept next to the till, one of the most popular citizens in the village.

Evie loved to go in and talk to the dog while Cora chatted to Callie, Cora inevitably picking up a jar of jam, or a box of shortbread she didn't need, to support Callie's business.

As Cora watched the gentle activity below, comforted by the familiarity of the scene, a figure outside the chemist drew her eye.

The woman was tall, with a blunt blonde bob tipping her collar, and she was standing with her back to the road. She carried a large, crocheted handbag, and her black padded jacket had a fur-lined hood which lay flat behind her shoulders. Her legs were shapely, her jeans tucked into long leather boots, and even inside the bulk of the jacket, Cora could see that she was lean, with a narrow waist.

As Cora watched, the woman dipped her head, taking a mobile phone out of her bag, then held it up to her ear, turning her head slightly to the right.

Cora caught her breath, something familiar about the profile making her lean in and press her palm against the cool glass.

'What is it?' Aisha was standing at Cora's side.

Cora watched as the woman slid the phone away and, without turning around, walked into the chemist. Cora's heart was thumping wildly, her palms suddenly clammy, as she pushed out a shaky breath.

'Nothing. I just thought I saw...' She halted.

There was no way. It couldn't be her.

Could it?

9

The whole way home, Cora's heart was thumping in her chest. She couldn't banish the image of the profile of the woman in the street from her mind, or the sense of foreboding that it had left her with.

Behind her, Evie and Ross were singing Michael Finnegan at the tops of their voices in the back seat, their cakes from Mackay's in a paper bag between them.

Cora glanced in the rear-view mirror, seeing Evie conducting them, with impressively good rhythm, as she dipped from side to side in her car seat. Ross, as ever, was mimicking her, his cheeks rosy and his sky-blue eyes locked on his sister's profile.

'My goodness, you two. That's the fourth time,' Cora mock-tutted as they started the song from the beginning again, while she pulled up in front of the house and turned off the engine.

She got out of the car and as she walked around the front of the Volvo, a movement on her doorstep made her halt. A dark-clad figure sat there, the blunt blonde bob tipping the shoulders of the woman Cora had seen outside the chemist, just a few hours ago.

Cora's heart faltered, and she gripped her keys so tightly, they bit into her palm. There was no mistaking who this was, now that she could see the full face, the pale-green eyes, the wide mouth, and the long legs that unfolded as the woman stood up.

It was Holly. A slightly slimmer, more polished version, but definitely Holly, and seeing her standing there punched the air from Cora's lungs.

She froze to the spot as a lone bird of prey called above her, the call turning into a blood-curdling screech that sent a disconcerting buzz across Cora's skull. Her face felt as if it were on fire, her heart now beating like a kettle drum, as she forced a breath in, and then out. How could this be, after all this time? Why now?

As Cora stayed completely still, trying to make sense of what was happening, Holly walked down the garden path and halted at the gate as Cora, subconsciously, held her palm up like a stop sign.

After what this person had done, Cora didn't want her at her home, or in her life, never mind the children's. This was Cora's worst nightmare come to pass. After everything that had happened; the shock of finding the children on her doorstep, getting past the dilemma of whether to keep them with her but choosing to focus all her energy on them, then the months of them living happily, as a family, with this woman's reappearance, it could all be taken away.

As Cora's heart was flooded with both outrage and fear at what might be coming, as quickly as she saw it all falling apart, through the pain, there was a split second when she had to acknowledge a flicker of nostalgia in the back of her mind for the gentle patterns of her old life, before the drama had taken over.

Trying to process the unexpected moment of ambiguity, her thoughts going back to Evie and Ross, she turned and looked in the rear window of the Volvo. The children were unbuckling the straps of their car seats, Evie immediately wriggling out of hers and trying to drag Ross from his. Seeing the progress they were making, Cora panicked. There was no way she would open the car door, get them out and say, 'Oh. Look, guys. Your mummy came home.'

She turned her back on the car again, attempting to shield the children from seeing Holly, who was now leaning over the gate, trying to peer in the back window.

Knowing that the next few seconds were critical, if she was going to protect Evie and Ross from further trauma, Cora swallowed hard.

Holly's eyes flickered as she met Cora's gaze. 'Hi, Cora.'

Cora battled to keep her voice level. 'What are you doing here?' she whispered, the face in front of her sparking a slew of painful memories.

Holly looked taken aback, as if Cora had asked her something absurd. 'I've come to see my kids, of course. I heard they were here.' She leaned over the gate again, squinting at the car.

Cora felt a force swell up inside her that threatened to blot out all reason, or even civility. She locked eyes with Holly, and spoke deliberately, not wanting her to misunderstand anything that was about to be said.

'First of all, where the *hell* have you been?' Her breath hitched. 'Second, regardless of wherever you *have* been, for almost a *year*, what made you think that just turning up without the decency of phoning first was remotely acceptable? Third, there's no way I'm going to let you waltz into my home out of the blue, and act like you just popped out for a loaf ten months ago.' Cora was aware that her voice was dangerously growly, but she was surprised when Holly took several steps back up the path. 'Is Fraser with you?'

'No. I haven't seen him since I left.' Holly shrugged. 'Listen, Cora. A lot has happened, and I'll explain, if you'll let me. But, first, I want to see my kids.' Holly's voice was softer than Cora remembered, her eyes flicking back to the car, where Evie now had her face pressed against the glass, her palms either side of her cheeks as she licked the inside of the window.

Cora took only a second to respond, her hands going to her hips. The gall of this woman to think that she could just come back and take up where she left off, after almost a year, was beyond belief.

'No, not like this.' She stood her ground as Holly began to ease her way towards the end of the path again. 'You need to leave, Holly. I won't do that to them.'

Holly's mouth tightened, as she flipped her hair over to the opposite side of her head, a trademark move that had always driven Cora mad.

'Look, I know it's been a long time, but once you hear what I have to say...' Holly gave a hopeful little smile that Cora wanted to slap right off her pretty, angular face.

'I'm telling you to leave, Holly. Phone me this evening, or tomorrow, and we'll talk then.'

Holly made to protest, but Cora stepped forward, her determination clear.

'Think about *them*, for once, please. You need to go,' Cora insisted, pointing towards the end of the street, where Holly had lived as a child.

Holly's eyes tracked Cora's finger, taking a second to register.

'I'm staying at the Ballater Arms until I get sorted out. Can you come there for a drink later, so we can talk?'

Cora shook her head. 'I can't come to the bar tonight. In case you forgot, I have two children to take care of.'

Holly's eyes narrowed, and her jaw took on the old, hard-set line that Cora remembered.

'Can't you get someone to babysit?' Her face suddenly softened again. 'Please, Cora. I really need to explain everything to you.'

Cora's head was about to explode, the flood of emotions rushing through her making her feel light-headed, so she dropped her chin to her chest and exhaled.

'Phone me. I know you have my number.' She looked up and met Holly's green eyes, the exact colour of Evie's, the reminder that the child was not Cora's like a hot needle piercing her heart.

Holly hesitated, then nodded.

'OK, I'll go for now, but you can't keep me from seeing them, Cora. They're mine, and you don't really have a say.'

Cora crossed her arms, the words shooting from her mouth like bullets. 'As their legal guardian, I think you'll find I do have a say, Holly.'

Holly looked shocked, her brow folding into a deep frown. 'Since when?'

'I'm not getting into it now. I have to take the children inside.'

Holly hesitated at the gate, taking in Cora's expression, before sighing again.

'Fine, I'll phone you. And when you listen to what I have to say, you'll understand.'

Cora stepped to the side, once again blocking the children from seeing, as Holly passed her and began walking towards the end of the road. Cora waited until Holly got to the junction with Albert Road, then turned right and disappeared, before she opened the door, and helped the children out.

'Who was that?' Evie asked as she skipped to the front door.

'Just a friend.' Cora's voice cracked, and her hands were shaking, as she ushered Ross up the path, hurried them both inside, and turned the lock on the door, twice.

. . .

'What the hell?' Aisha's voice was high-pitched, and Cora winced, lifting the phone away from her ear. 'What does James say?'

'I haven't told him yet.' Cora chewed her bottom lip. 'I'm still in shock, I think.'

Three hours had passed since Cora had sent Holly packing, and as Cora had fed, bathed, and put the children to bed, she'd half expected the doorbell to ring, Holly coming back for another try.

Now, with the curtains tightly drawn on the street, and a glass of wine next to her, Cora sat on the sofa, her stomach still knotted.

'So, what are you going to do?' Aisha asked. 'If she comes back?'

Cora shook her head in the quiet of the living room. 'I'm not sure. I mean, I can't keep sending her away, Aisha. I think perhaps I need to hear her out on neutral territory. Listen to whatever explanation she has for this past ten months, and then, if I think she's genuine, and not going to disappear again the next day, I'll check with the solicitor first, but I'll probably have to let her see the children.' She grimaced, the very idea making her feel queasy. 'But on my terms.'

She could almost hear Aisha thinking, picture her expression of disapproval, but Cora knew that what she'd said was true. Holly was their mother and had rights that would probably override the guardianship order, should she contest it.

'I'll come and sit with the kids, if you want to go over there.' Aisha spoke softly. 'I mean it. I'll come right now, if you want.'

Cora's stomach flip-flopped. While it made sense, to get it over with, the thought of sitting down with Holly and talking in a civilised manner, after everything that she'd done, was hard to imagine. Also, Cora hadn't had the chance to tell James yet, and agreeing to meet Holly without him knowing felt like a betrayal.

'Thanks, Aisha, but I need to talk to James about it first. I'll see him tomorrow, then perhaps we can figure out a time for you to sit on babies, while I meet her?'

'Sure. Whatever you need.'

'Thanks.' Cora sipped some wine. 'It'll give me time to prepare myself, too.' She nodded to herself. Whatever Holly had to say would have to be spectacular to excuse her actions and, for once, Cora wasn't planning on rolling over and taking any crap.

She'd done enough of that for one lifetime.

The following day, James's reaction to the news was disconcerting, taking Cora by surprise. Rather than being angry, or railing at Holly's audacity, as she'd expected him to, he was silent, his face blank, as if he were in shock.

'Did you hear what I said, James?'

He nodded, as she glanced out of the window, seeing Ross trotting across the back lawn, chasing Duchess. The big dog seemed aware of the child's limited speed, and had slowed her pace, allowing Ross to catch up with her.

'Shall we sit in here?' Cora gestured towards the conservatory, where Lochnagar dominated the view, its rugged slopes spearing the sky and seeming to watch over them all.

James nodded again, following her out into the bright room.

Despite the overcast day, and the drizzle they'd had that morning as Cora had dropped Evie at school, the conservatory was warm, the terracotta pots of sage, dill, and thyme that Cora had placed on the deep windowsill scenting the space.

James sat opposite her in his usual spot, linking his long fingers in his lap.

'So, when are you going to meet her?' He eyed Cora, his tone cautious but controlled.

She shrugged. 'I don't know yet. I told her to phone me, so I suppose I'll wait to hear from her.'

At this, James leaned forward, his hands gripping his knees and his eyes darkening. 'Now listen to me, Cora. As far as I'm concerned, there is *nothing* that she can say or do that will excuse her for pulling a Houdini act.' He shook his head. 'Absolutely nothing.'

Cora nodded, gauging his mood as being dangerously explosive, now that the seal had broken on his initial shock. The last thing she wanted was for him to have a stroke, or something worse, so she gave him a calming smile.

'Do you want me to come with you? Show a united front?' The tanned skin of his forehead folded into a concertina of concern.

'I think it'll be better if I go alone. This time, anyway.' Cora took in his subsequent nod. 'I won't stand for any nonsense, don't worry.' She saw his mouth pucker in response. 'I'll let you know as soon as the meeting is set up, and then I'll come directly to you afterwards and fill you in.'

'Aye. Good.' He sat back, letting his hands settle on the wicker arms of the chair. As Cora made to get up, he said quietly, 'What do you think she'll have to say for herself?'

Cora shook her head. 'Honestly, I can't imagine. But unless she was in a coma, or taken hostage by terrorists, I don't think I'll be able to forgive her.' She gave him a half-smile, hoping to both lighten his spirits and show him that she wasn't going to be intimidated.

To her surprise, he let out a sharp laugh.

'Right enough. I suppose being held in a cave somewhere might be considered mitigating circumstances.'

Cora chuffed through her nose, watching him rise stiffly from the chair, then wince as he put weight on his left leg. Sympathy swept through her, but, to preserve his dignity, she kept it from her face as she followed him back into the kitchen.

'You'll phone me whenever you hear from her?' James asked.

Cora nodded. 'I will. I've got this, James. It's going to be OK.'

He eyed her for a moment, then patted her forearm. His face slackening, showing his weariness.

Cora hated to see him look defeated by anything, and her determination to stand strong gained ground within her. Whatever Holly had to say, and whatever reason she had for her behaviour, this was about the children, and, most important of all, Cora was going to protect them.

Even from their mother, if necessary.

10

Two days later, the Friday night before Evie's party, Cora left the children tucked up in bed, and Aisha in the living room with a giant bowl of popcorn watching TV.

Having heard from Holly, to arrange it, Cora was scheduled to meet Holly, and Cora's stomach was in knots. The Ballater Arms was only a ten-minute walk from the house, but it being a bitter cold night, Cora had worn her grey Arran sweater and heavy black cords, tucked into her leather boots. She'd then wrapped herself in her grey wool coat, and her red, Munro tartan scarf was wound around her neck and covering her lower lip. Her hair was stuffed under a soft, red wool beret, but by the time she approached the inn, her hands were stinging inside her gloves.

The building was Tudor, thick black beams crossing the creamy white frontage, and two windows on the second floor cantilevered out above the street. The leaded windows, with thick bubbled glass, glowed orange and as soon as Cora opened the heavy wooden door, the noise from inside sent a thrum through her head. Her cochlear implant heightened certain frequencies that made environments like this difficult for her.

Sighing, she slipped her hat off and swept her fringe away from her eyes, waiting for her hearing to adjust.

Scanning the room, she saw some familiar faces. The parents of a child in Evie's class at school sat at a table against the window, and Queenie and her flatmate, Mara, were at the far end of the room, by the big fireplace. Harry Mackay sat at the bar, his broad back taking up more than one place, and as she smiled at those she knew, Cora's heart began to thump at the prospect of seeing Holly again.

Unwinding her scarf, Cora winced at Holly's raucous laugh rising above the general hum in the bar, the familiar rasp making the hairs on Cora's arms stand to attention.

Across the crowded room, Holly was at a table in the corner. She had two men with her, neither of whom Cora recognised, and they all had half-full pint glasses in front of them. The older man had thinning grey hair and wire-rimmed glasses, and was wearing a faded denim jacket, his hands wrapped protectively around his glass. The other looked like he could have been related to the older man, perhaps his son, the younger man's hair in a long dark ponytail, a rose tattoo on the side of his neck and a black leather jacket bunched up on the seat next to him.

Cora hesitated, considering turning around and leaving right then, but as she hovered between two tables that were occupied by some of the local cricket team, Holly looked up and saw her.

Holly raised her hand in the air, her blonde hair swinging just below her jaw and her wide-set green eyes glued to Cora. Then Holly leaned in and said something to the older man on her right. He glanced over his shoulder at Cora, nodded, then both men got up and moved away towards the dartboard on the far wall.

Relieved that she didn't have to deal with awkward introductions when her nerves were already frayed, Cora wove between the remaining tables, until she reached Holly, who was now standing up.

'Hi Cora.' She smiled, her tone seeming genuinely warm. 'Thanks for coming.' She half-shouted, as she often had in the past, unsure how to pitch her voice when she talked to Cora.

Cora tried not to wince; her head was already swimming with layers of noise that made it hard to hone in on one voice. Focusing on Holly's mouth in case she missed her saying something more, Cora slipped her coat off, draping it over an empty chair.

'Busy in here tonight.' She pulled a chair out and sat opposite Holly, who resumed her seat. Being here felt surreal, and exchanging vapid niceties seemed ludicrous given the circumstances.

'Oh, sorry. I forgot.' Holly flapped her hand at her left ear. 'It is pretty loud.'

Cora nodded. 'It's OK for a while. I don't have long, though. Aisha is babysitting.' She halted, aware that her reference to the children could be hurtful.

'I get it.' Holly nodded, her cheeks prettily pink, and her turquoise sweater making her almond-shaped eyes impossibly green.

The new, blunt haircut brought out her angular features and as she tucked it behind one ear, revealing a sparkling diamond stud, Cora's hand went to her own hair, the long dark strands slightly frizzy from the rain, and the static from her hat that she'd dragged off at the door. Her sky-blue eyes were devoid of make-up, and as for jewellery, she wore only the pearl earrings her mother had given her when she'd turned sixteen.

'What do you want to drink?' Holly leaned forward. 'The heavy isn't bad. A bit metallic, maybe.' She nodded at her glass. 'They probably need to clean the lines.' She shrugged, the irony of this having been her establishment before she'd disappeared not lost on Cora.

'I'm not thirsty.' She shook her head, the idea of drinking anything with Holly making her feel queasy.

Holly appeared nervous, her eyes flicking back and forth to the door as if she was planning an escape, but when she finally met Cora's gaze, there seemed to be no guile in her expression.

In the past, Cora had often felt that Holly was performing, playing a part that kept her encased behind her sarcasm, and sometimes harsh language. But there was something different in her manner, how she held herself now, the way she kept sucking in her bottom lip, and spinning the stained beer mat between her thumb and forefinger, that all smacked of vulnerability. Not something Cora recalled having seen in her before.

Despite wanting to be cool and unyielding with her nemesis, Cora now felt pity begin to swell insider her, the last thing she had expected. As she leaned her elbows on the table, Holly leaned forward too, keeping her voice metered this time.

'Are you ready to listen to me, Cora? Because I know I owe you an explanation.'

Cora's eyebrows jumped at the easy admission. 'Yes, you do.'

Holly nodded, then lay her palms flat on the table either side of her now empty glass.

'First of all, I want to thank you from the bottom of my heart. For taking care of the kids.' She paused, as, taken aback, Cora stared at Holly's mouth. 'Things weren't good between me and Fraser. They hadn't been for a while. We were fighting like cat and dog, and you know how he can be.' She dipped her chin, apparently waiting for Cora to meet her eyes.

Sensing that, Cora looked up, seeing Holly's hopeful expression, as if she was waiting for Cora to commiserate on the tiresome habits of their mutual friend, and Cora's erstwhile husband. But she hadn't come here just to dump on Fraser, rather to learn what catastrophic event he'd brought about that had caused Holly to leave her children on the doorstep and bolt, so, rather than speak, Cora refocused on Holly's mouth. Whatever else she had to share was too important to miss or misunderstand.

'Well, everyone knows he's no picnic, and after we'd been going at each other for weeks, something just snapped.' Holly sat back, letting her hands drop to her lap. 'I couldn't stand it anymore.'

Cora frowned. 'Stand *what*, exactly? And where is he, anyway?'

Holly shrugged again. 'The way he loped around all the time, never taking responsibility for anything. Fannying his time away in that poky room he called a studio.' She nodded in the direction of the door, then, seemed to recalibrate her thoughts. 'I had to get away, for the sake of my mental health.' She halted, seeing Cora's eyebrows lift. 'I was in a state, Cora. Not coping with the kids, or running the pub, never mind Fraser being like a third child rather than a partner.'

Cora let the last statement sink in, trying to decide whether it was entirely fair.

'I reached breaking point, and I had to go. It wasn't like I planned it, but once I got away, and into the treatment centre, it was such a relief.' She nodded to herself. 'I can't even tell you.'

Cora frowned at the casual referral to a treatment centre, unsure what she was supposed to say. But relief from what? Being a mother? Was she serious?

'OK...' Her comment felt devoid of compassion, but it was all Cora could come up with that wouldn't sound like a reprimand.

'I went through loads of one-on-one therapy, group sessions, and workshops.' Holly eyed Cora expectantly, then continued. 'I was almost catatonic when I got there, and the therapist told me that I had to cut off all communications with my triggers and focus on myself and healing. I wanted to phone, to check on the kids, but one day of feeling a bit better led to the next and then the next. Then I felt that isolating myself, until I was truly better, was better for the children, too. It was hard, Cora, and a lot of work, but I knew I had to focus on getting well before I could come back, get my life back on track, and be a good mother again.'

At this, Cora's defences surged, but before she could respond, Holly continued.

'I won't go into all the details, but I'm back, I'm better, and I want my kids, Cora.'

The words colliding inside her head amidst the clang of other voices behind them, Cora's throat tightened, the response she needed to find suddenly beyond her grasp.

'I know it was wrong to disappear like that, but I wasn't well, Cora. You have to try to understand.'

To Cora's amazement, Holly's eyes filled, and despite herself, Cora felt the long-held knot of anger at her core ease a little.

'I know what it's like to feel overwhelmed, Holly. Believe me. But to leave your children like that. I mean, how bad was it?' She couldn't let her off that easily, but the new vulnerability in Holly's manner was making Cora control her anger.

Holly tipped her head to the side and dabbed at her eyes with a tissue. 'Was what?'

'Whatever Fraser did to make you go off like that.' Cora held her breath, readying herself for him having another affair, running up credit card debts, drinking away his unhappiness, any of which she could accept as possible.

'It doesn't matter now, and that's between me and him, anyway.' Holly shook her head sadly.

Cora's jaw clenched at the casual dismissal of a critical factor of this last ten months, that was so much more significant than the fallout of a private disagreement between Holly and Fraser.

'How can you say that, Holly? It was about much more than

whatever went on between you and him. It involved *me*, too. In fact, it ended up being more about me and the children than about either of you,' she snapped, her hands beginning to tremble as adrenaline swept through her. 'This whole thing has taken over my life. And James's. Did you even consider him in all this? Never mind the utter devastation you created in Evie and Ross's lives.'

Holly looked shocked, perhaps at Cora having the temerity to fight back, or put herself and James into the equation.

'The point is, Cora, that Fraser is gone, but *I* am here now. And I want to make things right. To put my family back together, at least part of it.' She sniffed, her mouth dipping sadly. 'I never meant to stay away this long, but things being as bad as they were with me...' She placed her palm on her chest. 'It took longer than I thought to get to a healthy place.'

Cora tried to picture Holly in a group therapy session, sitting in a circle of people dealing with their challenges, in a mature and sensitive way, but the image wouldn't solidify. The Holly that Cora had known would have scoffed at the concept of sharing anything that would leave her appearing vulnerable. What she knew to be true of Holly, and what she was now hearing, was a puzzling juxtaposition.

As Holly talked on about how she was determined to repair things with the children, and Cora, too, despite feeling dubious, Cora tried to listen with an open heart. Being in a dark place, with little hope of change, never mind understanding or affection, was something that she could relate to, and while she was furious, and afraid of what Holly's reappearance would mean for her and the children, something deep inside Cora realised she couldn't completely condemn her.

As Holly described her path to recovery, Cora once again began to imagine a scenario where the children were back with their mother, and Cora returning to her ordered, serene life. The idea of that transition now sent a spiral of such searing loss through Cora that it made her blink away tears, but then, as she pictured the silvery river, the elegant arches of the Dee bridge filled in by a tangerine dawn behind them, the electrifying tug of her line as a trout took the bait, or the squelch of damp moss and leaf mulch under her feet, at the base of Craigendarroch as the sun began to set over the Cairngorms, a longing began to reawaken inside her.

Would it be so bad to go back to that life, if the children were happy, and safe with their mother? Could she possibly face giving them up, if it meant she got her life back?

The following morning, James slammed the fridge shut with such force that Cora jumped.

The kitchen at Locharden House was warm from the Aga, and outside, the December sun had made an appearance overhead, albeit watery, where the bouncy castle was tethered to the back lawn.

Cora had been working on the food for the party all morning, while Aisha had kindly taken the children to the park for a couple of hours, and now the countertops were littered with platters of miniature sandwiches, bite-sized savoury pastries, and ramekins full of sliced fruit. The giant blueberries looked almost black against the scarlet of the strawberries that Cora had bought at Mackay's that morning.

The unicorn cake sat under a cloche, the decoration a pastel triumph, including a rearing white unicorn under a rainbow, and a spray of golden stars in an arc beneath its hooves. Above the unicorn, *Happy 4th Birthday Evie!* was written in lemon icing, and tiny lemon-coloured rosettes circled the edge of the cake.

As Cora washed her hands and dried them, James walked over and sat at the table, his pale eyes hooded.

'She can go through all the damn therapy she wants, Cora,

but that woman walked away from her children, and her marriage, albeit to my feckless son. She deserves *no* consideration, or at least a lot less than you seem to want to give her,' he huffed.

Cora walked to the table.

'All I'm saying is that she seemed genuine when she said she regrets walking away, but that she's put the work in to get better and wants to repair things with the children. I went in there wanting to condemn her, to call her a damn waste of space and storm out, but I found myself believing her.' She paused. 'She's hurt us all so much, James, and I can't believe I'm saying this, but at the end of the day, good or bad, she *is* their mother.'

He made another huffing sound. 'She gave birth to them, but she's been no kind of mother,' he grumbled.

Cora met his eyes, her chest aching at both the depth of his anger, and from her own hurt. By giving Holly the benefit of the doubt, she was potentially putting the security of her role in the children's lives at risk, but what else could she do?

'I suppose we can't understand other people's struggles, James. Or what goes on inside their marriages, behind closed doors.'

His frown deepened. 'I know that's true, but being a bit overtired, frustrated by work, or having a lazy oaf of a husband – *none* of it is any justification for what she did.' He shook his head. 'I'm sorry, Cora, but even you can't persuade me that she is anything other than selfish and narcissistic.' He took a moment, then looked aghast. 'You didn't say she could come today, did you? I'll not have anything spoil this for Evie.'

'Of course not.' Cora shook her head. 'I'd never spring that on the children. I told her that you and I would talk about everything and that together we'd decide when she can see them.'

Cora's throat began to clog as she pictured the reunion, the picture-perfect moment when Evie recognised her mother, the hugs and happy tears as Holly kissed her daughter and promised never to leave her again. It was poignant, but cripplingly painful, the potential for the children's room to be empty again not something Cora could contemplate.

'I think it should be at my house, or maybe the park if we want somewhere neutral. What do you think?' She stood up and busied herself rearranging the platters on the countertop. Thinking about the meeting was overwhelming, her determination to be the children's advocate and protect them from any more hurt or disappointment making her hands shake.

'It should be at your house. Where the children feel safe and happy.'

Cora considered what he'd said, the sense of it making her nod.

'Right. Yes, of course.'

'When?' The single word held so much significance that Cora felt trapped by it.

'Monday, or Tuesday maybe? After Evie gets back from school.' She lifted a heavy platter with egg sandwiches on it and slid it into the fridge, the scratch of the ceramic against the glass shelf sending a tinny screech through her implant that made her grimace.

'I'd offer to be there, but Queenie is taking me into Aberdeen for X-rays that afternoon.' He patted his left leg. 'Not sure how late we'll be back, but hopefully that'll be me done with doctors for a while.'

'I hope so, too.' Cora nodded. 'I asked Holly about Fraser, but she didn't seem to know where he is.' She wasn't sure how James would react to this last piece of news, so she held her breath as he stood up and, using his stick, carefully walked to the sink.

'Do you believe her?' He squinted, as if asking himself the question.

Cora considered it for a moment.

'I'm not sure. But why would she hide it if she knew? I suppose it changes nothing at this stage, though, either way.'

'Aye, I suppose not.' He shook his head slowly. 'They were a mismatch from the start.' His eyes drooped, the knuckles of the hand on his stick turning white.

Concern for him bubbling up inside her, Cora moved to his side.

'How about you put your feet up for a bit, before the noisy mobsters arrive for the party?' She slid her hand under his elbow. 'Just have a nap in the living room if you prefer. Easier than negotiating the stairs without Queenie.'

She felt his arm tense, then he leaned his head towards her and spoke quietly, the citrus smell of his hair tonic making Cora hold her breath.

'You always know what I need, Cora. It's a gift.' He hugged her arm tightly, then let her lead him into the living room, where the morning sun streaming in the windows was creating a crosshatch design over the furniture and the wood floor. 'Just plop me in the chair.' He waggled his stick at a soft, damask armchair near the fire, its twin opposite it was where Rosemary had loved to sit and read in the afternoons. Then Duchess, who had followed them in from the kitchen, turned in three tight circles and flopped down at James's feet.

Cora helped James get settled, then draped a light rug over his knees, the sight of his drained face worrying her.

'I'll come and wake you in an hour or so.'

He smiled at her, then, as she was about to leave, he said her name. 'Cora?'

'Yes?' She halted in the doorway.

'Whatever you decide to do about Holly, you know I support you one hundred per cent, don't you?'

Grateful for the vote of confidence when she wasn't convinced that she knew what was best herself, she nodded. 'Thanks, James. I know that.'

He eyed her. 'One thing I'm certain of is that you will do what's best for the children, no matter what this mean old bugger thinks.' He patted his own chest, the veins on his hand standing out under the thinning skin. 'I have a habit of holding grudges, you know. Not giving folk the benefit of the doubt.' He paused, as if recalling instances in his past when he'd been less than fair, and taken aback at this spontaneous confession, Cora wondered if he was thinking about Fraser. 'I trust you implicitly, and your judgement is impeccable, so I'll accept whatever you decide to do.' His eyes looked heavy, as if keeping them open was an effort.

'Thanks, James. That means the world.' She nodded. 'But I'll not do anything without discussing it with you first. Be sure of that.'

He met her eyes, his now watery and bright. 'You are a good woman, Cora Campbell. My Fraser never deserved you.'

The reference to Fraser was confirmation that his son had indeed been on his mind, and Cora was surprised by the twinge of sadness that followed James's last statement. While she would not stand up for Fraser, she also knew that he wasn't a wholly bad person, just a troubled one.

When she considered the different ways they had been raised, the stark contrast struck her again, as it had when they'd decided to get married. She had moved from one foster family to another, then in and out of residential homes, never knowing from one month to the next when she might have to pack her little suitcase again. Fraser had grown up at Locharden House with both his parents, surrounded by luxury, and privilege that he seemed to want to shed, but rather than feel sorry for herself, or envy him that, she found she pitied her ex-husband.

One thing she had learned even before the Campbells had taken her in was not to judge other people when you had no experience of what they were dealing with. So, despite everything that had happened, she couldn't judge Fraser too harshly, when he'd grown up with a father who told him regularly what a disappointment he was.

In the time they'd been married, Fraser had been kind to her, caring, and even thoughtful. She knew he could do the right thing, which made this abandonment of his new family more puzzling, and heartbreaking, than disappointing.

Despite the deep scars he had left on her heart, Cora still held on to some of the good memories, just as she had learned to do as a hurt and lonely child.

11

The following Wednesday, it had been a miserable rainy December day, and Cora and Evie had both got soaked getting into the car at school. Now they were upstairs drying their hair, while Ross marched around Cora's bedroom, singing 'Twinkle, Twinkle, Little Star', the latest song that he'd learned.

Holly was due to arrive at Cora's house in half an hour, and Cora was nervous. She had decided not to tell the children about their mother's visit until now, and finding the right words was proving impossible. She had tried to construct a couple of gentle ways to mention their mother, find a way to bring her back into their young consciousnesses, but everything sounded forced, and confusing.

Having decided to let things unfold as they would, Cora played the hairdryer on a long hank of Evie's hair. Her eyes were closed as Cora dried the last section between her shoulders, the golden locks bringing Holly's image to mind more vividly.

'Your hair is so pretty, Evie. It's the same colour as your mummy's.' The words broke loose of their own accord, and Cora tried not to let her nervousness show as she concentrated on brushing, but when she caught Evie's expression in the mirror, it was pure confusion.

'No, your hair is brown.' Evie frowned.

Cora's heart contracting at Evie's sweet acceptance of Cora as the mother figure in her life, she smiled at the little girl.

'I know it's been a long time, Evie, but do you remember your mummy, Holly?'

Evie turned to face Cora, her lips pursing, then, after what felt like an eternity, she nodded slowly.

'Mummy, when we were Mummy and Daddy and us?' She pointed at Ross, who had stopped pacing around the bed and was staring at them both, his thumb now in his mouth.

'Yes, that's right.' Cora put the hairdryer and brushes away in the drawer of her dressing table. 'And do you remember when she went away, and you and Ross came to stay with me?' She worked to keep her voice light, with no trace of emotion, or agenda for the perceptive child to pick up on.

'I don't know.' Evie frowned. 'When did she go?'

Cora took a moment, then needing to feel her closer, drew Evie into her side.

'It was almost a year ago, chickadee, when you were still three, and Ross was just one and a half.' She looked down at Ross, who had also moved in next to her, his pudgy hand gripping her jeans.

Now two and a half, and increasingly chatty, usually singing, or humming to himself as he played, Ross's sudden silence was sightly unnerving. Cora hadn't been sure if he'd have any memory of his parents, having been so young when they'd left, and she thought it was possible that he was just picking up on Evie's tone, but Cora felt his grip tighten, so she laid her palm gently on his back to reassure him.

'I wanted to tell you both that something good has happened. Your mummy has come back here, and she would like to see you.' Cora felt Evie tense, a child now pressing in on each side of her. 'Do you think you'd like to see her?' Cora's throat was knotting, so she forced a swallow.

Evie took a moment, then shrugged.

'I don't know.' She stepped away from Cora and lifted her cardigan from the back of the chair at the dressing table.

Regretting that she had left it so close to Holly's visit to broach this, Cora leaned down and hefted Ross up onto her hip.

'What about you, Ross?'

He put a little palm on her cheek, his eyes locked on hers and mimicked his sister. 'Don't know.' His gaze flicked to Evie, then back to Cora as if he was seeking the right answer, from either of them, then he frowned. 'You're my mummy.'

Kissing him on the cheek, her heart feeling as if it might shatter, Cora mustered all the positivity she could.

'Well, I think it will be nice to see her, so let's go downstairs and put the kettle on. Evie, you can choose some biscuits for the tray, and, Ross, you can find your favourite engines to show her. How about that?'

Evie hugged the cardigan to her chest and, without answering, walked out into the hall. Ross looked unsure of whether to follow her or to cling to Cora, but then he snuggled in closer, and relishing the intensity and comfort of his hug, Cora went into the hall and followed Evie down the stairs.

In the kitchen, Cora put Ross down and then began setting a tray with mugs, and a delicate floral plate her mother had always used for visitors. It was hand-painted with irises and each time Cora used it, it reminded her of Eliza, and the way she would bake all morning if her friends from the lawn bowling club were coming for tea.

'Evie, can you get the biscuits please?' She pointed at the large, ceramic jar on the counter by the fridge. 'Can you reach?'

Evie was chewing the sleeve of her cardigan, her cheeks pulsing.

'Don't do that, love,' Cora chided her softly, seeing the slightly distant way Evie was staring out of the window.

Dropping the cardigan onto a chair at the table, Evie then stood on tiptoe and slid the jar towards her.

Nervous that she might drag it right off the counter, Cora stepped in and helped her carry it to the table.

'Now, you choose whichever ones you want to put on the plate, OK?'

Ross was standing at the opposite side of the table, his chin pressed up against the edge. 'I want a jammy one.' He pointed at the packet Evie was holding. 'Can I?' He looked at Cora, his eyes hopeful.

'Just one.' She smiled as she wagged her finger at him, and he clapped his hands together.

Evie handed him a biscuit, then hesitated.

'But *she* can't have any jammy ones. Those are our favourites.' Her mouth dipped as she put the packet back in the jar and replaced the lid.

Cora could almost feel the flash of anger running through the child, her shoulders raised towards her ears and her mouth set in a firm line. Perhaps she had more memory of Holly, and being abandoned, than Cora realised? That being the case, was allowing Holly to come here the right thing to do?

Holly sat on one of the chairs by the fire. She had arrived a few minutes earlier in a slim-fitting leather coat and long black boots, carrying a plastic bag from the gift store on Bridge Street. As soon as she'd walked into the living room, Cora had felt as if invading forces had stormed her favourite beach, the sensation bizarre and unsettling.

Cora was glad that she had put on a little eyeliner, the dark brown making her blue eyes glow, and the swipe of rouge she'd added highlighted her high cheekbones. Her cashmere V-neck sweater was camel-coloured and though slightly pilled, still made her feel more stylish than she did in her usual Arrans or sweatshirts.

When the doorbell rang, Evie and Ross had stayed at the kitchen table, and only after some concerted coaxing, and the offer of a trip to the play park at the weekend, had they followed Cora into the living room.

Evie was now close to Cora's side and Ross was behind her, his customary grip on her jeans making it hard to walk.

'Here we are.' Cora knew her voice sounded overly bright, but her nerves were getting the better of her. 'Who wants tea?' She looked down at Evie, who was staring at Holly as she stood up and made to walk towards the child.

'*Evie?*' Holly's eyes were wide, as if unsure that this was indeed her daughter.

As Holly stepped forward, her arms opening, Evie grabbed Cora's leg, her fingers pinching the flesh of Cora's thigh through the denim.

'Ow.' Despite herself, Cora winced, making Evie look up at her, her eyes questioning. Seeing the confusion there was like a vice closing on Cora's heart, so she immediately pivoted. 'Would you like to give your mummy a biscuit?' She lowered the tray, putting it within Evie's reach. Saying the word mummy was jarring, its significance immense.

'No.' Evie shook her head, moving a little further behind Cora's hip.

Holly's smile wavered as her arms dropped back to her sides, the difference she'd seen in Evie obviously having knocked the wind from her.

'You are so big now.'

Cora eased herself forward and put the tray on the coffee table, both children still gripping her jeans.

'She's a very big girl who goes to school now. And Ross is going to be as tall as a tree, soon.' She glanced down at Ross, who was sucking his thumb, his lips curving downwards around it as he stared at Holly from hooded eyes.

Holly turned her attention to her son, and her expression changed from one of surprise to disbelief. 'Ross. Look at you. I hardly...' She halted as her voice seemed to fail her. 'So grown up,' she whispered, her head shaking slightly.

Holly's unguarded reaction to seeing her son was touching, and Cora felt sympathy emerging under her nerves as she made her way awkwardly to the sofa. Releasing the children's grip on either leg, she sat down and helped them both settle in next to her.

Unsure where to go next, how to navigate this surreal meeting, Cora swallowed hard, wishing for inspiration. As she started to say something about the rain, Evie edged forward on the sofa and pointed at the bag at the side of Holly's chair.

'What's that?' she asked, blinking rapidly.

'Oh, it's for you, and Ross,' Holly gushed, as she leaned down and lifted the bag onto her lap. 'I brought you both a pressie.'

Evie looked up at Cora, silently asking for permission to cross the room, and as Cora nodded encouragingly, the child stood up, her hands in tight fists at her side.

'Come on then.' Holly smiled. 'They won't unwrap themselves.' She pulled out a long narrow parcel wrapped in paper covered in giant pink roses, then a small silver-wrapped box with a red ribbon around it.

Evie edged forward, glancing back at Cora, who was trying to smile.

'It's OK, chickadee.' Cora nodded again, as Holly's eyebrows lifted.

'*Chickadee?*'

Cora felt suddenly defensive, and it took all her willpower to keep that from her voice.

'Yes, it's just for fun.' She watched as Evie approached Holly, her eyes on the gifts on Holly's lap.

Refocusing on the little girl, Holly said brightly, 'Guess which one is yours?'

Evie was now standing directly in front of her mother, her scarlet sweatshirt looking oddly garish next to Holly's beige coat.

Evie pointed to the box. '*That* one!'

Holly shook her head and laughed, a raspy sound that took Cora back in time to the many occasions she had heard it in the past, its implication that Holly had won some unconscious battle or scuppered a clever plan to scam her.

'Nope. This one.' She held the long parcel out to Evie. 'I hope you like it.'

Evie took the gift from her hand and held it up to her chest, then turned and walked back to Cora, where she wiggled up onto the sofa again. As she started to unwrap it, Ross slid off the sofa and padded across the room.

'Me too. I want a present.' He held his hand out, and Cora couldn't help herself.

'Ross, it's not polite to ask.'

Holly's mossy eyes snapped to Cora's, and she clearly saw annoyance at her correcting him. 'He's fine, Cora. He's just a wee boy.' Holly handed the box to Ross. 'Want me to help you, matey?' She made to untie the ribbon, but Ross backed away, holding the gift behind him.

'No. I want my mummy to.'

The oxygen seemed to be sucked from the room as the word floated above them, like a helium-filled sword, its point aimed directly at Holly's heart. Cora sucked in a breath as Evie, seemingly unaware, tore the paper off her gift, revealing a rainbow-coloured, fluffy worm with big plastic eyes, each with a green disc inside that jiggled. Evie looked at the toy, then over her shoulder at Cora.

'This is for babies.' Her mouth dipped as she pushed the paper off her knee onto the floor and tossed the worm onto the sofa next to her.

'Evie. Say sorry.' Cora felt her face flush, and Holly seemed genuinely stung.

'You used to like those.' Holly pointed at the worm. 'You had an orange one that we put in the washing machine once, and it fell apart. Remember?' She looked crestfallen now and, despite everything, Cora's heart ached for her as Cora tried to imagine how it would feel to have your own children not know you, or even appear to want to.

Evie shook her head.

'Sorry.' Cora met Holly's gaze, seeing the pale-green eyes awash with hurt.

Holly then looked over at Ross, who had finally pulled the ribbon off the box, but couldn't get the lid off, so he handed it to Cora.

'Help me, Mumma.' He looked up at her, his blue eyes adoring.

Across the room, Holly audibly gasped. The sound, to Cora, was like the tide slapping on the riverbank, but there was no gentleness to it. Rather it was raw, grating both inside her head and her heart.

Evie's eyes snapped to Cora's profile, Evie's mouth forming an O shape as she leaned back on the sofa, as if she were choosing Cora, too.

Her throat knotting, Cora took the lid off the box and handed it back to Ross, who pulled out a blue plastic rattle in the shape of a dumbbell, his name etched on it in big red letters. He frowned, tapping the rattle on the sofa, then dropped it on the floor.

The last ten months seemed to have been lost on Holly, her having no sense of what stage her children were at, or currently engaged by. Witnessing it was sad, but then a tiny part of Cora felt almost gratified. Holly had given up these precious little people as if they were used books, or old toys destined for the village jumble sale. How could she waltz back in after almost a year and expect things to be just as they were when she'd walked away?

The children had sent a clear message. They considered Cora to be their mother, and even though she knew it had hurt Holly to witness it, Cora couldn't help but feel slightly less afraid that she'd lose them. All the love, and care, and attention she had given Evie and Ross over the past ten months had forged a bond between them that was strong.

Perhaps even stronger than Cora knew.

12

The children were now in the kitchen, where Cora had given them drinks.

'I'll be back in a few minutes, OK?' She pushed Ross's chair closer to the table. 'Be good, now.'

Evie bit into her Jammie Dodger and nodded. 'OK, Mummy.'

Cora smiled at her, grateful that Evie was reinforcing Cora's significance in her life. But, this time, Cora's conscience kicked in, making the victory she'd felt a few minutes earlier feel a little less shiny.

Holly was standing looking out of the window, her handbag slung over her shoulder and her arms crossed. The line of her back was taut, as if she were struggling to hold something in, something that was battling to free itself.

Cora hesitated in the doorway, then walked in and slowly closed the door behind her.

'Are you all right?'

When Holly turned to face her, her eyes were full.

'Well, I suppose I deserved that.' She shrugged miserably. 'I just thought they might be a bit more pleased to see me. How naïve of me.' She huffed through her nose. 'Evie is angry with me, that's obvious. But Ross, he doesn't even seem to...' She stopped, shaking her head.

Cora took a moment to compose herself.

'They are just children, Holly. They were little more than babies when you left, and they're anxious. Unsure of you. It's only to be expected.' She hoped she hadn't sounded condescending, but there was no kinder way of putting it.

While Evie had seemingly retained some memories of Holly, enough to have made her feel angry towards her now, it was apparent that Ross had no clue who Holly was, and it was clear that Holly knew that, too.

Cora wanted to get back behind the hard shell she'd had to grow as a child, and which the Campbells had gently worn away with their kindness, and love, but having spent so long without parents of her own, deep inside Cora there was a nut of acknowledgement that the current arrangement, while giving *her* something that she'd always known she needed, might not be what was ultimately best for the children. But until Holly could prove that she was back to stay, and that her mental health was stable and where it needed to be, Cora would hold her ground. She owed that to Evie and Ross.

Holly was staring at Cora, her eyes full of questions.

'So where do we go from here?' Holly hugged her handbag to her chest.

Cora shook her head. 'We take one day at a time, Holly. There are a lot of questions still to be answered. Things to be worked on and repaired.' She nodded towards the kitchen. 'But nothing will change as far the children are concerned. Not for the moment, anyway.'

Holly looked stricken. 'But I'm back.' She gaped at Cora. 'I'm their mum and they need to come home with me.'

Cora's insides folded over, her sense that the safe and

ordered life she'd created for the children was about to enter another phase of turmoil overwhelming.

'I know you're their mum, Holly. But there are other factors here. Much more in play than pure genetics.' Her voice was threatening to crack.

'But no court in the country would support you, against their *actual* mother, Cora. You must know that?' Her voice had the old, familiar edge to it.

The implication of the word 'court' sent a spike of fear through Cora, which instantly morphed into anger.

'No one is talking about court, Holly. The guardianship order is fully legal and was put in place on the basis that you abandoned them.' She halted, seeing the impact of her words widen Holly's eyes. 'I think you should go home now. Take a few days to get settled and then we'll talk about you seeing them again.'

Holly stood still, her full lips working on themselves as she blinked repeatedly. 'I'm not threatening you, Cora. There's no need to be so defensive.' She let her handbag drop to her side. 'I just want to see them. Be with them.' She shrugged. 'They're *mine*.'

Despite the calmer tone, Cora heard the determination in Holly's words, and rather than get sucked into conflict, Cora simply nodded.

'I'm not disputing that fact. I'm just saying it's not as simple as that, anymore.'

Holly took a few moments to process what Cora had said, then slung her bag back over her shoulder.

'Can I at least say goodbye to them?'

Cora hesitated, knowing she couldn't say no, and then opened the door.

'Of course you can.'

Holly walked past her, a waft of musky perfume lingering in her wake.

Cora followed, a few paces behind, and hovered in the kitchen door as Holly stood next to the table. Ross was intent on his biscuit and didn't look up, but Evie glanced at Cora, then met Holly's eyes.

'OK, kiddos. Mummy's got to go now, but I'll be back to see you soon.' She leaned in as if to kiss Evie, but the child instantly pulled away shyly.

'You're *not* my mummy.' Her voice was soft, but the handful of words were so cutting that, once again, Cora heard Holly gasp.

Cora held her breath, hoping that Holly wouldn't press this. Persist in establishing her rights when her daughter was so clearly confused. Just as Cora was about to move forward and intervene, divert the tension towards something less prickly, Holly stepped back from the table.

'Right, well... I'll see you soon then.' She lifted a hand and gave a wave as Evie took a few moments, then slid off the chair and padded out of the room.

Holly watched her go, and Cora caught the sadness in Holly's eyes, then she shrugged, and looked at Ross. Rather than try to kiss him, she simply patted his head. An awkward gesture that the child seemed unaware of as he munched his biscuit. Getting no response from him, Holly sighed, turned, and walked into the hall.

As Cora followed her, then opened the front door, Cora waited for Holly to say something, but she walked past Cora and then paused on the top step. Turning to Cora, her face was unreadable. The pale eyes empty of the anguish Cora had seen just moments before.

'Cora, I know this is difficult, and that you've been here for them all this time, but Evie and Ross are my family. They're all I have left, and I need them with me.' Holly paused, as an image of packing the suitcase with their belongings made Cora's heart ache. 'I don't want to argue with you or upset them.' Holly gestured over her shoulder. 'But I'm better now, and at some point, they're going to come home with me. I'll do whatever it takes to prove to you that I am the best option for them.'

Cora held her gaze, determined to keep her face impassive. If Holly was set on this path, perhaps she was genuine in her remorse and wish to reconnect with her children, but whatever happened next, the law was still on Cora's side. Until that changed, the children were going nowhere. There was no way she would allow Evie and Ross to go back to live with someone whom they didn't know or feel comfortable with. Genetics be damned.

Two days later, while Evie was at school and Ross was napping upstairs, Aisha and Cora were curled up at either end of the sofa, across from the Christmas tree at the right side of the fireplace. The tree was heavily wrapped with popcorn chains that the children had made with Cora, something the Campbells had introduced her to, and bands of silvery tinsel that glittered in the sunlight seeping in the window.

'So do you think she'll get a lawyer or something?' Aisha asked.

'No idea. I mean, I hope not.' Cora paused. 'The last thing I want is some legal battle. It won't be good for the children, or James. Any of us, honestly.'

Aisha nodded, her scarlet hair newly cropped close to her head.

'But if she does go down that route, what will you do? Do you think a court would support your guardianship?'

Cora shrugged.

'I've done some research, and it seems that if the birth mother can prove that she has sought help for her issues, is in a stable living situation and is able to support the children, it'd be a hard case for me to win...' Her words trailed as she felt the sickening tug of a potential separation.

'Well, that's bloody nonsense,' Aisha huffed. 'So, they just forget that she walked away from them? Dumped them, basically. She decides to come back, and all is forgiven?' Her chocolatey eyes were fiery.

'I know. But, Aisha, she is their mother. As long as she is truly healthy, and stable, and wants them back...' Old memories began to clog Cora's throat. 'If all that's true, then maybe she *is* the better option?'

Aisha put her empty cup onto the coffee table.

'That's crap. She's a selfish waste of space and always has been. You've changed your entire life for those kids, and they're better off with *you*, now.'

Cora stood up and lifted their empty cups, touched at Aisha's long-awaited endorsement of her decision to keep caring for the children.

'It's not that simple. I wish that it was.'

Aisha followed her into the kitchen, then stood at the back door looking out at the tiny garden, where the patio and planter boxes were all covered in a dusting of snow. Christmas was only days away, and the December sky was tinged a purply blue as a thick band of cloud slid across the horizon.

'Why are relationships such minefields?' Aisha sighed. 'How do you know that the person you care for won't hurt you, at some point?' She turned to face Cora. 'I mean, look at you and his lordship. On paper, Fraser was a good guy. A little up his own bum at times, but basically a good man. Right?'

Cora chuckled at the remark, then nodded.

'Everything is going fine, then bam.' Aisha smacked her palm on the countertop, making Cora jump. 'He blindsides you, cheats with what's-her-face, leaves you, marries her and pops out two kids, then buggers off *again*.' Aisha's eyes were wide.

'What on earth induces us to forgive that stuff? To trust enough to move on and open up to someone new?'

Cora was taken aback at this tangential, somewhat maudlin outpouring from Aisha, who always had a positive quip or jab of humour to counter negativity. But beneath humour there was often pain, and Aisha was obviously struggling with something she hadn't shared.

Cora felt guilt slide through her as, for the past few days, or more accurately, months, Aisha had supported her through the most turbulent time of her adult life, Aisha rarely bringing her own problems to the table. Now, seeing what looked like apprehension in the kind eyes, Cora flipped the narrative, and focused on her friend.

She studied the familiar face, the amber complexion, the long slender nose, and the splash of scarlet hair that had replaced the long mahogany locks of her childhood. Overcome with gratitude for all the years she'd had Aisha in her life, Cora cleared her throat.

'What's up? Are things with Bruce not going well?' Cora beckoned to Aisha, who followed her along the hall, where Cora noticed the pile of unopened post that she had left on the table by the door. Deciding to open it later, she walked into the living room, where the embers of the fire she had lit early that morning were still glowing.

Aisha flopped into her favourite chair.

'It's not that. Bruce is great. Not rushing anything or crowding me.' She pushed her palm away from the centre of her chest. 'What's freaking me out is that he actually *gets* me, I think.' She frowned.

'And that's a problem, why?' Cora tipped her head to the side. 'He seems like a good one, Aisha. And the way he was looking at you, at Evie's party, was really sweet. Like a soppy puppy with a new toy.' Cora laughed at Aisha's grimace.

'A better analogy, please.' She tutted, then continued. 'I'm scared of what might happen if I get in. You know? Really get in.'

Cora nodded. 'I understand, believe me, but you can't hide from love, woman. It's rare enough that we find someone we feel we could love, never mind have them love us back. When it happens, grab it. That's what I say.' Cora snatched at the air. 'You deserve it as much as anyone, and more than most.' She smiled, seeing Aisha's frown melt, and the warm eyes narrow as they always did when she smiled.

'Yeah, I suppose so.' Aisha shrugged. 'There are no guarantees in love. Or life in general.'

Cora squinted at her friend and leaned forward in her seat. 'Hold on. Did Aisha Pakram actually say the word *love* – and not in relation to a gin and tonic, or a day off?'

Aisha let out a sharp laugh.

'I'm not saying I'm *in* love.' She pouted. 'Just thinking about what might happen if I *did* fall for him. If things changed because of it.' She took a moment, then added, 'And then, if they did, what would happen to Mum.'

Cora sat back, running her fingers through the hair at her temple, this statement a clear indication that Aisha was wandering into uncharted territory with Bruce.

'Is she OK?' Cora frowned, picturing Priyanka, the tiny, pearly teeth, the same nose and honeyed complexion as Aisha's, but now Priyanka's dark-brown eyes vacant, and afraid.

'She's OK. No changes, anyway.' Aisha shrugged miserably. 'Sometimes I think she still knows me when I visit her, but mostly she talks to me as if I am an old friend. Someone she knows but can't place.'

'I know how hard that is, Aisha. I'm sorry.' Cora's heart ached for her friend. 'But why are you worrying about her relative to Bruce?'

'I'm just being daft. Imagining a future that probably has no chance of happening anyway and getting myself all twisted up about it.'

Cora frowned. 'Want to tell me about it?'

Aisha shook her head. 'No, not at the moment.' She swept her scarlet fringe to the side. 'Maybe later.'

Cora was suddenly struck that perhaps her own bad luck in marriage had had a deeper impact on her best friend than she had realised. Aisha was right when she'd said there were no guarantees in love, but Cora wanted her to trust in it. To believe that she could have a relationship that would last, despite life's curveballs.

'It's not daft to imagine the kind of life you want, Aisha, and what's really important to you. In fact, it's a necessity.'

As Aisha gave a half-hearted smile, and nodded, Cora realised that that was precisely what she had been doing with the children, the clarity of her vision for the future, and the new threat Holly represented to it, making Cora long to hold Evie and Ross close, and not let them go, for as long as she could.

An hour later, closing the door behind Aisha, Cora picked up the pile of post and went back into the kitchen. Sitting at the table, she sifted through the various envelopes, spotting her electricity bill, a bank statement, and a reminder to renew her subscription to a vegan cooking magazine.

At the bottom of the pile was a large brown envelope, the watermark smudged but half of the word Aberdeen still legible. There was a white slip on the front with tracking information, so, curious, she ripped it open and pulled out a single sheet of heavy white paper.

The shield logo at the top was unfamiliar, the three names listed next to each other not registering with her, but as she scanned the line at the bottom of the sheet, what she saw made her catch her breath.

Ferguson, Smythe, and Bolton. Solicitors at law.

13

The letter lay on the kitchen table, and Cora sat still, staring at it, her heart thumping wildly. While she had suspected something like this might happen, she hadn't expected it so quickly.

The solicitor's letter had informed her that Holly wanted to meet with her, and her solicitor or representative, to discuss the custody of the children. It only concerned Holly's claim to the children, with Fraser's continued absence screamingly obvious. The tone was formal and yet cordial, and they had requested that Cora respond within seventy-two hours.

As she folded the letter in half and slid it back into the envelope, images of Evie and Ross filled her head. Ross tucking his beloved Elly under his chin while Cora stroked his back to help him get to sleep. Evie with her stuffed unicorn sitting next to her on the patio, her mossy eyes wide as Cora showed her how to pat the soil down close to the base of a new seedling. Them both sitting at the kitchen table gleefully squeezing Play-Doh between their little fingers while Cora cooked, and the endearing, and surprising way they both seemed to understand that they couldn't screech around Cora, that it would distress her somehow.

They had become such integral parts of her day, her heart, and her life. Could she possibly go back to living without them? The concept was utterly overwhelming.

Two hours later, having picked Evie up from school, the children were kneeling at the coffee table in the living room at Locharden House with Duchess curled up next to them on the floor. The old dog loved the children, seeming to sense their need for comfort, and inevitably she would plant herself as close to them as she could get.

Cora had brought a Thomas the Tank Engine jigsaw puzzle, and they were both engrossed, trying to piece together Gordon, Ross's favourite engine.

Cora and James sat in the brocade armchairs either side of the fire, keeping their voices low.

'The main thing is not to panic.' James nodded sagely. 'Often, these solicitors' letters are just to get a reaction. Not an indication of real intentions.'

Cora sipped her coffee, her throat still tightly knotted.

'Well, it certainly got a reaction out of *me*. I can't afford to start a legal battle, James. It's not something I'm willing to put the children through. It'll be too disruptive and upsetting for them.'

He leaned forward, his blue eyes bright and elbows propped on his corduroy-covered knees. 'It won't come to that, believe me. She is bluffing.' He huffed. 'She doesn't have the wherewithal to go down that path, Cora. She's all talk and no action.'

Cora frowned, his dismissal feeling too glib. 'I don't think we can assume that, James. If you look at the facts, her situation, her rights as their mother.' She shook her head. 'We have to give this credence and be prepared for whatever she has in mind.'

He eyed her, then sat back and crossed his legs.

'If you feel that way, then we should at least try to take back the reins. Suggest something other than solicitors. We can propose mediation, maybe? A neutral party to consider all the facts and help reach a solution that works for everyone.'

Cora felt the lift of hope. 'Mediation? Do you think that could work?'

'It's worth a try. They're not legal eagles, per se, but they are trained to be impartial. Take both parties' position into account, and guide discussions. They help avoid conflict, too, which is critical here, and if we can't get one through the county, I'll pay for a private mediator.' He clamped his hands over his knees, the sleeves of his bottle-green sweater loose around his wide wrists.

His hands reminded her of Fraser's. The way the long fingers tapered at the ends, the same oval-shaped fingernails, in Fraser's case, often with dark arcs of paint beneath them. Each time she thought about her ex, she wondered where he was. How he could detach himself from his entire life and disappear like the proverbial puff of smoke. No matter how many times she had the thought, she couldn't rationalise it, even with everything she knew about him.

'What do you think?' James asked, jolting her back to the moment.

'I think we should suggest it to Holly and see what she says. But before we do that, shouldn't we know what it is *we* want?' She shrugged. 'And what we expect from her, as well.'

James nodded. 'Yes. Absolutely. We should write everything down. What we are willing to compromise on, and what we're not.'

Cora heard the edge in his voice that often appeared whenever he had talked to, or about Fraser, and Holly.

'So, our position is that we aren't willing to just hand the children over. That I should remain their guardian, and that we will consider negotiating some kind of visitation for her. Then, if she proves herself reliable, and the children begin to feel comfortable with her, maybe we can progress to some unsupervised visits, say at weekends?' She watched James's eyes darken.

'After what she and Fraser did, neither of them is fit to raise those bairns, if you ask me.' James frowned. 'They need to live with you for as long as you are willing to have them, and those two can take whatever concessions we give them.'

Cora sighed. While she understood his anger, her own simmering beneath her anxiety over what was to come, she also knew that making command decisions about Evie and Ross's fate was not as simple as James laying down the law, as he had throughout Fraser's childhood. There were rules to be followed, laws to be respected, and more than that, there was the need for compassion. If Holly had put in the work, got herself straightened out, she deserved the benefit of the doubt, regardless of how much that might hurt Cora to admit.

'Mummy, help me!' Ross held a large piece of puzzle out, his other hand beckoning to her.

Hearing the word still caused a lilt in Cora's heart, and she glanced at James, who was smiling at her.

'The child knows.' He shrugged. 'From the mouths of babes.'

That night, after spaghetti bolognaise and a bubble bath, Cora tucked the duvet against Evie's back.

The smell of cocoa butter soap and baby powder filled the room, and the little starfish-shaped night light was glowing amber under the window. Ross was snuggled under his quilt on the bottom bunk, and as Cora leaned in to kiss Evie, he patted Cora's thigh.

'Night night, chickadee.' Cora dropped a kiss on Evie's temple. 'Sweet dreams.'

Evie took Cora's fingers in hers, the child's eyes seeming to glow in the dimly lit room.

'Are we going to Grandpa's house tomorrow?'

Cora moved a strand of hair away from Evie's cheek.

'Not tomorrow, but the next day. Tomorrow is Saturday.'

Evie nodded. 'Can we go to the park?'

Cora smiled. 'I think that can be arranged. But remember that tomorrow morning, I'm going for a walk, and Auntie Aisha will be here to take care of you. But when I get back, maybe we can all go to the park together. OK?'

Evie considered this for a moment, then sighed.

'I want to go with you on a walk.'

'I know, sweet girl, but Craigendarroch is steep, and you'd get too tired.' Cora could almost taste the crisp air at the top of the mountain, see the sweeping view that she had missed over the past few months.

Aisha had said Cora needed a break, and that she'd watch the children, and while Cora had been reluctant to go, the lure of the mountain and some time to herself had won out. Albeit winter, the climb was doable with the right shoes, and the effort would be well worth it.

At just over 1,300 feet, it wasn't the largest of the Cairngorms range but was a favourite of Ballater folk. The name meaning the crag of the oaks, its steep flanks hosted many mighty oak trees, making the ascent an enjoyable, pretty, but still taxing walk.

On a clear day, you could see Monaltrie Park to the southeast, where the Ballater Highland Games was held each year. Due south, the River Dee wound through the valley below, the glittering river where salmon jumped and otters played, and where Cora had learned to fish, and to trust again.

Dominating the south-west skyline was the distinct shape of Lochnagar. The moody mountain had inspired artists, poets, writers, and kings for centuries – Cora's favourite quote, which her father had taught her, being by Lord Byron: *'Oh, for the crags that are wild and majestic. The steep frowning glories of dark Lochnagar.'*

She had read the children *The Old Man of Lochnagar* numerous times, them taking turns to turn the pages for her as she held them close. Reading was a part of their night-time ritual that Cora relished, and this night Evie had chosen *The Tale of Peter Rabbit* from the Beatrix Potter collection Cora's mother had given her for her ninth birthday. All the small hard-backed books slotted into a glossy case that Cora had loved to look at as a child, the illustrations so gentle in their simplicity. They had been the first books that had ever belonged exclusively to her, and their significance was no less important to her now.

As she bent down and kissed Ross's white-blonde head, then gave Evie another kiss, the little girl surprised Cora by putting her hands on her cheeks, Evie's gaze holding hers in the semi-darkness. There seemed to be a question she needed to ask, and Cora could sense some anxiety lurking behind her eyes.

'What is it, chickadee?' She stayed still, Evie's palms holding her gently.

'Are we going away?' Her brow puckered, then her eyes began to droop, as sleep tugged at her.

Cora's heart folded over. 'Go away where, sweetheart?'

Evie licked her lips, then released Cora's face.

'With another mummy.'

Cora felt as if the floor might give way beneath her at this heartbreaking observation, as she summoned every iota of willpower that she had to keep her face unreadable.

'No, darling. You're not going away.' She smiled. 'Sleep now, and I'll see you in the morning.'

On the bunk below, Ross tugged Elly closer to his face and

closed his eyes, his mouth clamping tightly, then instantly relaxing around his thumb.

Above him, Evie turned onto her side, her hands tucked under her cheek. The unicorn on her pillow seemed to be hiding between two long hanks of her hair.

'Night night, Mummy.' She surveyed Cora's face, the pale-green eyes, duplicates of Holly's, taking in every feature, as if recording them for posterity.

'Goodnight, my loves.' Cora kept her voice light, then blew them each a final kiss and walked out into the hall, pulling the door almost closed.

As she headed for the stairs, the tears in her eyes meant she could barely see where she was going, so she stopped at the top and took a few deep breaths, blinking hard. Evie had obviously understood far more of the conversation that day, with James, and going forward they needed to be more careful in front of the children. That Evie had processed what she and her grandfather had said and reasoned that it could mean that things might change was both impressive and heartbreaking.

The look of angst in her young face had been enough to unseat Cora, and now, more than ever, she was determined that nothing but one hundred per cent certainty in Holly's remorse, and new attitude, would induce Cora to part with the children. It was just unthinkable.

After soaking in the bath, writing her shopping list for the next day, and throwing a couple of new logs on the fire, Cora was curled up on the sofa in her pyjamas, her phone in her hand. The soft blanket that her mother would drape over her knees on winter nights was around Cora's shoulders and, across the room, the Christmas tree lights were glittering.

She had bought stockings with the children's names on them, to match the tartan one Eliza had ordered the first

Christmas Cora had spent here in this house. Mentally counting the handful of days she had left to finish her shopping, find something to give James from each of the children, then wrap everything up, Cora sighed. Time was galloping by, and it wouldn't be long before it had been a year since the two little souls had turned up on her doorstep, changing her life entirely.

As she tapped her phone looking for the number she needed, she pictured Holly's face, remembering the subtle changes she had noticed when Holly had come over a few days earlier. While much about her had remained the same, there had been a new uncertainty behind her eyes, perhaps an acknowledgement that she had screwed up and had a lot of ground to cover to regain the advantage she'd held over Cora in the past.

The old, slightly cruel rubbing of Cora's nose in the family unit that Holly had created with Fraser, her sense that she had won, and Cora had lost, was absent now. Or was it simply that, for the first time ever, Holly knew that, potentially, Cora had the upper ground?

Either way, nothing would sway her in terms of the children, at least not yet.

Holly was shouting into the phone, just as she used to, her voice a robotic monotone inside Cora's head. The clanging background noise was causing her to grimace as she tried to focus on what Holly was saying.

'Where are you?' Cora stared at the fire in her living room, a plume of smoke spiralling up the chimney, taking a spray of glowing wood particles with it.

'I'm in the Glendarron Arms. I've got a job, managing the Ghillie's bar.'

Cora pictured the classy Inn on Dee Street with a pricey bar and brasserie that attracted tourists, like bees to nectar. She had been in there a few times, with Fraser, and had appreciated the classic Victorian architecture and stylish Highland decor, a quieter environment than his usual hangout at the noisy pub where Holly had worked back then.

The Glendarron was not the kind of place she could see the old Holly fitting in, but perhaps this was another indication of how she had changed.

'Congrats.' Cora sucked in her bottom lip as Holly continued.

'I've rented a two-bedroom cottage on Golf Road. It needs a coat of paint here and there, but it's sweet.' She sounded excited.

Cora knew the road well, the pretty sandstone, terraced cottages were a five-minute walk from Mackay's, with a little park directly across the street.

'It's perfect for the kids. They can play on the green, and I've picked out new beds and duvet covers for them both.'

Cora's stomach was turning somersaults, anger building inside her at Holly disregarding what she had said about taking things slowly. As Cora stood up and walked to the window, then closed the heavy curtains on the starry night sky, Holly was prattling on about the plans she had for the cottage, but all Cora could think about was the solicitor's letter, and what she'd agreed with James.

As she sat on the arm of the chair at the fire, unable to listen anymore, she cut into Holly's monologue. 'Holly, look, slow down. You're getting way ahead of yourself. And we've got to talk about that letter.'

Holly went silent.

'Before you make any more plans, we need to discuss what's going to happen.'

'What do you mean?' Holly sounded puzzled.

'I don't want to involve solicitors, because I'm not going to drag the children through any more drama.' Cora halted, aware that that had sounded accusatory. 'I've talked to James, and we'd like to use a mediator.'

She waited for the refusal she was sure would come, chewing on her lower lip.

Then, surprising her, Holly replied, 'OK. That's fine, I don't want to upset them either, Cora. I just want to sort things so we can all get on with our lives.'

'Right. Good.' Cora frowned. This felt too easy. 'So, I'll text you the info when we decide who to use.'

'Fine. When can I see the kids again?'

Cora stood up and shoved the wrought-iron guard back against the bricks surrounding the fireplace, the heat from the embers coating her face and chest. This question wasn't unexpected, but it was nonetheless unsettling.

'Let me talk to James and I'll get back to you.' She switched off the lamps on the side tables next to the armchairs and straightened the little watercolour painting of the Dee Bridge that Eliza had bought from Fraser, for Andrew's sixtieth birthday.

The way Fraser had captured the light on the water was mesmerising, the depth of the river beneath a sheath of ripples seeming fathomless, and the current and eddies perfectly depicted by a few simple swirls of white. Cora had seen a lot of his work over the years and had always been impressed by the way he could perfectly catch the gold-tinged light of dawn, as the sky turned from grey to pink behind the peaks of the Cairngorms that hugged the town, a scene she had witnessed in person on many of her early-morning fishing forays to the river.

As she stared at the painting, recalling the day her mother had hidden it behind the sofa until her father got home from work, and the excitement of keeping Eliza's secret, made Cora smile. She missed her parents as much today as when she'd lost them, and that sense of loss made her think about Evie and Ross all over again.

Death was the brutal stripping away of people one loved. A hard inevitability that there was no choice but to live with. But what Holly and Fraser had done was crueller. They had left of their own volition, not taking into consideration the damage they were causing to their precious children, and that was something that Cora didn't know if she could ever, *truly* forgive.

'Cora, did you hear me?' Holly shouted again, making Cora start.

'No, sorry.' Cora draped the rug over the back of the sofa and turned off the overhead light.

'I said can I come over this weekend? I'm off on Sunday.'

Irritated that Holly was pressing the point, Cora checked the lock on the front door, flipped off the hall light and climbed the stairs.

'No, Sunday won't work. I take the children to James's on Sundays.'

'Can I come over there, then?'

Cora stopped short at her bedroom door, the idea of Holly showing up at Locharden House feeling invasive, and potentially incendiary. 'No, I don't think that's a good idea.'

She walked across the room, drew the curtains, and turned on the bedside light.

'Well, when *is* a good time?' Holly sighed. 'I don't want to leave it too long. They need to get used to me and get comfortable again before they come home.'

Cora clenched her teeth, the assumption that she would acquiesce, that she was nothing more than a stopgap before the inevitable return of the children, galling.

'I'll phone you on Monday and we'll find a time.' Feeling strangely empowered, she slid under the covers, the chill of the sheet beneath her making her shiver. Shifting to the middle of the bed, she rubbed her feet together to warm her toes. 'Bye, Holly.'

Before Holly had a chance to respond, Cora hung up and

switched the phone to silent mode. As she stared at the ceiling, the call having left her agitated, Cora consciously slowed her breathing down. Holly had always had a way of unsettling Cora, with her boisterous energy, her disregard for those around her, and by being decidedly brusque whenever they talked. But things had changed, and Cora's determination to hold fast, and put the children first was growing, regardless of whatever their mother was thinking.

As Cora's eyelids began to droop, she turned onto her side and removed the external processor of her implant. As silence filled her head, she felt her limbs grow heavy as sleep won out.

It was raining, the water running in rivulets down the outside of the living-room window.

Evie's golden hair was hanging below her shoulder blades, her jeans tucked into pink wellington boots. Beside her, Ross wore his all-in-one navy snow suit, and yellow wellingtons, and was on tiptoe, peering out through the grey of the morning, both of them pressing their noses against the glass, as if waiting to spot Santa's sleigh in the sky.

Ross patted Evie's back, the way Cora patted his to get him to drop off to sleep, and Evie tilted her head towards her brother, the tiny movement endearing, and enough to reassure him that he was not alone.

The fire was crackling in the grate and Christmas music was playing, though Cora couldn't identify what song. There was a sense of peace, of everything being just as it should be, then the doorbell rang, shattering the calm.

Across the room, Cora went to stand up but was frozen to the spot, watching the children looking for her and seeming to not see her sitting in her usual place at the end of the sofa.

Catching a flicker of panic in Evie's eyes, Cora tried to speak, to say her name, but no sound came out, as if her mouth were taped shut. To her horror, Evie walked into the hall and headed for the door, Ross trotting behind her.

Cora focused on her feet, planting them firmly on the rug, and tried to heave herself up from the sofa, but it was as if she were glued to it, her body leaden and her legs as weak as a newborn's. Then, ivy began to twist around her ankles, long strands of green waxy leaves curling their way to her calves, taut and restrictive, the tension close to unbearable.

As she tried again to call to the children, to get them to come back to her, she heard Holly's voice, the familiar pitch of it making Cora's heart begin to slam in her chest.

A few moments later, Holly walked into the room and began gathering things from the little table in the corner where Cora had set up a colouring station for the children. The ivy was twisting around Cora's thighs now, her flesh bulging between the vines as the binding became tighter and tighter. What was happening? Why could she not move?

'Let's get your stuff then. It's time to go home.' Holly crammed Ross's Elly into a big carrier bag and scanned the room, her eyes skimming over Cora, whose heart was now threatening to burst through her chest. Why couldn't she speak?

She opened her mouth and tried again, but nothing came out.

'I don't want to go,' Evie whispered, taking Ross's hand in hers, once again surveying the room as if looking for Cora.

I'm right here, chickadee. Why can't you see me?

Ross began to whimper, his chin wobbling in the way that tugged directly at Cora's heart.

Don't cry, sweet boy. I won't let her take you... Not yet...

'You have to come with me. I am your mummy.' Holly turned her back on Cora and lifted Evie's latest crayon drawing from the low table. 'We'll put this on the fridge at our new house.' She folded the drawing and stuffed it into the big bag.

Evie was backing away from Holly, easing herself in front of

Ross, who was now crying softly, his tears torturous to Cora, who felt herself being sucked back into the seat, the ivy now reaching around her waist.

'Our mummy is here. We want to stay here.' Evie glowered at Holly, who was obviously growing impatient.

'*I* am your mummy, Evie. Do you hear me?' Holly made to take Evie's hand, and the child whipped it behind herself.

'No. I don't like you.' Evie's eyes were full of tears, her lip quivering.

That's right. Tell her, Evie. Your mummy is right here!

Cora felt as if she might implode. She needed them to see her. To know that she would protect them.

Evie. I'm here!

But no matter how she tried, she seemed to be invisible to them all as the ivy made its way around her chest, making it hard to breathe. Her throat was clogged with fear, and her limbs locked inside the creeper's grip.

This feeling of being powerless, unable to control what was about to happen, wasn't unfamiliar to Cora, but it had been years since she'd felt this way, so utterly stripped of her voice, her will and wishes being overlooked as she became trapped somewhere she was meant to feel safe.

Look at me, children. I am here. I am here. No sound came out as she felt the ivy creeping up towards her throat.

As she saw Holly separate Ross's hand from Evie's, and then swing the little boy up onto her hip, Cora's head was now thumping as wildly as her heart. With every iota of her willpower, she commanded herself to stand, to stop what was happening, but her body was imprisoned by the vines, and her voice still stripped from her.

Holly took Evie's hand. 'Don't be silly now. Come on. We're going home.'

Evie's cheeks were glistening, tears rolling down the alabaster skin that Cora could feel beneath her lips.

You can't take them, Holly. They're not yours anymore.

Cora saw Evie jerk her hand free and run towards the hall, the fear in her young face like an arrow being released inside Cora's heart.

No! Evie, I'm here.

Cora's eyes shot open, and she stared at the bedroom ceiling, momentarily disorientated, as sweat trickled between her breasts. Her hand flew to her throat, feeling only smooth but clammy skin under her fingertips.

The street light outside her bedroom window was glowing, a sliver of orange light seeping in under the bottom of the curtains. Registering where she was, relief sloshed through her as she fumbled in the dark for the external processor of her cochlear implant and reattached it. Her breathing was ragged, as flipping on the bedside light, she threw the covers off and sat on the edge of the bed.

Her mind was racing, filled with images of the children, their faces contorted as they resisted Holly. Cora focused on controlling her breaths, getting her heart to return to a normal pace, as tears slid down her face. While she realised that she had dreamt the heartbreaking scene, there had been a tangible realness to it that was terrifying, and as she stood up, her legs were trembling.

Walking slowly across the bedroom, intending on checking on the children, she paused, grabbed the edge of the open door and took several deep breaths. Whatever happened next, she had to get a grip. The reality was that the children might well, in time, return to their mother and Cora would have no choice but to come to terms with that, but as she stood in the dark, tears still trickling down her face, she didn't know how she ever would.

14

While Cora packed a lunch to take on her hike, Aisha sat at the kitchen table, a box of treats from the bakery in front of her.

'Mine's the one with the chocolate goo. So, hands off, rug rats.' She pointed at an oblong, flaky pastry. 'You can choose any of the others.' She pulled a comical face as Evie, sitting next to her, giggled.

'I want the pink one.' Evie pointed at a ring doughnut covered in pale pink icing and rainbow sprinkles.

'Well, that's a shock.' Aisha feigned surprise. 'I thought Ross would want that one.'

Ross, who sat across from Evie, shook his head vigorously. 'I want chock-lit.' He went to take a chocolate brownie from the box.

'Did we check with Mummy if it's OK first?' Aisha widened her eyes, as Ross looked uncertain for a second.

Cora let the impact, and comfort, of the word Mummy calm her as she closed the backpack and hung it on the back of her usual chair, forcing away the residual ripples of distress that had been lingering from her dream.

'It's fine, little man. You ate all your breakfast.' She smiled at

Ross, who grinned back at her, his fingers clenching into a fist and opening again as if he were squeezing clay. 'Did you two say thank you to Auntie Aisha for bringing these yummy treats?'

'Thank you,' the children chimed in unison.

'You're welcome.' Aisha bowed her scarlet head. 'Well, dig in then.' She shoved the box towards Evie, who carefully lifted the pink doughnut out and put it on the small plate Aisha had placed in front of her. Then, as Ross grabbed the brownie, Aisha turned to Cora. 'Want one for your packed lunch?' She nodded at the box that still held two golden croissants.

'No thanks. Empty calories.' Cora patted her flat stomach.

'You could use a few, Saint Cora.' Aisha tutted, then pulled the box towards herself. 'But I suppose that means all the more for me, then.'

Cora squeezed her friend's shoulder as she passed behind her.

'You're a saint,' she whispered. 'I really need this break.'

Aisha nodded. 'Yep. No arguments here.'

Cora zipped her rucksack closed and set it by the back door. The prospect of the morning all to herself was thrilling and she couldn't wait to get out into the crisp cold of the December day. Knowing that the children were safely at home with Aisha meant that she could relax, let the outdoors in and recharge her me-time batteries.

As she lifted her waxed jacket from the back of the chair opposite Evie, a flash of her dream came back, Evie's tears as Holly had tried to take her hand. Suddenly, her happy abandon about the morning ahead of her faded a little. What if Holly came to the house while she was up the mountain?

Cora leaned in close to her friend's ear. 'If you-know-who turns up, don't let her in. OK?'

Aisha leaned away from her, her giant brown eyes wide beneath raised brows.

'Are you joking? She'll get a good-size portion of short shrift from me, and that's all.' She flexed her purple wool-covered bicep. 'Never fear. Aisha is here.'

Cora laughed, pulling on her jacket and zipping it up to her chin. She loved Aisha for her confidence, and Cora had no doubt that she would protect the children, but Holly was still something of a loose cannon, and until they came to a formal agreement about the children, Cora knew that she would likely feel anxious about leaving them, regardless.

Two hours later, Cora stood at the summit marker on Craigendarroch, soaking in the view of Lochnagar in the distance. The weather had been kind, and while it was cold, the sky had remained almost cloudless and the wind's gentle push at her back had helped her progress.

It had been almost a year since she'd done this climb, and her old boots that had taken on the shape of her feet had felt wonderful, and yet odd to pull on again. Her legs had grown heavy halfway up, so she had stopped for a water break and eaten something, then, feeling re-energised, had completed the climb in good time. Slower than her old time of just over an hour, but still very respectable.

The air was crisp, carrying the earthy smell of the moss coating the north side of the leafless oak trees she had passed on the lower slopes, and her lips still tingled with the tang of the orange she'd eaten after her sandwich. As she closed her eyes and listened to the distant call of a bird of prey, the sound turning into a robotic mid-tone in her ear, in the middle of all this beauty, Cora was suddenly overcome with sadness.

Opening her eyes, she swiped away tears, then shook the hair off her clammy forehead. She had missed this. The sense of peace she got from being outside, melding with nature, and letting herself disappear into her surroundings. Experiencing it again left her both invigorated and feeling somewhat empty, which she found hard to reconcile.

While she had grown to love Evie and Ross to the point where she didn't know how she'd be able to let them go, deep inside she still missed serenity, the ordered calm, the ease of the day, or even days, ahead, filled with promise but with no rigid plans she couldn't alter if she chose to.

As she hunkered down, then crossed her legs under her to sit on the cold, jagged rock beneath her, she shook her head. What was wrong with her? Pitting two perfect little souls enriching her life against the ability to climb a mountain, or fish at dawn? Laughing softly to herself as she heard Aisha's voice in her ear, Cora whispered, 'I know. I know. I'm only human, and everyone deserves some me-time now and then.'

As shadows of her dream began to fill her head again, she blinked them away. Whatever was to come would come and she and James would face it together. She was not alone in this and that meant the world.

Letting her head tip back, she watched a twist of cloud begin to roll overhead, the dark dots of a group of birds punctuating the message that it was time to head home.

Reluctant to leave just yet, she hugged her knees to her chest, took one more look at the dark outline of Lochnagar, the familiar shape of the upper slopes slicing into the sky like a group of old friends, and rested her forehead on her forearms.

The smell of the well-worn wax jacket brought images of her father back in a rush, his wavy salt-and-pepper hair and ruddy cheeks, his long legs in the waders he wore to fish, and the way he'd winked at her, his brown eyes twinkling behind his glasses, when she'd first refused to touch the hooks, or bait. A pang of loss was followed by a rush of love, and Cora took a deep breath and let herself fully feel every sensation that was rushing through her.

A few minutes later, checking the position of the sun as her father had taught her, Cora heaved herself up, adjusting the backpack. As she tightened the strap across her chest, she felt the vibration of her phone against her shoulder blade and heard a buzz as Bluetooth delivered the sound to her implant.

Slightly anxious, hoping it wasn't Aisha having a problem with the children, as Cora was at least ninety minutes from home, she slid the backpack off and dug inside it, pulling out her phone.

Seeing another unknown number, she frowned, her instinct to ignore the call, but as she was about to send it to voicemail, something held her back. The area code wasn't familiar and yet it tugged at her memory. Thinking back to the mysterious texts she'd received months earlier; she answered the call.

'Hello?' She frowned into the watery sunlight, using her palm as a visor as she scanned the outline of the summit of Lochnagar, dense clouds beginning to obscure it from view.

'Cora?' The voice was a man's, low and slightly gruff. The breeze was making it hard to hear clearly, but there was something in the tone that made Cora's skin prickle.

15

Cora pressed the phone to her good ear as a blast of cold air coated her face, lifting her hair in a dark veil behind her.

'Yes?' She turned her back on the view, her heart racing.

'It's me. Fraser.'

The breath left her in a rush, his name alone enough to make her press her eyes closed as a slew of questions, and painful memories, cascaded through her.

'*Fraser?*' She frowned, picturing his face, the messy blonde waves and the piercing blue eyes, rimmed with black, just like Ross's. The tiny scar above his upper lip that he'd got from a lacrosse ball hitting him when he was twelve.

'How are you?' He kept his voice soft, as he had always done when he talked to her.

Cora shook her head, her brow furrowing deeper as she walked carefully towards the track she'd come up. 'What's... I mean, are you bloody joking? How *am* I? Where *are* you, Fraser? Where the hell have you been?' Her voice threatened to splinter, her anger so fierce that she could almost taste it.

'I'm in Braemar, at a B and B. I need to see you, Cora. Please, can we meet?'

Cora leaned against a boulder, her stomach churning and her face beginning to feel numb from the cold breeze that was increasing in intensity.

'Oh, so you're back and want to meet. Just like that. No explanations, or *apologies?*' Her mouth gaped. 'What the hell are you doing in Braemar, anyway? Are you frigging serious with all this?'

'I know. You have every right to be livid, but I want to explain. So much has happened, and I can't do it on the phone. Please, Cora?'

'So much has happened to *you?*' Cora shouted, something she rarely did, the resultant buzz behind her ear disconcerting. 'You're damn right it has. While you've been away doing God knows what, the two precious children you abandoned have gone through heartbreak, have had to learn to live without not one but two of their parents. They've had to learn to trust again, and in the meantime, they've grown up, Fraser. They know only me as their parent now. They did nothing wrong, and they deserved so much better from you, and frankly, so did I.' She spat the last words, her anger now bubbling hotly in her throat. 'Wherever you've been, whatever the hell was going on, why didn't you contact me, or at least your father?'

'I know. Believe me. There hasn't been a day when I...' He halted.

'Don't you *dare* tell me you missed them, or that you thought about them all the time, because there is nothing that you can offer as explanation for the total radio silence, for almost a year, that I will ever, *ever* accept as reasonable.' She was shaking now, her insides in turmoil.

There was a pause, then he murmured, 'You don't know what happened, Cora. I can't explain it this way. That's why I need to see you. And I know that Holly's back in the village, too.'

Cora's eyebrows jumped. 'How do you know that?'

'I still have a friend or two in the area. I heard about it two days ago, that's why I'm here.'

Unsure what friend he could be referring to, Cora shook her head.

'So, now that *she's* back, you decide to reappear, too? Is it some kind of twisted competition between you? Honestly, you're both the bloody limit.'

'I know how it looks. Just please, please give me the benefit of the doubt, until we can talk.' He sounded desperate, as if afraid that she might hang up, and despite her wish to throw the phone off a cliff, and Fraser with it, she hesitated.

'I'm up on Craigendarroch, and I have to go. The children are with Aisha, and I need to get back.' She looked ahead of her at the track leading back down the mountain, where her little family was waiting for her, unaware of this next bombshell that had landed in their lives.

'That's fine. What about tomorrow?'

'I can't tomorrow. I'm taking the kids to your dad's for lunch, and to spend the afternoon there. It's a weekly routine.' As she thought about James and the way he would likely react to hearing that his son was back, Cora closed her eyes and pushed out a long breath. It would not be pretty, that was for sure.

'Don't tell him I'm here. Please, Cora. Not yet. I have things I need to do first, and for God's sake don't tell Holly, either.' There was a new quality to his voice that Cora hadn't heard before, a slight tremor that she guessed was coming from fear of facing the second wife he had walked out on.

Irritated that she felt even a flicker of interest in what he was feeling, she stared up at the sky, the wispy clouds thickening as they wove together overhead.

'I'd say that was *my* decision, Fraser. Your dad and I have been in lockstep since you left, caring for the children together. He deserves to know what's going on.'

She heard Fraser sigh.

'He always preferred you to me, anyway.'

Annoyed at the shift towards self-pity, Cora tutted. 'Oh, just stop with the *poor me* stuff, OK?' She took a moment to think about what she had scheduled, and if she could make this meeting work. As she mentally sifted through the next couple of days' events, the idea of seeing him again was surreal, and unsettling, but if it was to happen, it would be when it worked for her. 'Monday. I can do the morning, if I can leave the children with your dad. We'd only have an hour or so, though.' She stepped over a large stone and walked carefully on, keeping to the right of the path where there was gravel, and the terrain was flatter.

'Monday is fine, and maybe you could bring the kids with you?' He sounded hopeful, as Cora frowned. 'Can you come here to Braemar?'

There was no way she was taking the children anywhere near Fraser until she understood exactly what was going on with him.

'I'm not bringing the children, but I suppose I can come there.' She frowned. 'But is all this cloak-and-dagger stuff necessary? Why can't you come to my house?'

'Cora, please, I wouldn't ask if it wasn't important.'

Annoyed at having to change her plans for Monday, and now to drive to Braemar too, she tutted. 'Fine. Eleven o'clock. Text me your address.'

'I will and thank you. I owe you more gratitude than I can ever express, for this, for everything you've done.' His voice caught, making Cora's frown deepen.

'You're bloody right you do.' She stumbled slightly, taking a moment to steady herself. 'See you on Monday, and Fraser? Whatever you have to tell me, it better be good.'

Before he could reply, she ended the call and shoved the phone into her pocket. Her heart was pounding as she focused ahead, making sure to keep her eyes on her footing and letting the wind sweep the hair from her burning cheeks as she made her descent.

An hour and a half later, Aisha was standing in the open front door in her padded navy coat, her bag over her shoulder and a rainbow striped scarf wound round her neck a few times, the garish colours making the shock of scarlet hair seem even brighter.

The children were watching TV in the living room, so the women spoke quietly to one another.

'Are you sure you don't want me to come with you?'

'No, thanks.' Cora shook her head.

Aisha had been shocked when Cora had told her about hearing from Fraser, but more than that, she'd been predictably furious. Now, her tone was more cautionary.

'He's such a selfish arsehole, Cora. Always was. Just don't let him manipulate you with some pathetic sob story.' Her eyes flashed.

'I think I've come a long way since Fraser was able to do that to me, Aisha. Don't worry. I'm a lot stronger these days.'

Aisha surveyed her friend's face, then gave a half-smile.

'You are. I can see it.' She squeezed Cora's arm. 'Quite the mama bear now.'

Cora laughed softly, her role as a mother so precious, and yet now in question. 'Just less of a pushover.'

Aisha nodded, adjusting her scarf.

'Bruce and I are going to the Italian out on the Braemar Road tomorrow night. Can you come?' She hoisted the bag higher up on her shoulder. 'You could get a babysitter.' She wiggled her eyebrows, her chocolatey eyes bright. 'I'm sure Agnes Mackay would be happy to come over. Or maybe even Queenie, as the kids know her so well now.'

Picturing the rosy-faced Agnes, Harry Mackay's wife, and the local district nurse, Cora shook her head. 'Agnes is an absolute gem in a pinch, but it's too short notice, and I can't ask Queenie. It feels like imposing. Maybe next time?' She smiled as Aisha pouted comically. 'I don't want to be a gooseberry anyway.'

Aisha tutted. 'Don't be silly. Bruce really likes you, and three is never a crowd, with you.'

'Aww, thanks.' She hugged her friend. 'You two are still coming here for Christmas Eve dinner on Tuesday, right?'

Aisha nodded.

'Wouldn't miss it. We'll come after I've been to see Mum.' She sighed, then suddenly bellowed, 'Bye, rug rats,' over her shoulder, making Cora flinch at the grating sound. 'Sorry.' Aisha grimaced. 'Give me a ring tomorrow, OK? I want to know what's going on with Holly, the wench. And call me from the road on Monday, once you've met you-know-who.'

'I will. And thanks again for today. It was just what I needed.'

'Any time.' Aisha gave her a salute and walked down the path towards the road. 'Say hi to the old man tomorrow.'

The idea of seeing James, the next day, and not telling him about Fraser's return made Cora uncomfortable, but she'd sleep on it before deciding what to do.

The next morning, James was in the greenhouse with Duchess and Queenie when Cora arrived with the children, and seeing Queenie at Locharden House on one of her usual days off was a surprise.

She was wearing a Black Watch kilt and a dark-green V-neck, the outfit flattering to her tall form, and a contrast to the scrubs she wore when on duty. Her long, peachy hair was up in the ubiquitous ponytail, tangerine wisps framing her face.

Warmth radiated from her hazel eyes as she turned and saw Cora, with Ross on her hip, and Evie close behind.

'Hello, you two. Nice to see you, Queenie.' Cora smiled at her, then at James, who was standing behind Queenie, potting an orchid, his grey Arran sweater sleeves rolled up and his cheeks pink from the warmth of the greenhouse.

'Hello yourself.' Queenie smiled. 'Nice to see you, and the wee ones.'

'Ah, Cora m'dear. Perfect timing.' James beamed at her. 'We're just finished, and both famished into the bargain.' He met Cora's gaze, a glimmer of mischief in his eyes that made her heart lift.

She knew that he had become close to Queenie over the past few months, but there was a relaxed energy between them now that spoke of friendship more than professional courtesy, and perhaps even something more developing. That James might find comfort, or maybe even love with a new companion was an uplifting thought, and Cora instantly let herself imagine how that might affect her own life, if he were a bit less dependent on her. The image wasn't unpleasant, so she let it play out for a few seconds.

'Queenie's joining us for lunch, if that's all right with you, chef?' James set the orchid on the bench and rolled his sleeves down.

'Of course.' Cora nodded, putting Ross down. The little boy ran straight to Duchess and hugged her tightly around the neck, then to James, raising his arms to be picked up.

James chuckled and lifted Ross onto his hip.

'Oh, jeepers creepers, laddie. You weigh a ton.'

Ross snuggled into James's neck. 'Gampa.'

James's eyes seemed to become misty as he held his grandson close.

'And hello to you, Evie-bell.' He smiled at Evie, who was hanging on to Cora's jacket. 'So, what's for lunch?'

Cora took Evie's hand, feeling the slender fingers cool in hers.

'We've got lots of good things. Everything we need for an Italian meatloaf, and roasted veggies. Then Evie is going to help me make a trifle, aren't you, chickadee?'

Evie nodded. 'I like orange jelly best.'

James laughed. 'As do I, lass. Come on then. Let's away in.' He walked purposefully out of the greenhouse, and they all trooped behind him, a Pied Piper with his little band of followers in tow.

Lunch had been easy, a relaxed affair with much laughter, and the bubble of conversation around the big kitchen table, that Cora loved. Doing this for the children was so important, giving them the experience of being part of a functional family, and until they had started the weekly routine of Sunday lunches at Locharden House, Cora hadn't realised how much she had missed this kind of interaction herself.

Queenie seemed at ease, joining their merry group as if she'd been there all along. The children were very comfortable around her now, after months of seeing her at their grandad's house, and there was no awkwardness at her being part of their day.

Throughout the lunch, Queenie had caught Cora's eye a few times over the table and smiled, slightly coyly at first, but when Cora made a point of saying how lovely it was to have her here, Queenie had visibly glowed.

Now that the children were in the living room, where Queenie had offered to read them a story before they went home, James was helping Cora with the dishes. He rinsed the plates and handed them to her as she stacked them in the dishwasher, his big hands rosy from the heat of the water.

'I've got the contact details of a mediation group,' James said as he passed her the last plate, then dried his hands on a tea towel. 'They're based in Aberdeen, but they have a family mediator who lives in Banchory who is willing to meet either in person or do virtual sessions.'

'Oh, that's great. It would make it a lot easier if we could do it virtually.'

He nodded, rubbing the toe of one of his black brogues behind his other calf. His corduroy trousers were silver-grey and with the crisp white shirt he wore under his sweater, Cora registered the extra effort he'd made to dress smartly. Certain that this was for Queenie's benefit, Cora smiled at him.

'You look really well, James. It's great that you're not using your stick anymore, either.' She gestured towards the walking stick that was propped up against the wall near the back door.

'Aye, I'm feeling much stronger.' He nodded again. 'It's all the good care I've been getting.'

Cora held his gaze, noticing a slight flush in his cheeks. It was endearing, and with no wish to embarrass him, she said, 'Shall I give those people a call tomorrow then?'

James walked to the Welsh dresser opposite the stove, opened the drawer and pulled out a piece of paper.

'Yes, I told them you'd be in touch. Once you've had an initial chat, we can set up a meeting together before we bring Holly in on things.' His eyes darkened with the name. 'I must admit, I'm still surprised she was open to it.'

Cora nodded, lifting her bag from the back of the chair. 'Me too. But let's not look a gift horse in the mouth.' She shrugged. 'Holly seems set on getting the children back, James, and if she pulls out all the stops, sets everything up properly to have them with her, and proves that she is truly back for good, we'll have a battle on our hands.'

James leaned back against the Aga, gripping the long metal handle behind him.

'She will have to prove herself beyond any shadow of a

doubt before I'll budge an *inch.*' He glowered, his head shaking almost imperceptibly. 'An inch.'

Cora walked over, put her arms around his neck and hugged him.

'One step at a time.' She moved back, seeing his taut face begin to relax. 'We're a team, and whatever else happens, Evie and Ross will have us. We are always going to be their family.' As she watched him absorb what she'd said, Cora's throat narrowed, the prospect that that could potentially change, or be taken out of her control, making her queasy.

Suddenly, keeping Fraser's call and reappearance from James felt terribly wrong, so she checked that the room was still empty behind him before dropping her voice to a whisper.

'James, I have to tell you something...'

16

Two days later, just three days before Christmas, Cora parked in front of the Queen's Café in Braemar High Street. It had been a few months since she'd been in the picturesque village, with its eclectic collection of shops and homes, and it was good to be back.

Many of the iconic sandstone buildings in the High Street had tall sash windows with bubbled glass and elegant dark slate rooves, and dated back centuries, the history of the village and the age of the homes literally etched on the worn stone lintels above their heavy wooden doors.

Across from where Cora had parked, a pharmacy and a gift store with a golden canopy above the window were set back behind a small green, the gift store attached to the picture-perfect honey-coloured cottage next to it.

Cora's mother had liked to come to the butcher here, the whitewashed shop standing at the end of the High Street being something of a local institution, and after they'd done their shopping, Eliza would take Cora to the tearoom across the street, for a toasted teacake.

Flooded with happy memories, Cora took a few moments to

be present, and take in the familiar street, picturing her and her mother walking around eating ice creams, or sitting on the green while Eliza read the paper, and Cora daydreamed about becoming a chef.

On the way out of Ballater, Cora had passed the site of The Rookery restaurant, where she'd worked with Chef Eddie years ago. Seeing the characterful, Victorian building, still empty, and with a 'For Lease' sign in one of the windows, had made her sad – another glimpse at her life from before she had become entangled with the Munros – a simpler time that she was feeling more and more removed from.

The previous day, when she'd told James about Fraser, James's face had turned ashen.

'After all this time? What's he doing in Braemar? Why didn't he come straight home?' James's voice had cracked, as if he might give way to tears, which had shocked Cora.

'I don't know, but I'm going to meet him tomorrow. He says he wants to explain.' She'd seen James's expression shifting from shock to confusion, and then settling into anger. 'I think it's best I see him, face to face, and hear him out. Then you and I can decide what to do from there.' She'd hoped she'd sounded convincingly positive about the decision.

'Shall I come with you?' He'd frowned, dragging his fingers through his silver hair.

'No, I'll go alone this first time. Is it OK if I leave the children here for a couple of hours?'

James had taken a few moments before nodding.

'Well, phone me if you change your mind, and of course. Leave the wee ones here,' he'd said, just as Queenie had walked into the kitchen behind him.

Cora had hugged them both, loaded the children into the car and made her way home, her stomach beginning to knot at the prospect of seeing her ex-husband again. With his disappearance, each week and month that passed making it seem less likely that he'd come back, part of Cora had begun to hope he'd stay away forever. Now that he was here, the thought of facing him again brought with it memories that Cora had long since put to rest, but which sucked her back to the worst moment of her life, as if she were reliving it in technicolour.

On that night, close to five years before, he'd come home, two hours after he'd promised to. Rather than sheepishly ask for her forgiveness, as he often did when he'd stayed too long at the pub, he'd been sober and wild-eyed as he'd mumbled that he needed to tell her something.

Cora had numbly followed him through the dark living room into the kitchen, and had flipped the light on, the overhead bulb feeling like a searchlight as she'd watched him awkwardly shift his sodden feet. His rain-soaked jacket clinging to his slender torso, his thick, fair hair plastered to his head.

'I'm sorry, Cora. I never meant to hurt you, but Holly and I...' He'd faltered. 'We are in love.' He'd stared at her, unblinking, as if his own words were surprising him.

Thinking that she'd misread his lips, or that her cochlear implant was faulty, Cora had cupped her left ear. 'What did you say?'

Hurt had sliced through her as she'd tried to focus on his eyes, but he wouldn't meet her gaze, his avoidance heightening the prick of tears behind her own.

As he'd stood still, she'd tried to absorb what she'd heard, his words feeling as surreal as the steady *pat pat pat* of the water dripping from his jacket – already forming a tiny puddle on the ceramic tiled floor.

One word had surfaced above the others. *Holly.* It wasn't the name, a simple enough name that bore a disjointed context for Cora, but the *way* he'd said it – haltingly, but with undeniable affection – that had brought Cora's eyes wide as the face *behind* the name had begun to materialise.

Holly was the landlady at the Ballater Arms, the small pub

at the end of the High Street where Fraser liked to drink, was tall and blonde, with a raucous laugh, startling green eyes, and a crackly voice that Cora had put down to the cigarettes she had been smoking ever since middle school.

As Cora had pictured the person behind the destruction of her marriage, Fraser had bumped around inside their little home, stuffing an odd collection of clothes, books, CDs, and weather-beaten waxed jackets, into two backpacks.

Now, as Cora sat in the car park, she recalled the low buzzing that had filled her head at the time; the desire she'd had to rip out her implant, be deaf to this cruel twist that her life was taking, had been overwhelming. Forcing a swallow, she slid back into the memory.

When she'd asked him what she'd done to deserve this, Fraser had stopped what he was doing and stared at her.

'It wasn't anything in particular.' He'd shrugged sadly. 'But your attitude towards me changed. You see me like the old man does, now.' His face had sagged as he nudged the backpack with the toe of his boot. 'You never used to judge me, but he's... poisoned you towards me.'

Cora had felt blood begin to surge back into her numb legs. 'That's not true, Fraser. He hasn't poisoned anything. I just grew to understand him over time, and what worries him about the estate, and the future, that's all. It never changed the way I feel about you, though.' She'd instantly seen the shift in him, the slumped shoulders get yanked back, the square chin lifting defiantly.

'Bullshit.' He'd eyed her. 'Admit it, Cora. You see me as a waste of space, now, too. A lazy, selfish guy who wants to paint silly pictures rather than be lord of the manor – to earn my keep, and please my father.' His jacket was still saturated, but the dripping had stopped, and his wet hair had parted into thick twists, the skin of his scalp looking pink and vulnerable between them.

'I don't think that at all!' Cora had shaken her head, a tiny flicker of guilt making her lick her lips.

The more she'd grown to understand and even begin to sympathise with James, the more Fraser had grown resentful of the bond forming between his wife and his cold-hearted father. Looking back, Cora regretted letting that happen. Her fascination for the life James Munro led, all alone in the impressive mansion, marching across the land he presided over, visiting the various tenant farms, and watching the herds of Highland cattle that roamed the rough hills and glens on the estate, had blinded Cora to the resulting friction that was building between her and her husband. Was there some truth to what Fraser was saying? Had she not begun to subtly nod her head when James would tell her how disappointed he was in Fraser's lack of interest in the estate, his disregard for the family legacy that James had worked his entire life to sustain so that he might pass it on?

'I never meant to make you feel that way,' she'd said. This being the only reason he wanted to leave her seemed unbelievable. She had rounded the table, her chest aching as if she'd been punched. 'How long have you been with her?'

She remembered that Fraser had blinked repeatedly, as if calculating the exact date that he broke his wedding vows, or perhaps the first time he realised that he wanted to.

'A few months.'

Months. As reality had begun to sink in, she'd felt her entire life slipping away.

'What does it matter now?' He'd shrugged. 'It's over between us, Cora. I think we've both known that for a while.'

'Don't speak for me. Don't you dare do that.' Her voice had shaken. 'You could have talked to me. Told me how you were feeling.' She had pressed her palm onto the cool tabletop, seeing a row of tiny crumbs lined up along the grout between two tiles. 'You could have tried to make it work rather than just throw us away like trash.'

'It wouldn't have changed anything.' He'd shaken his head miserably. 'Besides, Holly and I, well...' He'd halted, then closed his eyes. 'We're just better suited, Cora. She gets me. I feel like myself with her. Not trying to be someone I'll never be.'

'Better suited? That's rich.' She'd gulped. 'I've never made you feel as if you weren't enough. I always supported your choices, and your art, even if...' She'd stopped herself as his eyebrows jumped.

'Even if what? You thought it was a waste of time?'

As she'd tried to protest, he'd lifted a backpack and slung it over his shoulder.

'Look, I don't want to argue, or hurt you anymore, so I'm going to go.' He'd scrubbed his palm over the back of his neck.

Cora had taken a moment to gather herself, instinctually touching the implant behind her ear.

The movement had caused him to frown, then take a step towards her.

'I'll check on you tomorrow, OK?'

Fury had seeped into her chest like smoke, shoving out her willingness to admit that she might have contributed to this mess.

'Don't bother. I was fine before you and I'll be fine *after* you.' Her words had been bitter on her tongue, but she'd wanted them to sting.

She'd watched him cross the kitchen, hesitate in the doorway, then make his way through the living room, towards the hall, and Cora had felt tears crawl down her cheeks. Wiping them away, she'd turned her back on the scene that was tearing her in two – him walking away from her.

Her chest aching from reliving those life-changing moments, Cora twisted the rear-view mirror towards her and checked her face. Her green wax jacket was making her eyes look bluer than usual, and the dark-brown fringe that had grown out was tucked neatly behind her ear. As she touched her fingertip to the cochlear implant, feeling a slight buzz fizz across her skull, she noticed the new lines around her mouth, like parentheses that framed the full lips, speaking to time passing, and all that entailed.

She ran a thumb under each eye, where her mascara had begun to smudge, then pulled her shoulders back, whispering, 'You're OK. You've got this.'

As she locked the car and approached the door of the café, her heart was pounding. It had been so long since she'd seen Fraser that she wasn't sure how she'd feel. Aside from her anger that was simmering dangerously close to the surface, she was desperate to learn what had motivated him to walk away from his wife and children, something that Cora just couldn't reconcile, no matter how hard she tried.

The café was mercifully quiet, with only three tables occupied inside the low-ceilinged space. At the far end was a long counter with a glass display cabinet housing various cakes and pastries, and there was a sophisticated coffee machine dominating the top of it, along with stacks of shiny white cups next to an old-fashioned cash register, there purely for decoration.

Cora could hear music playing in the background, but it was quiet enough not to cause her problems. As she scanned the room seeing a mother with her young daughter at one table, and an elderly man reading a newspaper at the other, she spotted Fraser sitting in one of two armchairs in the far corner, next to a bay window that overlooked the narrow garden at the side of the building.

Fraser looked up just as she saw him and raised his hand. His fair hair was shorter than she'd ever seen it, cropped closely to his head, and even from across the room, the piercing blue of his eyes drew her gaze. He wore a round-necked beige sweater and dark-blue jeans, and a leather jacket was slung over one arm of the chair.

Her stomach twisting with both nerves and frustration, Cora walked over to him, then hesitated as he stood up and made to hug her. On a reflex, she pulled back, her hand coming up in front of her, and she saw a flicker of embarrassment in his eyes.

'Sorry. Old habits.' He dropped his eyes momentarily to the floor, then looked up again. 'Thanks for coming.' He gestured towards the other chair and, as she took off her jacket, he sat back down, nervously running a palm over the back of his head, something he did whenever he was uncomfortable.

As soon as she sat down, he stood up again, startling Cora.

'What can I get you? Coffee? Tea?' He pulled a slender wallet from his back pocket.

'Decaf latte, please.' She set her bag at her feet, noting her battered trainers and how ugly they looked next to the smooth suede boots he was wearing. Annoyed at herself for caring, she shifted back in the lumpy chair as he walked to the counter and spoke quietly to a petite redhead, who blushed as she took his order.

Women getting flustered around Fraser was nothing new but being reminded of how she'd once felt about that was enlightening. As she watched the interaction, Cora felt nothing other than angry with him, and the realisation that she was well and truly over Fraser Munro was a revelation. She had come a long way since he'd shattered her heart and now, in a position of strength, and with new-found self-belief, she knew that she could deal with whatever he had to say.

Fraser sat across from her again, his eyes flicking between the counter and the door, as if he was expecting someone else.

'So, where should we start?' She eyed him as he propped an ankle up with the opposite knee.

'First of all, I want to say thank you for everything you've done for Evie and Ross. I know what a massive responsibility it was, and you took it on. Honestly, Cora, there was no one else I'd have trusted with the kids.' He frowned as, confused, Cora remained silent.

A thank you was not what she wanted. She was waiting for the bombshell, the revelation that would make this past ten months make sense, but there was something in his manner that set alarm bells ringing inside her. She knew his body language too well, and as soon as he started to speak, she sensed he was editing what he was saying.

'I didn't take it on. It was handed to me.' She worked to keep her voice even. 'It's been really hard, dealing with the heartbreak, building their trust back. I suppose you know I'm their legal guardian now, right?'

His eyebrows jumped. 'I thought Dad was, actually, but it makes sense.' He nodded. 'I never intended on being away this long, Cora. But I knew they were safe with you, and Dad.' As he said the last word, his jaw seemed to stiffen.

'That's not reason enough to disappear from their lives without a word. They needed you, and their mother. I did the best I could. And James has been amazing. But you owe me, and him, an explanation. Never mind those sweet children, when they're old enough to understand.' Her pulse ticked at her temple. 'Where the hell were you all this time, and why didn't you at least contact us?'

'I've been in London. I was a mess when I got there, and I wanted to pull myself together before I got in touch. I was ashamed, afraid of what you and Dad would have to say to me.' He paused, as if picturing his father's disapproval being reinforced yet again. 'I stayed in a hostel at first, just sleeping all the time, until my money ran out.' His eyes slid to the tabletop. 'I ended up sleeping rough for a couple of weeks, not something I recommend in London.'

Shock jolted through her as she pictured him huddled in a

shop doorway, perhaps sharing a rough shelter under a bridge with other souls in the same position. Despite her anger at him still overwhelming, sympathy for his predicament made her stay silent.

'I got a job in a coffee shop, then I moved into a house-share in Putney. It was pretty crappy, but at least I had a roof over my head.' He nodded sadly. 'I met a good guy who worked with the homeless, who got me the place in the house. He helped me get into counselling and then, when I was beginning to feel like I could try living again, I moved to where I live now. My housemate is great.' He halted, seeing Cora's frown.

The last thing she wanted was to hear about his latest partner, or how wonderful she was, and even with what Cora knew now, his silence all this time was still unforgivable.

'When you were getting back on your feet, why didn't you get in touch? A phone call or even a text, Fraser. They were your children.' Her voice threatened to crack, but determined not to get emotional, she clamped her mouth shut.

'I know that, and as I started to rebuild a life, and started painting again, I realised just how far I still had to go. One month just kind of seeped into another.' He paused, his face a mask of misery. 'I am deeply ashamed that I didn't phone or message you, apart from that one text a while ago.'

Taken aback, Cora frowned, remembering the cryptic message she'd received months ago, presuming it had been from Holly. 'That was *you*?'

'Yes.' He nodded. 'It's taken me a long time, but I've finally got my life together, Cora. I live in a nice place now, and my art is being shown in a pretty prestigious gallery in Kensington, and it's selling enough to pay the bills.' He took a moment, then continued. 'I'm using the name Frank Campbell on my work.'

Cora was shocked that he'd chosen to use her surname, but part of her was annoyingly touched. 'Why?'

'Because I didn't want Holly to find me, and she would have if I'd gone on using Munro.'

Cora couldn't believe the ease with which he said it. That he seemed at peace with using her name to hide from his wife, and his children, his father, and even from her. As she suddenly pictured a smart art gallery on a leafy London street, with his paintings hanging on its pristine walls, scenes of his home, the place where he not only grew up but where his children were growing up without him, something inside her snapped.

'What is *wrong* with you, Fraser? Are you seriously telling me that you've been setting yourself up in a lovely life, living with someone, and taking care of number one with barely a thought for who you left behind? I know you're selfish, and sometimes thoughtless, but I didn't think you were a heartless narcissist.' Her voice crackled in her ear, a sign that she was close to shouting.

'It's not like that, Cora.' His eyes were hooded, a glow of shame colouring his smooth cheeks.

'Then tell me what it *is* like. I'm all ears.' She lowered her voice and flapped a hand at her temple.

'I can't, without...' He halted, replanting his raised foot on the ground and nodding at the young woman who approached and set their coffees down on the table between them. 'Thanks.' He pulled his cup closer to him, stirring the frothy drink as the redhead smiled shyly and walked back to the counter.

'Without what?' Cora ignored her coffee, her throat too tight to swallow. 'Why can't you just tell me what happened?'

He scanned her face, as if reminding himself of her features.

'Look, I will tell you everything, I promise, but I need some more time. I know I don't deserve it, but I'm asking you... no, *begging* you for that. I know I treated you badly, Cora. And that I hurt you deeply. But I would never have walked away from my children unless I felt it was in their best interest, at the time.' He shoved his cup away, the coffee untouched. 'Let's just say that things were falling apart at home, and then it all came to a head with me and Holly. The environment was toxic. A bad place for children to be.' He held her gaze. 'Please trust that I never meant to abandon them. And I am truly sorry.'

Cora watched him, his mouth dipping at the edges, the slightly sunken cheeks, and the deep frown on the high forehead that she had loved to trail her finger across when he slept with his head on her chest. There was something behind his eyes, a deep-seated sadness that seemed to have taken over his whole face, and despite her frustration at being given half the story, she found herself wanting to believe that his actions might not have been entirely selfish.

'What do you want from me, Fraser?' She lifted the cup and swallowed some coffee over a nut of tension.

'I want to see the kids, but I can't see Holly.' He leaned forward, his elbows on his knees.

'Just like that? You want to see them, oh, but not *Holly*.' Her voice caught. 'What makes you think that after all this time you can turn up, and just pick and choose who you see or don't see?'

Ignoring her question, he blinked nervously. 'What does Holly want?' Fraser asked uncertainly.

Cora frowned. *Was he serious?*

'She wants her children back, Fraser.'

At this, he dropped his chin to his chest. 'Oh, God.'

'What? She says she has had treatment for some problems she was having, and, honestly, Fraser, she seems calmer than I remember. More centred.' Cora hesitated as he slumped back in the chair and linked his hands on top of his head – a gesture of despair.

'She has a new job in the village, and she's rented a place for them all to live.' Cora pictured the terraced cottages near the park, the image cutting into her anger and making her pause. The heartbreaking thought of Holly taking the children back was still not something Cora could reconcile.

Fraser dropped his hands to his knees and his eyes locked on hers. 'They can't go back to her, Cora. That *can't* happen.' He shook his head – a series of tiny but emphatic movements.

Cora could once again see fear behind his eyes, enough so that she softened her voice a little.

'Look, nothing has been decided yet. She's only seen them the once, and it didn't exactly go smoothly, but I'm going to let her come back again on Boxing Day. Also, we got a solicitor's letter saying she wants to officially discuss custody.' She took another sip of coffee, hoping the warm liquid might ease her throat.

'Seriously?' His face paled.

'Your dad and I suggested that we use a mediator instead, and she's agreed, so I'm going to have an initial talk with them.'

Fraser exhaled slowly, his fingers gripping his knees. 'Please, Cora. Before anything else happens, I need to see them. I miss them so much.'

The pain in his voice so real, and disarming, Cora's anger faded a touch more as she took a moment to consider what to do.

'I suppose you could come to my place, but I'll have to prepare the children, first. It was awkward when Holly came over. She's virtually a stranger to them, so you'll have to be ready for that reaction, too.'

He nodded. 'I totally understand. I won't do anything to pressure them or make them nervous. I just want to see them.' His eyes were glittering. 'But I can't come into the village. Not yet.'

Puzzled, and more mildly irritated at more conditions, Cora sighed. 'Why not?'

'Because I still don't want Holly to know I'm here, and if I go to your house, someone will see me, and it'll get back to her. One hundred per cent.'

'Then what do you suggest? A clandestine meeting in a car

park somewhere?' The continued mystery surrounding this was infuriating.

'I know I said not to tell him yet, but could you maybe talk to Dad? Let him know that I'm here, and ask if I can stay at Locharden House, just for a few days?' He sounded tentative, as if knowingly taking the first step onto paper-thin ice. 'If he agrees, then I could see the kids there.'

Cora's patience was wearing dangerously thin. Fraser was many things, but, in her experience, he had never been a coward. However, this wanting to hide from Holly, and the rest of the village, wasn't adding up. As she stared at him, unable to understand what would prompt such behaviour, she couldn't help but think of Evie and Ross. Seeing their father might spark memories for them, at least for Evie, and if it went even slightly better than it had with Holly, then it could be a positive, even rewarding thing for the children.

Putting her own feelings aside, despite the pain it caused, she closed her eyes briefly and took a deep breath.

'OK, I'll talk to him. But I can't promise anything, Fraser. He's understandably furious with you. As am I. And he's very protective of the children. As am I.' Stating both points felt good, as if she was reinforcing the position that she and James were a team, and not to be messed with.

'Understandable. You both love them.' His eyes met hers, his steady and clear. 'As do I. That's why I did what I did.'

His pointed words weren't lost on her but having to accept not being given the whole story yet, and having to resume her old role as the conduit for communication between him and his father, was maddening.

'Fine. Phone me tonight and I'll let you know what he says.'

Fraser got up, tugging his sweater down at the front as she stood and slid on her jacket.

'Thank you, Cora. You really are an exceptional human being, and friend.'

She could think of nothing to say to that except, 'Talk to you later.'

As she walked out into the street, the sky had darkened, and heavy rain was falling, almost obscuring the whitewashed fascia of the butcher's shop behind her and the features of the sandstone cottages that lined the street on either side.

Surprised that she hadn't noticed the change in the light, and yet unsurprised that she hadn't heard the rain while inside the café, she pulled her jacket tightly around her and ran towards the car park.

She had no idea how James would react to this partial, and, frankly, inadequate explanation of where his son had been all this time, but what she did know was that there was more to this story.

Fraser was hiding something, and she needed to find out what.

17

The conversation with James had been tense, his anger giving way to the inevitable disappointment that peppered his tone whenever Fraser came up.

Cora had tried to present the little information she had gleaned as impartially as she could, but when she'd asked if James would allow Fraser to stay at Locharden House, the reaction had not been at all what she'd been expecting.

'Why would he even ask that?' James had frowned. 'This is his home, after all.'

Cora had taken a few moments to respond.

'James, you know he has always had a problem being honest with you. He's ashamed of what's happened.'

James had paced across the living room, the slight limp he had developed since his fall appearing a little more pronounced than it had been recently.

'That boy has never faced up to anything that was remotely difficult in his entire life. He turns and runs at the first sign of trouble, or hard work, be that at school or within this family. And what he did to you, and then to that Holly, and those wee children...' He'd swung around, his eyes on fire. 'I want to shake him until his teeth rattle. Tell him that he's got to stand up and be a bloody man, once and for all. Part of me is glad his mother never lived to see the mess he's made of everything.' James had slumped into his chair by the fire.

Cora had been conflicted; her fondness for James, and her understanding of his frustration, surprisingly diluted by a pinprick of sympathy for the Fraser she had seen earlier that day.

'I understand, James, but think about this. He *has* come back. He wants to see his children, and he is asking if you will help him. Don't you think that is him facing up to things, in a way?'

James had looked startled, probably thinking that, after everything, she was taking Fraser's side, and wanting to squash that thought, she'd continued.

'There's a lot that he's done that we might never understand, or feel we can forgive, but him wanting to come home and face me, and you, when he probably knows how we feel about everything, is brave. Don't you think?'

She'd held her breath as James's brow had creased, then smoothed again, and a look of tired resignation had washed over him.

'Honestly, Cora, I'm tired of being angry. I just want him to sort himself out. And if staying here for a few days is what it takes, then that's fine.' He'd shrugged. 'Who knows. Perhaps he's finally grown up.'

Cora had said she thought he was making the right decision, had hugged him, and had taken Ross and Evie home via Aisha's flat. She couldn't wait to bring her friend up to date with everything that had happened.

. . .

Evie had Aisha's headphones on and was glued to *Frozen*, playing on Aisha's laptop. Aisha sat with Ross on her knee, the little boy flipping the pages of a picture book about dinosaurs. He had Nutella smears on his Thomas sweatshirt and his cheeks were rosy from the heat pulsing from the fireplace.

'F is the limit, really.' Aisha helped Ross turn the page. 'But James said it was OK?'

Cora nodded, grateful that Aisha had remembered to use just the first initial of Fraser's name, in front of the children. She didn't know if they remembered their father's first name, but she didn't want to risk it.

'Yes. It was as if, through the anger, he was hurt that F felt he had to ask to come home. It was actually sweet.' Cora shrugged, standing with her back to the fire and letting the waves of heat coming from the gas flame warm her calves.

'I wonder what H will think. Does she know F's back?'

'Mumma, come.' Ross held out a hand to Cora, his fingers grabbing for her.

Touched, Cora crossed the room and sat next to Aisha on the sofa and squeezed his pudgy leg.

'I'm not going to tell her yet. He seemed quite spooked about her finding out, which was weird. I'm not sure what's going on there.'

Aisha tutted. 'They were always an odd couple, if you ask me.'

Cora wiped a fleck of Nutella from Ross's cheek.

'I suppose we'll eventually find out what truly went on between them. Though I'm not sure I want to know.'

Aisha moved Ross to Cora's knee and stood up. Her scarlet sweater topped by her vibrant hair was a shock of festive colour against the creamy walls of her living room.

'When is she coming back to see the rug rats?' Aisha walked into the open kitchen area and refilled the kettle.

'I'm going to suggest Boxing Day. I don't want anything to

spoil Christmas for the babes.' She sniffed Ross's neck, the salty, powdery scent of his skin good enough to eat. He squirmed, his throaty giggle sending a spark of love through Cora that snagged her breath.

'Good plan.' Aisha rinsed out their mugs and dropped two new tea bags into them. 'Do you want me to bring anything tomorrow night? Apart from wine, of course.'

'No. But thanks. I'm all organised.' Cora moved Ross's blonde fringe out of his eyes. 'You need a haircut, young man.'

Ross nestled in against her chest, his fingers resting on the open book. 'Love you, Mumma.'

Cora looked up at Aisha, the two women locking eyes above his head.

'Oh my God,' Aisha mouthed, her palm pressed to her chest.

'I know,' Cora mouthed back, her eyes stinging.

That evening, Cora had phoned Fraser and told him that James had agreed that he could stay at Locharden House. Fraser had sounded relieved.

'Thanks, that's great. Should I phone him, then?'

'Fraser, he's your dad. Regardless of everything that's happened, he cares about you, and he wants you to be happy. So, yes. Phone him. He won't bite.'

Fraser had made a soft, snorting sound. 'He won't bite *you*, maybe, but I've still got a few scars.'

Cora realised, not for the first time, that even after all the time she and Fraser had been together, she likely did not know everything that had gone on between father and son. Fraser had told her a lot, but as had happened in the café in Braemar, she sensed that there was more he was hiding from her.

'He's fine about it. Look, just talk to him. You two might find that a few days under the same roof will be a good thing.

You might even gain a little more understanding of each other.' She'd stopped herself, not wanting to patronise him.

'I will, and thanks again. Cora the great to the rescue, as ever. You're a saint.'

She'd felt a surge of irritation at him canonising her this way. She was far from perfect, and she'd have preferred him to acknowledge her humanism, or compassion, rather than make her out to be some kind of do-gooding automaton, but Fraser had never been good at saying the right thing at the right time.

Evie was sitting on the floor by the Christmas tree in her pyjamas, her legs straight out at a ninety-degree angle and her fluffy slippers bobbing in time to the music. Noddy Holder's raspy voice was wishing everybody a merry Christmas as Evie ate some sliced pear from a plate that Cora had put in front of her.

'So, can we open our presents tomorrow?' Evie popped a piece of pear into her mouth.

'No. The day after tomorrow.' Cora checked the time. 'Right, eat that up, then we'll do our teeth.'

'I don't want to go to bed,' Evie pouted.

Cora stood up and lifted an already sleeping Ross from the sofa into her arms.

'Come on, chickadee. Let's go upstairs now. Ross is already zonked out.' She felt Ross's warm breath on her neck as she helped Evie up and watched her carefully carry the empty plate into the kitchen. Evie slid it onto the counter by the sink and turned to Cora.

'Well done. Good girl.' Cora smiled at her. 'Now let's count the stairs on the way up.' Evie loved numbers and Cora was encouraging her to count at every opportunity.

'But I know there are thirteen.' Evie shrugged. 'It's boring.'

Cora couldn't help but laugh. 'Well, sorry it's boring, but if you want to be a clever girl you'll need to know how to count up to really big numbers.' Cora walked to the stairs, Evie close behind her.

'I can use a computer,' Evie reasoned, as she followed Cora up the stairs, Evie trailing her fingers along the top of the banister.

Amused at the mature logic of the statement, Cora wiggled her eyebrows at Evie. 'That's true, you could, but what happens if there's a power cut?'

'I'd have a holiday instead.' Evie's mouth dipped at the edges and Cora laughed once again.

'Well, that's a very good plan.'

She walked across the landing and into the children's bedroom, pulled the covers back on the bottom bunk and carefully laid Ross down. Covering him up and tucking the quilt along his sides, Cora then leaned in and kissed his forehead.

Behind her, Evie was hopping from foot to foot.

'Right. Teeth.' Cora took Evie's hand and led her to the bathroom. As Evie suddenly took the loaded toothbrush from Cora and began scrubbing her own teeth, surprised, Cora sat on the edge of the bath and let her give it her best shot.

Evie made a good job of the front, then Cora helped her with the back ones, then held Evie's golden hair behind her as she spat the foam into the sink.

'Nicely done, Miss Evie.' Cora smiled at her in the mirror.

'I'm a big girl now.' Evie wiped her mouth on a flannel. 'I can do things.'

'You certainly can.' Cora took the flannel and tossed it into the wicker laundry basket in the corner. 'Will you help me wrap some presents tomorrow, for Auntie Aisha, and Bruce?'

Evie tipped her head to the side, a tiny frown creasing her brow.

'What is it, love?'

'Is Auntie Aisha my family?'

Cora's eyebrows jumped, the question not something she'd been prepared for and one that needed a thoughtful response.

'Not really family, but a very special friend.'

Evie blinked several times, her brow still furrowed. 'Who *is* my family?'

Cora beckoned to Evie and drew her close, Cora's mind spinning. This was a minefield that she was nervous about navigating. What she said next could be confusing, and potentially damaging, but one thing she would never do to either Evie or Ross was lie to them.

'Ross is your family, and your mummy and daddy are too. And Grandpa, of course.' She felt Evie relax into her, Evie's silky hair smelling of coconut.

As if reading Cora's mind, Evie lifted a long hank of hair from Cora's shoulder and wound her finger through it, seemingly dismissing the mention of Holly and Fraser.

'And *you* are. But why is your hair and my hair different colours?'

Cora swallowed hard, her chest beginning to ache.

'I'm not really your family, Evie. I love and adore you, and I'm taking care of you, but your mummy and daddy are your family.'

Evie pulled back from Cora, Evie's green eyes piercing. 'I want *you* to be my mummy.'

Cora felt tears pressing in.

'When we love someone a lot, like I love you and Ross, that's a special kind of family. Let's call that the family of our hearts.' She placed a palm on Evie's little chest. 'And we can invite anyone we love into that family.' She watched as Evie's frown faded, and the child's expression seemed to brighten. 'So, I am in the family of your heart, and so is Auntie Aisha.'

Evie nodded, then placed her palm on Cora's chest, the gesture so poignant and touching that Cora had to blink repeatedly to hold back tears.

'Who is in your heart family?' The crystal-clear innocence in Evie's eyes was heartbreaking.

Cora smiled fondly at her. 'You and Ross, and Grandpa James. Auntie Aisha.' Cora paused, then deciding that she must do this for Evie, to begin to prepare her for what might be coming, Cora added, 'And your mummy and daddy, too.'

18

Christmas Eve had been fun, Aisha bringing a train set for Ross, a miniature stroller for Evie's dolls, and a beautiful hamper from Mackay's for Cora.

Cora had excelled herself making a succulent pork roast with all the trimmings and a pavlova covered in paper-thin kiwi and strawberry slices that Bruce had had three helpings of. After dinner, Evie had entertained them by dancing around the living room with tinsel wrapped around her shoulders like a glittery boa.

Ross had made a nest of wrapping paper and then banged on a little drum that Bruce had bought him until Cora had to take the drumstick away. When Ross had begun to cry, Cora had cuddled him close, with Elly tucked under his chin, watching as his golden eyelashes flickered and he finally fell asleep on her lap.

Bruce had been relaxed, his brown eyes following Aisha around the room, a gentle smile on his face that Cora approved of. He seemed like a kind man. A thoughtful man, who obviously cared deeply for Aisha, and if Aisha was happy, then Cora was too. He had brought his guitar with him and, after dinner, they'd sung carols around the fire. Having the house full again had been wonderful, but perversely had heightened Cora's loneliness, a strange side effect of the warmth and joy of the evening.

Cora had let Aisha help her tuck Ross and Evie in, read them *The Night Before Christmas*, and hang their stockings at the end of their beds. Evie had been excited, saying that she could hear Santa's sleigh bells, hugging Ross and saying, 'Can you hear it, Rossy?'

Ross had nodded enthusiastically, his little toes clenching the fibres of the soft rug at the side of the bunks.

Back downstairs, the adults had talked for a while over coffee and brandy, and now Aisha and Bruce were saying their goodbyes. The following day, Cora was taking the children to Locharden House, while Aisha was spending Christmas Day with Priyanka, and had prepared a feast of Indian treats that she knew her mother would enjoy.

Cora had also made a dish of *gajar ka halwa* – a sweet mixture of carrots, sugar, milk and tons of dried fruit – that Priyanka had always made for them as children, around Christmastime. When Cora handed it to Aisha as she was leaving, Aisha instantly burst into tears.

'Oh, God, even the smell brings back so many memories.' She passed the dish to Bruce and hugged Cora so tightly that Cora winced. 'Will you come and see Mum next week, after all the Christmas madness is over?'

'Of course. Give her a hug and tell her I'll see her soon.'

Cora waved her friends off and closed the door on the frigid night, the rich smell of their dinner, and the images of the fun evening they'd had filling her head.

As she tidied up the living room, she thought about the way she'd described Aisha to Evie, and as she arranged the children's presents under the tree, turned off the overhead lights taking a moment to whisper a merry Christmas to her parents, as she had every year since they'd passed, Cora's loneliness began to melt away.

Reminded of her decision about Holly's next visit, and that she had included both her and Fraser in her family of the heart for Evie, Cora grabbed her phone and texted Holly: *Want to come over on Boxing Day? 3pm?*

Cora was relieved that after the phone call a few days earlier, Holly had not pushed it by contacting her again, and she respected Holly's restraint. No sooner had Cora acknowledged that than Holly replied: *Yes. See you then!*

Seeing the response sent a shiver through Cora. She still didn't fully trust Holly and, based on the last visit, this next one didn't bode well, either.

Two days later, with a successful Christmas Day at Locharden House behind them, Cora was anxiously waiting for her doorbell to ring.

Evie was sitting on the living-room floor wearing new jeans and a sweatshirt with a dolphin on the front – her new favourite animal. Ross was lying on his back on the sofa, Elly on his stomach and his thumb in his mouth.

Cora had explained that their mummy was coming back to see them, and while Ross had stared at her blankly, Evie had said, 'The one from my heart family?'

Cora had nodded, impressed that the little girl had retained not only the term but had understood its meaning so profoundly.

Now, as Cora caught her reflection in the big mirror over the fireplace, she blew out a long breath to calm her nerves. She had put on some mascara and rouge, and had washed and dried her glossy dark hair, smoothing out the long fringe and tucking it behind her ear. She had picked out her best black wool trousers, a soft grey cashmere sweater, and she wore the pearl earrings her mother had given her on her sixteenth birthday, the colour of the sweater bringing out the opalescence of her blue eyes.

Her decision to look put together, a bit more stylish than usual, felt important. She wanted Holly to see how on top of everything she was, a swan gliding across the surface of parenting, rather than the mad scrambling duck she felt like under the water.

As she stared at herself, her heart-shaped face slightly flushed, the doorbell made her jump.

'That's your mum.' She turned to the children, as Evie stood up and nervously put her fingers to her mouth.

Ross rolled onto his tummy and tucked Elly under his chin like a pillow, his eyes glued to Evie, looking for a cue as to what he was supposed to do.

Cora managed to smile at them both, then walked along the hall to the door.

Holly's cheeks were pink, her fair hair swinging at her jaw. It looked slightly shorter than the previous week, soft brown eyeshadow making her eyes look impossibly green. She held a big plastic bag with some wrapped presents in it.

'Hi. I'm not late, am I?' She breezed in, Cora catching a whiff of musky perfume that smelled expensive.

'No, not at all. You're fine.' Cora took the long beige coat that Holly held out to her and hung it on a hook behind the door. She was wearing a cream cable-knit sweater and black jeans, and she looked toned and healthy. There was a glow to her skin and Cora couldn't discern whether it was from well-applied make-up or just from general well-being.

'The children are through here.' She gestured towards the living room.

Holly carried the bag in front of her and walked into the room, ahead of Cora.

'Hello, you two.' She set the bag down next to the Christmas tree and turned to face the children.

Evie stood at the side of the sofa, and Ross was now behind her, his fingers gripping Evie's waistband. They both looked at Holly, then simultaneously over at Cora, who smiled encouragingly.

'Say hello to...' Cora hesitated, then steeling herself, said, 'your mummy.'

Evie eyed Holly, then she looked at the bag by the tree.

'Did you bring us a present?'

Cora tutted. 'Evie.'

'Oh, that's OK.' Holly flapped a hand. 'Yes, I did. And I think these ones are better than the last ones.' She winked at Evie, who took a moment, then, to Cora's surprise, smiled coyly at Holly.

'Can I open it?'

Holly crouched down by the bag and pulled out two parcels, one long narrow one and a giant oblong box with a big red rosette on the top.

'This is for you.' She put the larger gift on the rug rather than hand it to Evie, and for a second Cora pictured a hunter leaving a trail of breadcrumbs to attract their prey. Shaking the melodramatic image away, she watched Evie walk towards Holly, Evie's eyes glued to the gift.

'What is it?'

Holly laughed, a deep, throaty sound that thrummed in Cora's ear, and made Ross twitch as he took a couple of steps backwards, Elly dangling at his calf.

'You'll have to open it to find out.' Holly nodded at the box as Evie sat cross-legged on the floor and began tearing the paper off.

Cora crossed the room and, on a reflex, lifted Ross onto her hip, her need to give him comfort obliterating any thought of Holly's potential reaction. Catching the movement, Holly glanced over at them, a flicker of anxiety crossing her face before she replaced it with a practised smile. Cora walked to the window as Ross clung to her neck, his legs wrapped around her and his fingers in her hair.

Evie ripped the final piece of paper off to reveal a box covered in illustrations of a Barbie mansion. While Cora thought it a little grown up for her at just four, Evie squealed.

'Barbie!'

'Do you like it?' Holly beamed at her daughter.

Evie nodded, already trying to get the box open.

'Do you want me to help you?' Holly sat on the floor next to Evie and began opening the box. Then, as if sensing Cora looking at her, Holly turned to Ross. 'This is for you, Ross.' She lifted the long parcel and held it out. 'Would you like it?'

Ross tightened his grip on Cora and shook his head.

Holly's smile faded as she put the box on the rug. 'It's there if you want it, pal.'

Cora thought she could see disappointment in her eyes, but that Holly just turned back to Evie, rather than persevere with Ross, was puzzling, and hurtful.

Cora walked over to the rug and tried to put Ross down, but he wouldn't release his grip on her, his fingers now tugging at the back of her hair and his cheeks looking flushed.

'All right, sweet boy,' Cora whispered, shifting him higher up on her hip. 'We can open it later. OK?'

Ross nodded, his thumb going into his mouth as he lifted Elly and jammed his face into the threadbare fur.

'I think he's tired.' Cora put her hand at the back of his head and gently rubbed his hair, something that calmed him when he was distressed.

Holly was staring at her now, a distant look in her eyes.

'You're very good with him.' Her voice was wistful, peppered with what sounded to Cora like regret. It made Cora sad for a moment, then the anger that she'd been keeping at bay threatened to erupt, bringing with it a slew of long-buried accusations and vitriol. If Holly truly wanted to form a bond with her son, she'd have to try a little harder than this.

As Cora took a few moments to collect herself, with Holly's help, Evie tugged the giant pink mansion from the box.

'Look, Mummy. It's *pink*.' Her face was alight as she spoke not to Holly, but to Cora.

Cora's heart lifted, while Holly instantly looked defeated, hurt cloaking her features as she turned her face towards the window.

19

Sympathy and frustration were doing battle inside Cora. She was annoyed that she and the children were in this uncomfortable situation, in her home, their safe place, but corralling her emotions, she found a smile for Evie.

'Yes, chickadee. It's a lovely house.'

Holly's shoulders visibly shifted backwards, and when she turned back to Evie, she was smiling.

'Maybe we can put it in your new bedroom?' Holly said suddenly.

Evie was engrossed with her new toy and seemed not to have registered what Holly said, but Cora flashed her a warning look that obviously hit home.

Holly looked flustered, running her hand through her hair several times, then sitting on the edge of the chair next to the Christmas tree.

Cora felt Ross's grip loosen, so she set him on the ground, and no sooner was he free than he ran out of the room.

'Where's he off to?' Holly made to get up, but Cora held her hand up, palm out.

'I'll go. You talk to Evie.'

Holly visibly regrouped and simply nodded, as Cora went into the hall in search of the little boy.

There was something odd in Holly's manner when it came to Ross, a deeper disconnect than there was with Evie. Cora scanned the kitchen, seeing no sign of him, then she crossed the hall and climbed the stairs two at a time. As she walked across the landing, towards the children's bedroom, Cora reasoned that Ross had been eighteen months old when Holly had left him on the doorstep. It was understandable that the child had no memory of her, and that Holly felt more connected to the now four-year-old girl she had walked away from than her baby son – a sweet natured boy who was now nearly two and a half, and whose character was forming so beautifully.

Spying him sitting on the bedroom floor next to the toy box, Cora exhaled in relief.

'There you are.' She smiled at Ross as he gave her a coy grin and raised his arms, letting her pick him up and wedge him onto her hip. His wiry legs gripped her side, and he circled her neck with his arms, the force of the child's embrace speaking volumes. Although he was still a baby in many senses, Cora adored his spirit, his gentle but strong will, and the way he openly adored his sister. That his mother knew nothing about any of that was confounding, and heartbreaking, but it made Cora even more determined that, from now on, she would need to see a more concerted effort from Holly before any decisions were made about the children's future.

The rest of Holly's visit had been relatively peaceful. Cora had kept Ross close, and he had remained quiet and detached, avoiding Holly unless she talked directly to him. Even then, he hid behind Cora, or the sofa, mumbling a word or two, and eventually Holly had given up trying.

As she'd observed Holly interacting with Evie, and the

obvious joy on Holly's face, Cora had begun to question her own reservations. Holly was here, putting in the effort both in fixing her life and in setting herself up to take care of her children. The missing piece of the mystery was Fraser, and how he fitted into this whole, bizarre disappearing act of theirs.

Thinking about Fraser, Cora wondered whether he'd phoned his father yet, but rather than call James to ask, she would stay out of it. They were grown men who needed to put their differences aside, talk to one another, and work together to repair the damage that had occurred in their relationship and had left them close to being strangers for much of Fraser's life.

During Holly's visit, Cora's decision to keep Fraser's presence a secret had solidified, but she felt conflicted, particularly as she still didn't know exactly what he was hiding.

Aside from the awkwardness with Ross, Holly seemed genuinely happy to be with the children, and until Cora could observe how things progressed between them, and then gauge the children's response to Fraser, there was nothing to be gained in betraying his trust.

Holly left around 5 p.m. and Cora had been pleasantly surprised that Evie had given her a shy hug goodbye. From Cora's hip, Ross had waved, that in itself being progress – unless, of course, Cora wondered, he had simply been happy that Holly was leaving.

Now that the children were in bed and Cora had cleared up the kitchen, and stoked the fire, she sat in the armchair that had been her mother's and stared into the flames.

The whole situation had become so complex that Cora's head was reeling. Evie, Ross, James, Holly and now Fraser were a set of delicate plates that she was spinning on bendy rods, each needing her constant attention so as not to come crashing down on the ground and shattering into so many pieces that they might never be put back together. It was exhausting, and had it not been for Aisha, her rock, Cora would have been utterly overwhelmed.

Just as she thought about her friend, as if divining her presence, Cora's phone chirped next to her. She turned it over and read the text from Aisha, Cora's lips moving silently.

How was the visit from you-know-who?

Cora began to type OK, then stopped. She owed Aisha truth, so she started again.

Weird. Awkward. Sad, and a bit scary. I can't lose them, Aisha.

Cora watched the ubiquitous dots as Aisha typed her reply, Cora's chest aching dully as if it were bruised. As she looked at the words she'd typed, they took on weight. What if she had to give Evie and Ross back? Would she survive that kind of loss?

Aisha's reply appeared on the screen, and it instantly made Cora's eyes fill.

You'll always have me.

Three days later, while the children were watching their morning cartoons, Cora received a phone call from James.

They had not been to Locharden House since Christmas Day, and she was in the kitchen, having made Eliza's fruit dumpling that she intended to take with them that day. The intense smells of fresh ginger, cinnamon and cloves had brought with them poignant images of making the aromatic pudding with her mother.

Licking some of the remains of the fruit mixture from a wooden spoon, savouring the sharp and yet sweet combination of the orange peel and the juicy raisins, Cora answered the call.

'Hello, m'dear. How're things?'

She wedged the phone under her jaw and washed the spoon in the sink.

'Fine. I just made some dumpling to bring over.'

'Oh, lovely. You do spoil me.' His voice was full of warmth, then he cleared his throat. 'So, Fraser's here. He arrived yesterday.'

Relief flooded through Cora.

'Good. How's it going so far?'

'We're finding our feet. He's out in the greenhouse with Duchess. Said he wanted to help me with the orchids.'

Cora dried her hands and sat at the kitchen table, trying to picture Fraser in James's long greenhouse, amidst the rows of delicate blossoms, the steamy temperature making his skin tacky as it did to hers whenever she was in there for more than a few minutes.

'That's great, James.' She smiled to herself, then dived straight into the difficult stuff. 'Have you two talked about what happened, his life in London, and why he's back?'

'Not in so many words. He just said that he will tell me everything soon but must get some things worked out first.' He halted. 'It's strange, but he seems... different, Cora. More centred.'

Cora considered the word and realised that she agreed. The Fraser she had met a few days earlier had lost the nervous energy that used to emanate from him, the habits of picking at his cuticles, stretching his neck awkwardly, and clearing his throat before he spoke.

'That's exactly the right word, James. I hadn't put a label on it, but that's it.'

'He's really keen to see the children, so I was thinking today would be as good a time as any, if you agree, of course.'

Cora let the question linger for a few moments, swamped by an unsettling image of walking into the kitchen at Locharden House and Fraser standing at the far end, anxiously waiting for some sort of recognition, at least from his daughter, just as Holly had.

Cora tried to imagine the children's reaction to their father, a relative stranger, coming back into their lives so soon after their mother had, and as she put the scene together in her mind, once again Cora was overcome with a sense of loss so profound that it gripped her heart like a vice.

Glancing at the clock on the cooker, she calculated that she would only have an hour or so to get the children ready, and talk to them about seeing their father, the short timeline making her anxious.

'Um. I think that'll be OK. But I'll need to prepare the children first, James, so give me an extra hour or so. We could be there at one instead of twelve.' She looked over her shoulder, catching the familiar music of *Thomas the Tank Engine* floating into the hall.

'Perfect. I'll get Fraser to help me set the table and get things ready for you.' He sounded pleased, a lilt of excitement in his voice that was sweet, and somewhat unexpected.

'Good. See you soon, then.'

'Thanks. And, Cora, it's going to be all right. Nothing is going to change unless you and I decide it is.'

James sensing her anxiety was touching, and his reassurance was exactly what she needed.

'Thank you.'

'Of course.'

'Bye for now.' Cora ended the call and draped a clean tea towel over the pudding.

The time it would take to cool was all the time she had to tell the children that in the space of ten days, not one but both of their parents had come back.

Fraser stood near the door to the conservatory, just as Cora had imagined he would, his hands in his pockets. His thick Arran sweater was almost a duplicate of the one his father wore, and seeing the two of them together for the first time in several years was surprisingly emotional for Cora.

Evie had rushed into the kitchen ahead of her and Ross, and now the little girl stood completely still, a few feet from her father, her fingers twisting a length of her hair into a golden coil.

The conversation with the children earlier that morning had been less jarring than when she had talked to them about Holly, and while Evie had seemed more curious than spooked, Ross had remained quiet, his big blue eyes glued to his sister, and his thumb plugged in his mouth, as usual.

'So, our daddy who went away?' Evie had tipped her head to the side, taking Ross's hand in hers. The protective gesture had sent a wave of maternal pride through Cora.

'Yes, chickadee. Your daddy who had to go away.'

Cora had waited for more questions, but, oddly, Evie had just nodded.

'OK.'

'Do you want to ask me anything about him?' Cora had gently probed.

'No.' Evie had shrugged, then led Ross out of the room and into the kitchen, leaving Cora flabbergasted.

Now, as Evie stared at Fraser, James stepped forward.

'Hello, Evie-bell.' He beamed at his granddaughter. 'Give your old grandpa a love then.' He opened his arms wide.

Seeming to snap out of a trance, Evie walked into his arms and hugged him tightly around the middle.

'Hello, Grandpa.' She spoke into his stomach, then turned her head and once again stared at Fraser.

Fraser met Cora's gaze, as if asking for her permission to speak, so she nodded. He stayed back, taking his hands out of his pockets, but as soon as Evie stepped away from her grandfather, Fraser spoke softly.

'Hello, Evie. I like your coat. Is that a rainbow on the back?'

Evie took a second to register, then twisted her head around trying to see the back of her jacket.

'Yes, a rainbow and a unicorn.' She looked straight at him. 'Do you like unicorns?'

Fraser seemed surprised to be engaged in a conversation so easily, but he rallied immediately.

'As a matter of fact, I do. Are they your favourite thing?' He took a cautious step forward as James moved around the long table and lifted Ross up onto his hip.

'Unicorns and dolphins are my favourites.' Evie's voice was clear and strong. 'And Rossy's favourite is trains.' She gestured towards her brother, who was straining to get out of his grandfather's arms.

James set Ross on the ground as Cora put the bag of food on the counter and shrugged her coat off. As she watched, Ross walked over to his sister and gripped the hem of her jacket, his eyes boring into Fraser's face.

'Trains, eh? Well, that sounds like a sensible thing to like.' Fraser took another step forward as James moved in next to Cora, his arm going protectively around her shoulder. Cora felt the weight and support of it, and the message of solidarity was clear, and welcome.

As the children and their father faced each other, Cora and James hung back until, eventually, Evie closed the gap between her and Fraser, her little brother following slightly behind her.

'Are you our daddy?' Evie's question was razor-sharp and yet there was no guile there. Just innocent curiosity.

Fraser took a moment, once again meeting Cora's eyes, before he nodded.

'Yes, Evie. I am your daddy.' He spoke quietly, his eyes beginning to glisten.

Evie surveyed him, taking in the fair hair, the long nose, the angular jaw and the oval-shaped eyes.

'You look like Rossy.'

Fraser's face visibly brightened.

'I know. We do look like each other. That happens with dads and their children.' He smiled at her, then, shockingly, Ross let go of Evie's coat and moved in front of her.

Across the room, on a reflex, Cora reached for James's hand and squeezed his fingers, her heart beginning to race.

Ross took another step forwards and, seeming to sense that he needed to meet him at his own level, Fraser hunkered down on his haunches. Ross hesitated for a second at the movement, then gingerly walked up to Fraser, his little hands making fists and releasing at his sides.

'Hello, wee man.' Fraser's voice was low, and fractured, the tenderness in it making Cora's throat narrow. 'You're such a big boy now, Ross.' Fraser slowly opened a hand and waited, like a birdwatcher might wait for a hummingbird to land on its finger.

Evie stayed still, giving her brother the floor, and when Ross took hold of Fraser's index finger, Cora audibly drew in a breath.

James tightened his grip on her fingers, and she forced a swallow.

'Hi.' Fraser smiled at his son. 'That's quite a grip you've got there.'

Ross took him in, then tugged at Fraser's hand.

'Come see Thomas.' He pointed towards the little TV room; his eyes glued to Fraser's face. The child then blinked several times, a tiny frown creasing his brow, as if testing this mysterious new person in his life.

Fraser stood up, locking eyes with Cora above Ross's head. Sensing that he was asking for guidance, she nodded towards Evie and gave him a half-smile.

Picking up the cue, Fraser held his free hand out to his daughter. 'Shall we all go together?'

He waited as Evie seemed to consider whether this was a

good idea, then she nodded, took his hand, and let him lead her and her brother into the next room.

Cora released her breath, and turned to look at James, whose mouth was slightly agape.

'I can't believe it. He wouldn't go *near* Holly.' Cora pulled a chair out and sat at the table. 'That's... I mean... I don't know what to say.' As she watched James sit opposite her, a cocktail of shock mixed with a healthy dash of jealousy rushed through her. Ross being so open to Fraser, feeling confident enough to engage with him so quickly was extraordinary, but the fact that Ross hadn't felt the need to check with Cora, and had even walked ahead of his sister, was even more confounding.

'Did you see the way he made his own mind up?' James's face was pale, but there was pride behind his eyes. 'Just walked right up to him.'

Cora nodded. 'I know,' she murmured.

They sat in silence for a few moments, then, still shaken, Cora stood up and took the food out of the cooler bag. She had decided to make risotto, so she'd brought arborio rice, fresh chanterelles and hedgehog mushrooms, a head of garlic, some skinny asparagus and a block of earthy parmesan. As, on autopilot, she laid the ingredients out, then took the dumpling from the bag and set it on top of the Aga, a single tear cut its way down her cheek. Seeing it, James spoke quietly.

'Nothing is going to change unless you and I decide it is, Cora. Remember, that's our mantra.'

She swiped at her cheek, ashamed of her self-centred response to the touching scene of a few moments ago. She wanted the best possible outcome for the children, regardless of how it might affect her, but seeing them walk willingly away with Fraser had still hurt.

'I know. I think I'm just shocked. They were so different with Holly. Even Evie was cautious, only really opening up a bit as Holly was leaving the last time.' Cora put the empty bag in the pantry and closed the door. 'Should I check on them?' She looked over at the door leading to the TV room, hearing Evie's lilting voice over the mellow hum of the TV.

'I think they're fine for a few minutes.' James smiled kindly at her. 'Now, what can I do to help you?'

Lunch had been relaxed, the children sitting in their usual seats and eating the creamy risotto, that Fraser seemed shocked at them enjoying.

Cora had explained that she had always encouraged them to try new flavours and textures, and that they were both great in that respect, trying new things like champions. Fraser had nodded, obviously impressed.

'Wow. Well, good for you two. I lived on fish fingers and macaroni and cheese until I was about fifteen.' He'd laughed softly, then louder when Evie had chimed, 'Fish fingers are icky. We like smokies the best.'

Cora had laughed too at the little girl's reference to the smoked haddock that Cora would poach in milk, then flake through angel hair pasta for them, adding a few strands of saffron and a light broth.

Now, with the kitchen clean and the children out in the conservatory with Fraser, doing a jigsaw puzzle of a giant peach filled with lots of colourful worms, Cora pulled on her coat and met James's eye.

'So, what's your take on everything? Things seem calm between you two.' She gestured towards the conservatory. 'And he seems, I don't know. Confident.'

James nodded, then lifted both hands up as if he was carrying a tray. 'I'm conflicted. He seems more together. Says he has his life sorted out and wants to make amends, but I still...'

'*Amends?*' Cora felt a zap of anger run through her. 'Was he in a twelve-step programme or something, that I don't know about?' She knew she sounded bitter, but deep down she was still so angry with him for what he'd done – and now with the notion that he could swoop in after ten-plus months and just resume his place as their father, pushing Cora out of the new family she had built, and come to love.

James laid his hand on her forearm. 'I know how you're feeling, and it's completely justified. You and I need to talk alone, Cora, because I've learned a few things about my son that I didn't know and, well, let's just say I'm more than a little ashamed of myself. He's stronger than I knew.' He dropped his hand and turned away from her.

Shock ricocheted through her. What could possibly have made James question himself, sound so humbled, so camp-Fraser all of a sudden?

'What do you mean?' she whispered, her insides churning. Was he going to jump ship on their partnership? Leave her out in the cold after everything that Fraser had done, and that James had promised her?

'Can you phone me this evening? Once the wee ones are in bed and we can have a proper talk.' His eyes were full of concern.

'Yes, OK.' She zipped her jacket closed and lifted her bag from the back of the chair she'd been sitting in.

Just as she was about to ask James for an inkling of what he'd discovered, Fraser came into the room. He was giving Ross a piggyback, and Evie was holding onto the bottom of Fraser's sweater.

'Hello. What's happening in here?'

Seeing the ease with which he was relating to the children, the level of comfort that they had reached with his presence, his touch, and so quickly, was once again difficult to witness, and Cora took a second to find a smile.

'Not much. Just getting ready to go. Right, you two, coats

on.' She held out a hand to Evie, who released her father's sweater and moved to Cora's side. 'Have you had fun today?'

Evie nodded.

'Can you come to our house?' She looked directly at Fraser, her hand slipping into Cora's.

Cora's heart faltered as she considered, first, how she would feel about that, and second, what Fraser might say. As she played with a couple of potential scenarios, he smiled at his daughter.

'If it's OK with Mummy Cora.'

Cora blinked, this new title catching her by surprise, and despite its recognition of her position in their lives, it still created a tiny distance between her and the children. Within a matter of days, she was now competing for the role that she'd held exclusively for almost a year, and it felt unfair, and frightening.

Evie looked up at Cora, her green eyes pleading. 'Can he, Mummy?'

Cora felt as if her heart might implode as she cupped Evie's warm cheek.

'He can, but not today. It's getting late, and we have lots to do.'

'When then?' Evie said, beginning to pout.

'We'll see. Maybe on Sunday, after lunch?' She looked at James, who was buttoning Ross's coat. He didn't meet her eye, so she focused on putting Evie's jacket on, her cheeks burning.

As they hugged James goodbye, and she walked the children out to the car and put them in their car seats, Fraser was lingering at her back, and as soon as she'd buckled Ross's seat belt, he leaned in and waved at them.

'Bye, kids. See you soon.'

Cora could smell the musky aftershave he used, almost feel his warm breath on her cheek, a tinge of garlic on it. His proximity making her sense another incoming threat, she closed the back door of the Volvo and turned to face him.

'Let's take it slowly, Fraser. They did well today, but I don't want to overwhelm them.'

He dipped his chin, his eyes on hers. 'I understand. I'll go at your pace.'

As she was about to open the driver's door, he leaned in closer to her.

'Whatever I have to do to prove to you that I am able, and ready, I will,' he whispered as she frowned at him. 'I want them back, Cora.' He paused. 'And I'll do *whatever* it takes.'

This new amenable, steady version of her ex-husband was intriguing, but underneath her hope that he had indeed found himself in London, was in a place to be a better father, there was a lingering fear. What if she let him in? Let him get close to the children, and then he disappeared again?

20

As they stood opposite each other, next to the car, Fraser's statement gripped Cora's heart, the forceful way he'd said *whatever* separating itself from the other words.

'What?' She checked that the children had not heard him, but they were both absorbed in a book, their heads close together.

'I want them with me, not Holly. They need to be with me.' He pressed his palm to his chest.

Cora looked beyond him to see James standing on the top step, Duchess next to him, her tail swishing in circles. James smiled and waved at the car, then, seeing her and Fraser's body language, perhaps sensing the intensity of their conversation, he turned and walked back into the house.

'It's too soon to talk about that, Fraser. You've literally just got back,' she whispered.

'Look, I didn't mean to hijack you, and we can talk about it more. I'm so grateful to you for today, and for everything. All I'm saying is, please don't give them to... *her*.' His mouth sagged. 'She's not...' He halted.

Cora took in his expression, the slightly rheumy eyes, the tight line of his full mouth, tension palpably oozing from his pores. She knew this man well, or at least the version of him that he had let her see all these years, but something in his tone set alarm bells ringing inside her. He sounded genuine in wanting the children, but the veil around his concern about Holly was disturbing.

'If you want to talk more, we can. Just not now.' She nodded behind her. 'And I want to know everything that happened. None of this *I can't tell you* crap.'

'OK, that's fine. I promise to tell you everything, when the time is right.'

She eyed him, irritated that he was continuing to dodge the issue, and controlling when he'd finally tell her what was going on.

'We're starting mediation on Monday, so if you want to be a part of that you'll need to let Holly know you're back.'

He closed his eyes briefly.

'Not yet. Maybe you can give me the lay of the land after your first meeting. Let me know what she wants. What she says.' He shrugged.

'She wants the children, Fraser. It's that simple.' Frustrated, Cora held her palms up. 'She's apparently done the work to get the help she needed, whatever that was, and she wants them with her.'

He dragged his fingers through his hair, then turned to look at the house as if it might offer him the answer he was looking for.

'I can't join you on Monday, but if you can give me a couple more days, I'll try to join your next meeting.'

Annoyed at his reluctance to be fully involved, a rush of adrenaline finally made Cora snap. 'What's the problem, Fraser? Don't you want to present your case in person? I mean, you're not exactly the model candidate for custody. You disappear without a word, abandoning your children to move on with your own life, personally and professionally. Then you only turn up because you hear that Holly has come home and wants them back. Let's face it. Your propensity for abandonment is not exactly stellar. You might want to consider that before you choose not to be there.' The words were bitter, tinged with past hurts, and frustration, but the sentiment was spot on. If he couldn't man up and face Holly, then how could he be a good parent? What if he disappeared again when things got tough, which they inevitably would – something Cora knew only too well and had lived through more than once in her life.

He looked wounded, his eyes becoming watery as Cora's rapid heart rate ticked at her temple.

'They need to grow up with their father, Cora. I have to be in their lives.' He moved in sightly closer and spoke close to her ear. 'You of all people know how important it is for them to have a birth parent around. You lived in foster care, being shunted around between homes for years, then when you were adopted, you never located your birth parents.' He halted, then frowned. 'I never understood why you didn't try.'

His words cut her deeply, the reference to her childhood below the belt – a weapon he should not have used against her. Her decision not to try to trace the people who had abandoned her was hers alone and he had no right to throw that in her face.

'That has nothing to do with this situation.' As she bit back at him, she was flooded with memories of feeling unwanted, displaced, the impermanence of moving around so often, and not growing up with a proper family, for so many years. The memories were painful to relive, and that pain was just as powerful now as it been when she was a child.

'Cora, you have the power to change that for Ross and Evie.' He pointed at her heart. 'If you can't see that I'm the better option for both of them, then at least let me take Ross. I'll prove myself to you. I give you my word.'

Horrified, Cora sucked in a breath. 'What the hell are you talking about? They're not pick-and-mix sweets, Fraser. How *dare* you even suggest it? I can't believe you.' She shook her head. 'Would you seriously separate them because it's easier for *you*? If you think for one second that I'd allow that, you're out of your mind? Are you insane, or just inhuman?' Her voice snagged in her throat, the forced whispering robbing her of the freedom to scream at him like she wanted to. 'They are inseparable. Ross relies on Evie. She's literally his security blanket, which is hardly surprising given that his parents walked away from him when he was an infant. That stuff sticks, Fraser. Kids know when they're not wanted or have been left behind. Believe me, deep down they know.'

He was staring at her, his big hands now laced together as if in prayer, and his fingers white at the ends. 'You don't understand. It's not what you think. I don't want to separate them, but it's for the best. At least for a while.'

Cora shook her head, unable to comprehend what she was hearing. 'I'm not listening to this. I'm taking them home. You need to take a long look at yourself, Fraser, and decide what you really want. But cherry-picking between your children is not an option. I won't let it happen.' She opened the car door and got in, her hands shaking as she clipped her seat belt on.

'Don't go like this.' He put his hands on the rim above the open door. 'I'm sorry. I still need to talk to you.'

She met his gaze, seeing desperation behind the sky-blue eyes, but her anger was quashing her desire to understand him anymore. He had pushed her too far this time.

'Contact me when you've decided what you're doing about the mediation. I'm talking to Holly tomorrow to finalise the details of Monday's meeting. So, you have until then.' She slammed the door, turned on the engine and drove away, a spray of gravel from the back wheels making him jump backwards as she swung the car around and headed for the gate.

Later that night, Cora was in the living room with the lights out and the fire blazing in the grate.

She hadn't been able to stop shivering since she got home, the shocking conversation with Fraser playing over and over in her mind. Could he have been serious about separating the children? The notion was not only inconceivable, but the more she thought about it, the angrier she became. He might appear to be more centred, but, apparently, he was just as selfish as he had ever been.

When James eventually called, she considered telling him what Fraser had said, but something held her back. Her anger had cooled over the last couple of hours, and when she'd replayed the scene at the car in her mind, something had bothered her. The look of desperation she'd seen in Fraser's eyes, and the way he'd clasped his hands together as if he was begging for her to trust him without telling her why she should, had melded together making her more convinced than ever that there was much more going on between him and Holly than she realised.

Down the phone, James's voice was low in her ear, the timbre of it having always been easier for her to hear with her implant than Holly's, or even Aisha's.

'Fraser told me a lot about his time at boarding school. It opened my eyes, Cora. I had no idea what was happening at the time and when he explained, I must be honest, I was shocked.'

Cora hugged her cocoa mug to her middle and leaned her head back against the back of the sofa.

'What was going on?'

'He was bullied, fairly brutally, it seems. Rosemary and I were completely unaware, because whenever he came home for a visit, or in the holidays, he always said school was fine. He was quiet at times, but then Fraser was always a quiet boy. Not one to make a fuss, or demand attention.' James hesitated, then said, 'We should have asked more questions. Dug deeper.'

Cora sat upright, the image of Fraser being miserable at the prestigious boys' school he'd attended in Aberdeen was shocking. She had always assumed that he'd enjoyed his schooldays, all the privilege, the excellent education and facilities that so many children would have given their eye teeth to have at their disposal. 'God, really? He never mentioned anything to me either. How bad was it?' She leaned forward and put her mug on the coffee table.

'He wouldn't go into too much detail, but it sounds as if he was locked in a cupboard on several occasions, for hours sometimes. Then he had his meals taken from him by an older boy. He'd have to buy them back with his pocket money.' James paused. 'I used to tell him off when he asked us for more money. I couldn't understand what he was doing with it. God, Cora. Can you imagine? The poor boy.'

Cora's eyes instantly filled, a memory of being tied to a shed door handle by two girls in a residential home, making her shudder.

'James, you didn't know. If you had, you'd have stopped it.' Her throat was tightly knotted.

'Aye, but we were his parents, Cora. We let him down. *I* let him down.' There was raw emotion in his voice that heightened the ache in Cora's heart.

'I wonder why he never told you.' She stood up and walked to the window, drawing the heavy curtains on the starry sky.

'Maybe because I was always so hard on him. Judging him because he wasn't like me. Pushing him to do things he didn't want to, like play rugby, and lacrosse. Things I thought would make a man of him.'

Cora nodded sadly, the truth of this revelation being too cruel to corroborate.

'Anyway, I've learned more about my son in the past few days than I've known in years. It's just so sad that it's taken this long.' He paused. 'Cora, do you think it's too late to mend things between us?'

She turned her back on the window, looking down at her thick socks, their ribbed wool reminding her of her father, and the way he'd stuff one of his socks as a Christmas stocking for her mother. The gentle and easy acceptance and affection of Andrew Campbell was something that Cora would never forget, and that Fraser had never had that with his own father had been a source of pain for her ever since she'd first become close to Fraser, and oddly, it still was.

'It's never too late, James. If you're both willing to try.'

'I hope you're right, Cora.'

'Is he going to join the mediation meeting?'

'I don't know.' James sighed. 'He seems reluctant. He wants to stay incognito as far as Holly is concerned. In the past, I'd have called him a coward, but I think I must withhold judgement this time.'

Surprised, and wondering if she too needed to give Fraser more credit for what he *had* done so far, Cora nodded.

'Agreed. Maybe we both need to give him the benefit of the doubt. For now, at least.'

Cora had heard no further word from Fraser and the first, joint meeting with the mediator had gone smoothly. They'd all agreed to do it virtually, and after Holly had presented her case, and the mediator had responded with a few starter questions, Holly and James had left the call.

Cora had stayed online to talk further with the round-faced woman called Anabelle, who looked to be in her mid-fifties, with an impressive head of red hair, deep brown eyes and stylish, green-rimmed glasses.

'In cases like these, Miss Campbell, the law would generally lean towards the mother, unless there is categorical evidence of her unsuitability to parent. Particularly as Holly is now stepping up. She looks and sounds healthy, has got herself a new job and is being co-operative with you as the children's guardian. Though it's early days, it sounds as if the children are also becoming more comfortable with her, under your supervision.'

Cora nodded. 'It's just been two visits so far, but Evie did seem to warm to her a little, the second time. Not so with Ross, as of yet.' She hesitated, picturing him clinging to her, refusing to talk to Holly unless Cora encouraged him to.

'And that could take time. It's a lot for children this young to absorb.' Anabelle nodded to herself. 'May I ask if you believe that, in time, Holly can be the mother that Evie and Ross need?'

Cora was taken aback, not expecting to have to weigh in on this already. This was like being asked to be the judge at her own trial.

'Honestly, I don't know. It's too soon to say.'

Anabelle nodded again.

'Then let me ask you this. Are you more confident in her ability to parent them than in their father's?'

A weight settled on Cora's heart, her last conversation with Fraser coming back to her with alarming clarity. *Let me take Ross.* The words circled her mind, just as haunting and upsetting as when she'd first heard them.

'If I had to choose right now, I think, with the right support, Holly could be the mother they need.' As she said it, a sliver of Cora's heart broke off and floated up, lodging itself in the back of her throat.

'And why do you think that?' Anabelle's face remained impassive.

Cora hesitated, feeling disloyal to Fraser, which, given the circumstances, was illogical. But if they wanted this process to work, she had to be honest.

'Based on what I've seen, she seems more rational than Fraser. She's taking all the right steps. Being practical about having the children and what that means, whereas he seems emotionally committed, but that's about it.' She paused. 'He wouldn't even join our call today.'

'But we can't use that against him. There could be extenuating circumstances, things we are unaware of that influenced that decision,' Anabelle said.

Cora nodded, impressed by this woman's compassion and insight. 'Understood, and that's true. He did say he'd join the next one.' She watched Anabelle take some notes. 'Is there any benefit to having these meetings in person? I mean, does it help the process along at all?'

'In fact, yes. Having all parties in the same room can sometimes speed things along. If people are at odds and struggling to find common ground, being face to face can make the small stuff seem less critical, so, roadblocks can often be removed more quickly. It could be purely circumstantial, of course, but, in my experience, we've often reached agreements faster that way.'

Cora leaned back and adjusted the angle of the screen on her laptop.

'If I can get Holly and Fraser to agree, would you be open to doing it in person some time next week?'

'Absolutely. If we do that, I'd suggest you all coming to my place in Banchory. Being on neutral ground also helps everyone feel equally represented.'

'Makes perfect sense.' Cora smiled. 'Thanks for today. I know it was very much a getting-to-know-you conversation, but it feels good to have started the process.'

'I'm glad, and you're welcome.' Anabelle smiled, the dimples in her full cheeks deepening. 'Any other questions before we call it a day?'

'No, thank you. I'll talk to Fraser, and fingers crossed we can all gather in person next week.'

Cora closed the laptop, filled with a new determination to get this family round one table, and finally put some plans in place that made sense for the children, and for everyone involved. Not knowing how it would all end was like an immutable hangnail that sent frequent zaps of pain through Cora, but she knew that there was no way forward other than through.

21

The following week, having persuaded Fraser that he needed to attend the meeting in Banchory, Cora was standing at her living-room window. The sky was mostly clear, a few frothy clouds forming a shroud around the distant summit of Craigendarroch, which, in Cora's opinion, only served to make the mountain look more majestic.

Aisha was keeping Ross at her flat for the morning and was ready to pick Evie up from school if Cora wasn't back in time. Evie had been excited at the prospect of Aisha coming for her, and Cora had hugged her friend extra tight when she'd left Ross with her an hour earlier.

James had said that he and Fraser would come and pick Cora up so they could all travel together in one car. Holly was driving herself, and as it would be the first time that Fraser and she had seen each other, Cora believed that was the best plan.

When she'd talked to Fraser again the previous day, at Locharden House, he'd reluctantly agreed that he'd tell Holly he was back, and that he would come to the meeting if it helped them reach a resolution.

'I'll come, Cora. But I won't get dragged into a tug of war

with Holly. She doesn't play by the rules, and my children are not chess pieces to be shoved around a board of her making.'

Cora had been surprised by the vitriol, seeing him reverting to his old habits of stretching his neck awkwardly and clearing his throat before he spoke.

'There will be no tug of war, believe me. Neither James nor I will allow it.' She had seen him acknowledge that he'd pushed a dangerous button. 'The whole point of mediation is to resolve things before they escalate. The last thing we all need is for this to go to court.'

Fraser had nodded, his shoulders slumping forward inside his sweater. Cora had left with the children, frustrated, but relieved that finally he was going to face Holly.

Now, as she watched the street, she saw James's Land Rover come around the corner, so she grabbed her long woollen coat from the back of the sofa and checked herself in the mirror above the fireplace. Her hair was in a tight ponytail, the dark fringe tucked tidily behind her right ear. The turquoise of her sweater made her blue eyes sparkle, the thick dark lashes emphasised by a touch of mascara, and her cheekbones glowed, not from rouge but from nerves. So much hinged on this meeting, it had to go well so that they could come to an arrangement that worked for them all. Her stomach fluttering, she gave herself a determined nod, then headed for the door.

Outside, the air was heavy with mist, an early January morning that smelled of damp moss. As she pulled the door behind her, Cora squinted into the car. James sat alone in the front, the passenger seat empty.

A swoop of disappointment was quickly replaced by irritation as she walked along the path and approached the car, and when James leaned over and opened the door for her, his face was drawn.

'Where's Fraser?' She climbed into the seat, tucking her bag behind her calves. 'He promised me he'd come.'

James pursed his lips, then waited for her to put her seat belt on.

'I know. But when I got up this morning, he'd left the house. There was a note on the kitchen table saying he was sorry, but something had come up and he wouldn't be joining us. He asked me to take notes and that he'd catch up on everything that went on, this evening.' He checked his mirror and pulled out into the street. 'He left me some questions to ask, but his position is that he wants full custody.'

Cora stared out of her window, picturing Fraser's nervous neck stretching and hearing his shocking words again, about taking Ross. If he couldn't find it in him to sit in a room with his family, for the sake of his children, then Cora didn't think she could support him, or what he was asking of her.

James was unusually quiet, neither offering his opinion nor asking for Cora's, so she stayed silent, too, afraid that if she told him what she was thinking, their alliance might find itself on shaky ground. She needed James on her team, so, for now, she'd keep her own counsel.

The half-hour drive to Banchory was peaceful, neither Cora nor James talking much.

As she watched the familiar scenery unfold, the road densely lined with towering Scots pines on either side, and following the path of the River Dee, Cora was transported back to fishing trips with her father, when he'd take her to a secret spot by the Bridge of Feugh, where they'd often see salmon leaping.

Whenever she and her parents went to Banchory, though there were three bridges they would cross, spanning the Dee, she loved the narrow Bridge of Ess the best, with its small stone tower at the start, where Eliza had told her a beautiful princess lived. Cora would gaze out her window at the low stone walls on either side, topped with an intricate wrought-iron railing, and, for fun, her parents would tell her to hold her breath until they reached the other side.

Her mother, Eliza, had also told her that between 1946 and 1986, there had been prolific fields of lavender in Banchory, and that industry had made the place world famous. Now, as the bands of tall pines began to thin, replaced by more delicate birch trees and tall privet hedges, they passed the clutch of tidy sandstone homes that sat on the outskirts of the town, the peaks of the distant, green-black hills of the Cairngorms the perfect backdrop.

Cora smiled to herself, imagining a time when the air would have been heavy with the scent of lavender, long before you reached the town. She must have sighed, because James looked over at her.

'Are you all right?'

She shifted in the seat, the memories filling her with the customary mixture of calm, and sweet nostalgia.

'Yes, just reminiscing.' She looked out of her window again, and as the mixture of small shops and homes around them increased in density, she saw the sign for Raemoir Road, where she knew they must turn left. 'This is it.' She pointed at the junction in front of them, the proximity to their destination, and what lay ahead, extinguishing her moment of peace.

Holly was already at Anabelle's house when James and Cora arrived. Holly wore a stylish, long cream coat and her hair was up in a tight French roll, making Cora wonder at the copious amount of hairspray that she must have used to keep it in place. Holly looked smart and businesslike, as opposed to Cora's more mum-ish outfit.

Holly smiled warmly at Cora when she and James walked into the entrance hall of the Georgian, semi-detached house.

'Hello, Cora.' She looked beyond Cora then, seeing her former father-in-law. 'James.'

'Holly.' James's tone was formal but polite, just the way Anabelle had advised them, before they'd all met online.

Anabelle was taller than Cora expected, a full head taller than her own five feet five. She wore a Stuart tartan skirt with pale-blue sweater that complemented her brown eyes.

James was hovering at the door, taking longer than was necessary to brush his feet on the mat, his grey wool trousers, crisp white shirt, and navy sports jacket looking well put together.

'Come on through, everyone.' Anabelle gestured towards the back of the house, then led them across the hall and into a bright room, set up with two leather sofas facing each other and a long wooden coffee table in the middle. There were five teacups and a plate of biscuits on a tray, and a small vase of gerbera daisies sat in the centre of the table. The informality of the room was a relief to Cora, who had expected an impersonal office or conference room-type setting.

The big bay window overlooked a leafy back garden, with a terraced lawn, two steps up from the semicircular patio outside the French doors that were offset from the middle of the sitting area.

'You have a lovely home.' Cora slipped off her padded jacket and draped it over the back of the sofa.

'Thanks. We've been here a long time.' Anabelle sat on the end of the sofa facing the window, so Cora sat next to her, letting James and Holly settle on the opposite one. 'I'm glad we're meeting in person today.' Anabelle smiled at them each in turn, then focused on James. 'Fraser was unable to come, I take it?'

James nodded. 'I'm afraid so, yes.'

At this, Holly's head whipped around, and she stared at James, her mouth gaping slightly. 'Fraser's *back*?'

Cora's breath caught, her assumption that Fraser had been true to his word, and phoned Holly to say he was in town, suddenly making Cora feel foolish. Since when had Fraser ever been true to his word? Today was obviously no different.

What *was* different, though, was that this time, Cora was done protecting him.

22

Cora hugged Ross close to her and breathed in the sweet, powdery scent of his hair. She had got home in time to go straight to Aisha's flat where they were having a quick cup of tea before Cora went to pick Evie up from school.

'I can't believe F was a no-show.' Aisha drained her mug and put it on the floor next to her chair. 'What a waster.'

Cora sniffed Ross's neck until he giggled and wriggled lithely out of her arms.

'I don't know why I'm surprised. He's certainly not earned back any trust so far, despite all his pleas and promises.' Cora watched Ross reaching for another chocolate biscuit. '*Ah ah*! Did you ask Auntie Aisha first?'

Ross pinched his fingers together in mid-air and looked over at Aisha.

'Please?'

Aisha mocked serious consideration, then grinned.

'Sure, wee man.'

Ross lifted a biscuit and bit into it, then walked to the bookshelf by the fireplace and plopped down on his bottom, his free hand touching the spines of a row of cookery books.

'So, what now?' Aisha tapped the arm of the chair, her blue nail varnish clashing with the green velvet.

'Though I hate to say it, on paper, H looks like the better bet. Not that I'm saying sign here and they're all yours.' Cora frowned. 'I just think she is more serious about it.'

'I never thought I'd say this about that useless baggage, but she might be.' Aisha grimaced.

'I need to talk to Anabelle, though. My gut is telling me that there's something Holly's not saying. I swear it's like playing detective with that pair.'

'What do you think it is?'

'I don't know. It could just be that there's part of me that wants her to screw up. To make it easy for me to say no to her, because I don't know what my life will look like if the children aren't in it anymore.' Cora's heart felt weighted, vulnerable, and she was decidedly nervous to hear the *I-told-you-so* that she knew she'd earned.

Aisha frowned.

'Even if they are with her, some, or eventually all the time, you'll still see them, Cora. If you do reach an agreement, you need to stipulate that. Can you?'

Cora shrugged.

'I don't know but I can ask Anabelle.' Cora considered the question, the thought that she might have to negotiate having time with the children chilling, and hard to believe.

Evie was standing in the playground near the gate when Cora pulled up across the road from the school. Ross was in his car seat running a tiny green train back and forth across his stomach, humming the theme tune from Thomas.

'Come on, sweet boy. Let's get your sister.' Cora smiled at him as she undid her seat belt, got out, opened the back door and lifted Ross into her arms. Then, looking over at the playground, she caught sight of a blonde head, someone kneeling in front of Evie. Cora's heart rate instantly sped up as she locked the car and dashed across the road.

Holly was pulling up Evie's sock, her back to the gate. Evie's teacher, Angela, was standing a few feet away and when she saw Cora, she smiled and waved but looked slightly anxious. Understanding why, Cora shifted Ross higher on her hip, raised a hand in reply, and as she reached Evie, Holly stood up.

'What are you doing here?' Cora snapped.

Holly looked startled.

'Just saying hello. Evie and I were having a little chat while she was waiting for you.'

Cora took Evie's hand and protectively eased her away from Holly.

'You just *happened* to be passing the school?'

Their eyes locked, a flash of irritation in Holly's making Cora pull her shoulders back, clearly standing her ground.

Seeing her expression, Holly visibly checked herself, speaking softly.

'I didn't mean anything by it, Cora. I just wanted to see her.' The left side of her mouth lifted in a half-smile, then she turned to Evie. 'I hope you enjoy the book, Evie, and I'll see you soon. OK?'

'Book?' Cora frowned.

'It's in her backpack. It's all about butterflies. She likes it.' She gestured to the pink pack hanging behind Evie's shoulders.

'It's pretty. All the butterflies have stars and dots and things on them.' Evie looked up at Cora.

'That's nice, chickadee.' Cora found a smile despite the fizz of anger that was coursing through her. 'Right, let's go. We need to get home.'

Holly hesitated, then leaned down and hugged Evie, the child awkwardly hugging her back with one arm.

'Bye, Holly.' Cora's heart was clattering in her chest as she led Evie to the gate. Ross's grip tightened around Cora's neck as she turned and waved again at Miss Dunn, who was visibly relieved.

As Cora put Ross, and then Evie into their car seats, and closed the back door of the Volvo, her hands were shaking. Holly showing up like that was unnerving, and as Cora drove home, her decision to speak to Anabelle took deeper root.

As soon as they got into the house, Evie dumped her bag inside the door and rushed into the living room.

'Can I watch cartoons?' She lifted the remote control from the coffee table.

Cora was keen to get the children settled, and occupied with something so she could make a phone call, so while she didn't like them staring at the TV endlessly, this would make things easier.

'Yes, OK. Let me turn it on for you.' She took the remote as Evie climbed onto the sofa and Ross, who had followed his sister as always, climbed up next to her.

Cora found something suitable, then gave them each a drink in a cup with a straw. Satisfied that they'd be fine for a while, she went into the kitchen, found her phone and called Anabelle, who answered on the second ring.

'Oh, Miss Campbell. I'm so glad you phoned. I was just going to call you.'

Cora's stomach instantly somersaulted. 'Why, what's happened?'

'I wanted to let you know that after our meeting, Mrs Munro phoned me. She said that she's decided that mediation isn't going to work after all, and she wants to go through the court to petition for full custody.'

Cora felt the air leave her in a rush, her worst fears realised.

'Oh, God.' She gripped the phone tighter, glancing behind

her to ensure that the children were still in the other room. 'Is there anything we can do to prevent that?'

'All we can do is try to persuade her to give mediation a little longer before she goes down another route.'

Cora's vision blurred, her throat beginning to burn. She'd been naïve to trust that Fraser would do the right thing, and right to doubt Holly's intentions, and being stuck in the middle of them, trying to figure out the better of two less-than-ideal individuals, was excruciating. Cora's own wishes felt as if they were getting scrubbed out as the children's parents looked likely to begin a painful, and inevitable, tug of war with poor Evie and Ross at its centre.

'Can you please talk to her again? Try to make her stick with it?' Cora whispered.

'I'll do my best, but we should be prepared for her to walk away. I think you need to prepare yourself, Miss Campbell. While I'll do everything in my power to help you, it could be taken out of our hands.'

Cora pressed her eyes closed as a single tear crept down her cheek. She couldn't let the children be distressed by this, to be made to feel unsafe, or uncertain of what was happening to them. As she racked her brain as to what to do, Fraser's face materialised behind her eyes. If he knew Holly's intentions, maybe he'd finally see the seriousness of what was happening, and the need to face her.

As Cora found his number in her phone, her chest was aching. She was still unsure how James really felt about Fraser not following through that day, but for now she couldn't focus on what James felt. Things were escalating, and for the first time in a long time, Cora felt strong enough to tackle this alone.

'Hey.' Fraser sounded casual, as if letting her down earlier had washed right off his back.

'What happened to you today, and why the hell didn't you contact Holly like you promised?' Cora snapped. She walked to the sink and looked out at the back garden, seeing the brown twigs of the rosemary plants sticking up from the otherwise empty planter box.

'I know. I'm sorry. I let you down. Again.' This time, there was genuine remorse in his tone.

'Look, I don't have time to try to wheedle out of you why you did what you did. I have something important to tell you.' She turned her back on the window and once again glanced towards the empty hall, the sound of the TV a metallic buzzing in her ear.

'OK. I'm listening.'

'It seems Holly wants to stop the mediation and go straight to court, to apply for full custody. She just turned up at the school today, too.'

'Jesus, we have to do something to stop her.'

Cora winced at his raised voice, startled at him forgetting about her issues with hearing clearly on the phone.

When she'd first been dating Fraser, he had asked her openly what it was like to hear through the device, and Cora had been a little taken aback at his directness.

'It's like listening to a fight between the different sounds. You are fine, because I'm next to you, and I can see your lips, of course. But anything behind me, or over there,' she had pointed towards the bar at the far end of the pub they'd been in, 'it's like static.'

He had just nodded, then thanked her for telling him, at the time leaving Cora unsure whether he was judging her or just trying to understand her better.

'Don't shout, Fraser! You know that makes it difficult for me.' She touched her implant, feeling the external processor warm beneath her fingers.

'Sorry. I know you've tried your best, but perhaps if I talk to her, maybe I can get through.'

'You have to *try*, Fraser. She could drag us all into a legal mess if you can't get her back to the negotiating table. And be there yourself, too. I honestly don't understand why you haven't taken a stand yet. Really shown up for the children.'

A few moments passed as she lifted a cloth and wiped the spotless surfaces, then tossed it into the sink.

'Are you there?'

'Listen, Cora. I get the message. I'm here. Fully engaged. I will talk to her and do whatever I can to keep things civil between all of us.'

Relieved, Cora nodded. 'Good. Let me know as soon as you've spoken to her. We can't waste any more time, Fraser.'

'Agreed.'

She was about to end the call when he said, 'Cora, could I take the kids out tomorrow? Just for an hour or so, to the park or something.'

Surprised by the request, she frowned, the next day being Saturday when she had them at home all day, with no particular plan.

'It's freezing outside, Fraser. The park?'

'OK. To get a hot chocolate, or a milkshake or something at the café. I just want to spend a little one-on-one time with them.'

Cora walked across the hall and peered into the living room. Ross's head was on Evie's shoulder, the two of them transfixed by the purple dinosaur on the screen. As Cora stared at them, every fibre of her being committed to doing whatever could potentially make them happy, she sighed. With everything that she was dealing with, Cora was utterly exhausted, so the thought of a couple of hours to herself the next day was tempting.

'All right. But just for an hour or so. You can pick them up at eleven. I normally give them lunch at one, so if you have them home by then, that's fine.'

'Thanks. That's great, and I will.'

She waited, unsure if there was more, but instead he said, 'See you tomorrow' and ended the call.

Frowning, she slid the phone into her back pocket, a voice inside her whispering that maybe this wasn't a good idea, but remembering how well the children had responded to him at Locharden House, some more time with their father could be good for them.

Couldn't it?

The following afternoon, Cora stood in the living room, looking out at the big, wet snowflakes falling into the street, and the purplish grey sky – typical of early January. The pavement was already white, and the windscreen of the Volvo parked at the end of the path was opaque, and crystallised.

She checked her phone for the umpteenth time, seeing that it was 1.24 p.m.

Fraser had been cheerful when he'd picked up the children, his face ruddy beneath a red woollen hat, and his eyes twinkling when both Evie and Ross had greeted him with a hug. He'd only stayed in the house five minutes before bundling them into his Volkswagen Golf, careful to show Cora the car seats that he'd installed.

'See you soon.' He'd waved at her as he'd closed the car door and trotted around to the driver's side.

In the back, Evie had waved, then pressed her palm against the glass, her fingers splayed wide. Seeing the small palm in a farewell gesture had snatched at Cora's heart, but she'd smiled broadly and waved back as the car pulled away.

She checked her watch again. It was 1.26 p.m. She'd give him four more minutes before she phoned and read him the riot act. Turning away from the window, she crossed the room and carried on taking the last ornaments off the Christmas tree. The box she'd started filling earlier was almost full, and the remaining tinsel and lights would go in a big canvas bag that she kept in the attic. Dismantling the tree was a task she'd dreaded each year since she'd come to live with the Campbells. The reminder that another festive season was over left her melancholy, so getting it done while the children were out having fun had seemed like a good use of time.

As she closed the flaps on the box and looked around the room, it was eerily empty. The light and energy the children brought was palpable when they were here, and now, in their absence, even the air felt stale.

Cora carried the box upstairs and put it on the ground, then pulled the stepladder down using the rope with the toggle on it that her father had installed. As the ladder slid down towards her, she was overcome with memories of helping Andrew put the decorations away. He'd climb the ladder, then reach down to where Cora was allowed to climb, only two steps up from the ground, and he'd take the bags from her and stow them until the following year.

She'd finally been allowed all the way up into the attic when she'd turned ten, and she and her father had spent a few weekends that spring clearing out years of detritus, as he'd called it – faded clothes that smelled of mothballs, battered suitcases, numerous pairs of old boots with flapping soles, or holes in the toes – that Cora couldn't understand them keeping in the first place.

'A tidy home means a tidy mind, Cora,' Andrew had often said, his propensity for purging growing as he got older.

While they worked, her mother would stand at the bottom of the ladder and hand them up sandwiches, and biscuits, knowing that they'd prefer that to coming down. Eliza had always been so thoughtful that way, giving Cora exactly what she needed without needing to ask, something that Cora was proud to acknowledge that she was able to do for Evie and Ross.

Memories flooding in, of Christmases that had been happier

than Cora could ever have dreamed of, she lifted the box and carefully climbed the ladder, sliding it onto the plywood floor, then shoving it back against the rafters to the left, under the eaves.

'Until next year,' she whispered, then backed down the ladder and went to get the canvas bag.

Back in the living room, she glanced out of the window one more time, then seeing that it was 1.39 p.m., she pulled her phone out of her pocket and phoned Fraser. It rang four times then went to voicemail, the message short and to the point. *Can't talk now. Leave a message.*

Staring out at the empty street, the snow now accumulating on top of the hedge that ran along the inside of her front wall, Cora spoke slowly and clearly. 'Fraser, where are you? It's almost two. Call me back.' She hung up, staring at the phone as if expecting it to ring right away, then anxiety gripped her insides as she pictured his car, upside down in a ditch somewhere.

Knowing that Aisha was at work, she called James.

'Hello, m'dear. How are you today?' He sounded chipper, then she heard Queenie's voice, faint in the background. 'Queenie says hello.'

'Yes, I heard. Hello back.' Cora looked out at the street again, but there was still no sign of the Volkswagen. 'James, I don't suppose Fraser and the children are there, are they?'

James took a moment to reply, Cora picturing him frowning.

'No, they're not. Were they supposed to be coming over?'

Cora's heart rate began to pick up and her breathing became jagged as she replayed the image of Fraser driving away with the children.

'No, but he took them out for a bit and he's late bringing them back.' She touched the glass of the window, the surface cool against her clammy palm. 'He's forty minutes late, and with this weather, I'm getting worried.'

'You've phoned him, I suppose?'

'Yes, I left a message just now, but something feels off. I'm not sure what to do, James.'

James's voice became muffled, Cora guessing he'd covered the microphone, then he spoke deliberately.

'I'd give it a little longer, Cora, as he might just have lost track of time. If he's not back by two, then phone me again. I'll come over and we can drive around and look for them. They can't have gone far on a day like this.'

Cora nodded, feeling slightly nauseous. 'Right. You're probably right.'

'Try not to worry. I'm sure the children are safe with him.'

Cora's eyebrows lifted, this endorsement something she hadn't expected. Hearing it was surprising, and yet reassuring, too, just the balm her frayed nerves needed. James was calm, so she should be calm. Fraser wouldn't do anything to put the children at risk. Despite his actions two years ago, he had been a good father to them, at least until he'd disappeared.

At 2.25 p.m., James pulled the Land Rover up behind her Volvo. She watched him get out, then round the car and help Queenie out, the two of them linking arms and walking carefully up the snowy path to her front door.

Having Queenie come too felt reassuring, her gentle, steady presence something Cora needed right now. She had left two more messages for Fraser with no reply, so when she opened the door, letting a gust of snow blow in with James and Queenie, Cora was near to tears.

'Still nothing.' Cora gulped. 'Something's happened to them, I just know it has.'

James shook the snow from his jacket and brushed Queenie's back with his gloved hand.

'Hi, Cora.' Queenie smiled. 'I hope you don't mind, but I wanted to help.'

'Of course not. I'm glad to see you.' Cora tried to smile.

'All right. Let's make a plan.' James took Cora's hand in his. 'All will be well, m'dear. You'll see.' He smiled kindly at her, but there was an odd tone in his voice that sent Cora's anxiety up a notch.

'Should we phone the police?' Cora walked ahead of them into the living room.

James went to the window and looked out at the street.

'It's fairly coming down now, but I think we should take a drive and see if we can see them anywhere. Where was he taking them?' He turned to face Cora as Queenie perched on the edge of the sofa.

'He said he might take them to the café in the village, for a hot chocolate or something.' As she said it, Cora was flooded with regret. She had trusted him to drive the children away without knowing exactly where he was going. How could she have been so stupid?

An hour later, Cora, James and Queenie walked back into the house, having driven around all the likely places Fraser could have gone. James had stopped the car at a few spots, including the café, where Cora had run in and asked if they'd been there, but the young man behind the counter had shaken his head.

'No, I haven't seen any kids in here today. We're closing now 'coz of the weather.'

Cora's heart had sunk as she'd darted back to the car and jumped in the back, the snow falling even more heavily.

Now, as James and Queenie spoke quietly together just

inside the front door, Cora took her coat off – for once grateful that she couldn't clearly hear what they were saying.

'I'm going to phone the police, James. It's been long enough.' She draped her wet coat over the end of the banister.

James and Queenie hung their coats on the rack as Cora headed into the living room.

Just as she took her phone out of her back pocket, it vibrated in her hand, making her jump, and as she looked at the screen, a text message appeared.

Her hands shaking, she read the message, then read it again, unsure that she had seen it clearly. As James approached her, she turned and wordlessly showed him the screen.

23

James frowned, then took the phone from her, pushing his glasses further up his nose as he read out loud, 'I'm sorry, Cora. I'm taking the children home with me. She can't get them. They are fine. Happy. I will take care of them. Will phone when we get to London, and you can talk to them. Thank you for everything.'

He let the phone drop to his thigh, his mouth agape, as Cora's legs gave way, and she sank onto the arm of the chair by the fire.

'Oh my God.' Her voice cracked as tears filled her eyes. 'How could he do this?'

'I can't believe it.' James lifted the phone and re-read the message as Queenie walked over to Cora and put her arms around her.

'Oh, sweetheart. I'm so sorry.' She held Cora for a few moments, then stepped back. 'He won't hurt them, Cora. You just have to see him with them to know that.' She twisted her long fingers into a knot. 'I'll make some strong tea while you two talk.' She lightly touched James's arm as she passed, then he pointed her towards the kitchen.

Cora watched her go, willing her words to be true, but Fraser had done something so unfathomable that Cora had no idea who he was anymore, or what he might be capable of.

Later that evening, Aisha stood in front of the fire, a glass of wine in her hand and her damp jeans rolled up at the ankles. She had come straight from work and brought some French bread sandwiches that were left over from an event at the distillery, but Cora couldn't get anything past the knot in her throat.

'I'll frigging *kill him*, Aisha. I mean it. This is the last straw.' Cora sipped some wine, letting it sit on her tongue.

'I'll hold him down.' Aisha frowned. 'Seriously, though, does he think he's living in a bad B movie or something?' She swirled the wine in the glass, the dark-red liquid glowing in the firelight. 'Kidnap is a crime, even if it's your own kids, right?'

Cora shook her head. 'I don't know. I've phoned him so many times, but he's still not picking up. He said he'd call from London, and they must be there by now.' She glanced at the clock on the mantel. 'If they left right from here, then that was eleven o'clock. It's almost eleven now, so even with stops, they should be there.'

Aisha drained her glass.

'Yes, I'd think so. Want to try him again while I top us up?'

Cora nodded, lifting her phone from the cushion next to her.

'I'm staying tonight, by the way,' Aisha called from the kitchen, the higher-than-normal pitch of her voice grating in Cora's ear.

'Thanks.' She searched her outgoing calls and phoned Fraser, expecting to be diverted to voicemail again, so when he answered, she gasped.

'Hi. I'm sorry. We just got to the house.' He sounded out of breath. 'The kids are fine. Tired, but OK.'

Cora's throat was tightly knotted, her hand trembling.

'How *dare* you? I trusted you. How could you do this, Fraser? You lied to me!' Angry tears began to trickle down her face.

'I know, and I'm sorry, Cora. You don't understand, though. I had to keep them safe.'

Cora swiped angrily at her eyes as Aisha came back in with the bottle of wine.

'Is that him?' she mouthed, so Cora nodded.

'What are you talking about? They were perfectly safe with *me*.' Cora swallowed a sob, as Aisha sat next to her and put the glasses on the coffee table.

'Yes, they were, but if Holly got them back...' He stopped mid-sentence.

'Then what?' Cora hiccupped, taking the tissue Aisha held out to her and wiping her nose.

'I had to make a decision. It was impulsive, I know, but you need to trust me. It was the right thing to do.'

Cora shook her head. 'You keep saying that, but how can I ever trust you again. Are you out of your mind?'

'Look. Come down for a few days. You can see where we are, see the house. I'm going to make the spare room theirs, and make it really special for them.'

Cora stood up, anger now shoving the ache in her chest deeper down inside.

'They have a room here. A home, with me. You had no right.'

'They are my children, Cora. I know it's been a roller coaster this past year, but they are still mine.' His voice was low, and she could picture his face, the pale eyes, duplicates of Ross's, the heavy brow, and the cropped fair hair, him sucking in his cheeks as he did when he was feeling nervous.

'You gave up that right when you walked out on them, Fraser! I am their legal guardian now. They are not goods to be shuttled around or lost property to be reclaimed whenever you feel like it. They are little children, human beings, with feelings, and rights of their own.'

Aisha's eyes were wide as she handed Cora another tissue. Cora wiped her nose and scrunched the tissue up in her fist, her nails biting into her palm.

'Come to London, Cora. As long as you come alone, you are always welcome.' He paused. 'I know they'll miss you.'

Cora closed her eyes, picturing the empty room upstairs, the image gut-wrenching – the wardrobe filled with little jeans, sweaters and dresses, the pile of soft toys on top of the toy box in the corner, then she sucked in a breath. Elly. He had taken the children with nothing but the clothes on their backs, and Ross hadn't slept a single night without Elly in almost a year. He would be inconsolable without his beloved elephant and there was nothing Cora could do about it, which sent a new needle of pain through her shredded heart.

The decision came less than a moment later, the choice crystal clear.

'I'm coming tomorrow. They need their things. Send me your address right now.' She stared at Aisha, who was nodding encouragingly. 'Fraser?' Cora snapped.

'Why not wait a few days? They're perfectly fine, and I'll get them whatever they need here.'

'No, Fraser, I'm coming tomorrow.' She nodded to herself, already thinking about stuffing a few clothes in a bag, taking a few essentials for the children, and driving down the M1 alone.

'If you really want to, that's fine. Just come on your own.'

Cora frowned, thoroughly sick of the lack of information, and ridiculous mystery and theatrics that he was creating around this entire situation.

'I'll come on my own, but I'm telling Holly what you've

done. She has a right to know where her children are. She is their mother.'

He didn't say anything for a few moments, then he sounded defeated. 'OK, just don't tell her *where* we are. Please, Cora.'

Cora could picture his face when they'd talked at the café in Braemar, the shadow that had filled his eyes when he'd talked about his marriage. She'd go to London and demand that he tell her everything, then she'd pack up the children and bring them home. Whether he liked it or not.

A few minutes later, she phoned James to tell him that she'd spoken to Fraser and that she was heading to London the next day. James was relieved but concerned about her going alone.

'Do you want me to come with you? Present a united front?' He sounded tired, and again she heard Queenie's voice in the background. Cora was surprised that she was still at Locharden House this late, then pushed away an image of Queenie, sleeping in the big four-poster bed with James, in the spot where Rosemary had once lain.

'No, thanks. I'll be fine, and I'll call you from the road and keep you updated.'

James sounded dubious. 'All right. Just take your time. Be careful on that blasted motorway and keep in touch. I can't have anything happening to you, Cora. Or the children. You're all...' He halted, his normally mellow voice sounding fractured in her ear.

Understanding him completely and overcome by the honest sentiment of this gruff old man, whom she'd come to consider as a father-figure, she swallowed hard.

'I know, James. I feel the same way. You're my family. I'll only be gone a day or so and we'll all be back before you know it.'

. . .

Rather than wait and phone in the morning when she'd want to be getting on the road as early as possible, Cora decided to call Holly straight away. While it was after midnight, if she'd been working, she'd likely still be up, and if she wasn't, then this was important enough to wake her for.

Aisha had gone upstairs to change the sheets on the bottom bunk, and Cora, now in her pyjamas and thick bed socks, sat on the floor in front of the fire. As she searched for Holly's number, rather than feel nervous, Cora was charged up, focused on her journey the next day and at peace with her decision to go.

Holly answered the phone immediately, and, as usual, shouted the first hello, making Cora wince.

'I can hear you, Holly.'

'This is late for you to call. Is everything all right?' She lowered her voice, but it still sounded raspy and robotic to Cora, who held the phone away from her ear.

'Listen, Holly. I need you to stay calm, but something has happened.'

Holly was silent while Cora explained what Fraser had done, saying only that he'd taken the children down south with him. Even as she held back the exact location, anger flared inside Cora, at once again being tugged between these two people who had turned her life on its head, not once but twice now.

'I don't know what's happened, Holly, but I'm going there tomorrow. I'll talk to him, demand the full story about everything that's gone on, what made him do this, then I'll bring the children home with me.' She stood up and turned her back to the fire, locking eyes with Aisha, who had come back into the room and was wearing an old, cotton robe of her mother's that Cora kept behind the bathroom door.

'Hang on, Cora. I don't think chasing down there is the best idea. Let's just take a breath.'

Cora frowned, shocked at this wishy-washy response. She'd

expected outrage. Anger at Fraser, and perhaps even for Holly to insist on coming with her, but Holly putting on the brakes was baffling. 'I one hundred per cent disagree.'

Cora shook her head as Aisha mouthed, 'What is she saying?'

'I am still their legal guardian, Holly, and he had no right to take them without my permission.' Cora sat on the arm of her chair, the cooling fire smelling musky behind her.

'He's their dad, Cora. They'll be fine with him for a while. Once things settle down, we'll get them back and then...' She paused, as Cora frowned, waiting for what came next. 'I want to go through the court, Cora. If Fraser wants them, he'll have to work for it.'

Cora's lip curled in distaste at the implication that the children were a prize to be battled over, the spoils to the winner.

'I know you do. Anabelle told me you'd phoned.' Cora took a second to edit what she was about to say next, not wanting to make promises she couldn't keep. 'I believe that if we can get you and Fraser at the same table, with James and myself, we can come to some arrangement that will work for everyone.'

Holly made a snorting sound that grated in Cora's ear. 'That'll be the day hell freezes over. He has no backbone, Cora. You of all people should know that. He'll never sit down like an adult, face to face with me. The old man was right about him.'

'Well, I am going to try, Holly. You and Fraser will have to face each other at some point, and unless James and I are there, and on board, nothing is going to change the current arrangement.' She clenched her teeth, ready for battle, instead Holly just sighed.

'Fine. You do you, Cora. I'll be here waiting for him to come to his senses.'

Cora closed her eyes briefly, trying to process what was happening. After everything Holly had said, all the effort she'd made in getting herself ready to be a parent again, spending time with the children, and saying all the right things, her response to the current situation was beyond Cora's comprehension. All it did was muddy the waters, and Cora was exhausted trying to figure out either of their motives, or genuine intent.

All she wanted was to get the children back home where they belonged.

24

The ten-hour drive had been mostly uneventful. Cora stopped only twice: once for fuel and once for a hot drink and to use the bathroom.

By the time she left the motorway and approached north London, it was just after 4 p.m., and her anxiety began to rise as the roads filled up around her. She hadn't driven in this city since her culinary school days and the volume of traffic was overwhelming. Thankful that she had the GPS that James had given her with the car, she crept along, the navigator telling her she was thirty-eight minutes from the address in Kensington that Fraser had texted her.

She had spoken with both James and Aisha, checking in so they wouldn't worry, and as she focused on the road, the trail of black cabs surrounding her, bicyclists weaving between the cars, and the red double-decker buses – a trademark of the city – oddly, her nerves began to ease. The chaos around her was making her inner chaos quieten, an unexpected sensation that she appreciated. The closer she got to the children, the calmer she felt, like a mother bird nearing the nest after hours of foraging for worms.

Soon, the navigator announced that in one hundred yards she should turn left, and then her destination would be on the right. Easing the car into the left lane and waving to a driver who kindly let her in, Cora steered the car into Holland Street, for the first time allowing herself to look at the buildings she was passing, take in the environment. What she saw took her by surprise.

The road was narrow, thankfully one-way, with a row of cars parked nose-to-tail along the left side. The vehicles sat in front of a series of grand, two-storey Georgian homes with white stone walls enclosing their front courtyards, many with holly trees, and other evergreens she couldn't identify, softening the urban gardens.

To her right was an elegant, brick-fronted row of terraced homes, again what she believed to be Georgian, running all the way to the junction of the next road she could see up ahead. The building was pristine, the bricks clean, with bright white stonework detailing around the big sash windows and the wrought-iron balconies on the second floor. Wrought-iron fencing also enclosed the front courtyards and many of the homes had thick hedges behind the fences, and long-established ivy climbing around the front doors. Some of the front gardens had tall trees, reaching well above the first floor, hollys shaped into tidy ovals and what Cora recognised as chestnut trees, now bare until the spring.

Knowing that one of these glossy wooden doors on her right was Fraser's home, and praying to the parking gods, Cora almost yelped when a white transit van indicated and pulled out of a space slightly ahead of her. She waited for the van to leave, then parked her Volvo, careful not to nudge the back of a sleek Jaguar.

As she got out of the car, she saw that she had parked in front of a flower shop with a giant display window, a chic black canopy fluttering in the cold wind that carried the smell of ground coffee with it.

Next to the flower shop was a bookstore, with Victorian metalwork resembling a fire surround framing the impressive door, and stained-glass panels running above it, and down each side of the frame. Cora stood for a moment taking in the scene, the staccato sound of a dog barking somewhere nearby making her cover her implant with her palm for a second.

She turned to face the terraced homes behind her, and quickly spotted the house number she was looking for, to her right. The panelled front door was dark green, the numbers on it shiny brass. To the left of the door was a large sash window with a long window box underneath it, whatever plants that had once occupied it now brown and shrivelled. There were two further windows above, one with a balcony with decorative metal railings.

The front courtyard housed an ornate wrought-iron table, and two chairs that were now covered up, and clumps of thick privet poked through the fencing that enclosed the space. A metal gate stood half open, an invitation to the brick path that led up to the door.

Cora crossed the road and then halted at the start of the path, her previous sense of calm beginning to waver. In her rush to get here, to get to the children, she hadn't given any thought to Fraser's living situation. He had told her he was living *with* someone, which hadn't surprised her given his history, but now that she was standing outside the house, was she ready to meet the new woman in her ex-husband's life?

Cora took a moment to ready herself, as a car passed behind her, sending a pulse of wind up her back that made her shudder. She smoothed her ruffled hair and put the upturned collar of her jacket down, then the door opened.

Fraser stood in the opening, his head only inches from the top of the frame and a tentative smile on his face. Seeing him again sent her back to the place she had been the day before, as fury once again roiled inside her. How dare he smile at her?

'Hi.' He stepped out onto the path, his feet in dark moccasins. 'You made it, then.'

'Cut the niceties, Fraser. This could well be the shittiest thing you've ever done, and it's a long list.' Her voice was shaking as she tried to see behind him, craving a glimpse of Evie or Ross.

A slight flush coloured his cheeks as he briefly dropped his chin to his chest.

'Just come in, OK? You'll see that they're fine.' He moved back and held the door open.

'Where are they?' She looked behind him, into the hall, desperate to see their faces.

'Come inside, Cora.' He waited for her to enter, then closed the door behind them.

Cora followed him into a surprisingly bright foyer, with a black-and-white tiled floor. On her left was the room with the large window she'd seen from the front. It was a spacious sitting room with a fireplace and stylish, modern furniture. A low-profile linen sofa and chairs faced the fireplace and there was a series of leather cubes pushed together in the centre, that she presumed they used as tables when required.

Ahead of her, the staircase was impressive with a Persian-style runner and a glossy wood banister that curved to the right at the top.

Fraser was watching her look around, his expression wary as if waiting for a bigger storm to hit.

Suddenly feeling drained, all her energy now focused on getting to the children, she couldn't bring herself to tackle him further on his fleeing with them, so she cleared her throat.

'Just take me to the children, Fraser.'

'Come through. They're in the kitchen.'

She followed him down the hall, passing another room on

the right, this one with a long wooden dining table, and chairs with backs made of driftwood, and on the wall behind the table, a large painting. She stopped in her tracks, the outline of Lochnagar unmistakable, as was Fraser's style of painting. The perspective was from the summit of Craigendarroch, the view that Cora had seen recently on her hike. The wintry sky was strewn with feathery clouds and a shawl of mist obscured the summit of Lochnagar, the atmosphere he had created not gloomy, but darkly ethereal. As she stared at the work, Cora was surprised when her eyesight blurred. The depiction of a view from a place she treasured, hanging here in this stylish and yet somewhat clinical house, was maddening, making her want to take the painting back with her, to see it where it truly belonged.

As she blinked her vision clear, Fraser said her name.

'Cora. Are you OK?'

'Yes. When did you do that one?' She met his eyes.

'Last year. It's one of a series. The others are in the gallery, but I couldn't part with this one, for some reason.' He shrugged, then gestured towards the back of the house.

She nodded, then overcome with needing to hold the children close, she followed him into a large, sunny kitchen.

Everything was pristine and white. The cabinets, the backsplash, the cool marble countertops, the long island that sat in the middle of the space, even the floor was laid with white ceramic tiles – obviously not a kitchen that had been designed with children in mind.

As she scanned the room, seeing French doors in the centre of the back wall, and beyond them a surprisingly large garden, almost the same size as hers on Montague Road, Evie ran towards her. Her hair was in a messy ponytail, and she wore the same clothes Cora had dressed her in the previous day.

'Mummy!' She launched herself at Cora, her arms going around Cora's neck as she bent down. 'I missed you.'

'Oh, I missed you, too, chickadee.' The world instantly righting itself on its axis, Cora hugged her tightly, lifting her off her feet, and as Evie's legs circled Cora's waist, tears of relief pressed in. 'Are you all right, my love?'

Evie's face was tucked into Cora's neck, but the child nodded.

'Daddy made pancakes. Ross ate three.'

Letting the tears come, Cora looked over at Fraser, whose face had paled. He had moved back to the door to the hall and his hands were clasped in front of his middle. She had wanted to throttle him for what he'd done, but seeing him now, looking uncomfortable and almost displaced in what was now his home, she couldn't help but feel a little sad for him.

Before Cora could say anything, Ross galloped around the island and clung to her leg like a limpet, his fingers gripping her jeans so tightly he pinched her skin.

'Mumma. You came for us.'

Cora's heart so full it felt fit to burst, she reached down and patted his back, the child beginning to climb up her leg as if she were a tree.

'Yes, I came, sweet boy. I'm here.' Her voice caught in her throat, as, laughing through her tears, she helped him up onto her hip, Evie shifting slightly to make room for him.

As the weight of the two children made Cora feel more grounded than she had in the past twenty-four-hours, she closed her eyes and gently swayed from side to side, as her own mother had done to comfort her as a child. Cora never wanted to let them go again.

She wasn't sure how long they'd stood there, wrapped around each other like vines, until Fraser spoke quietly, almost reverently, behind her.

'Want to take your coat off, and have some tea? Maybe a bite to eat?'

Cora eased Ross and then Evie back onto the ground, then smudged the tears from her cheeks with her thumb.

'Yes. That'd be good.'

The children stayed close to her as she slipped off her wool coat and draped it over one of the tall stools at the island. Evie's hand then slid into Cora's as she watched Fraser move deftly around the kitchen, his soft grey sweater the colour of a Ballater sky.

'So, Evie, tell me what you've been doing today?' Cora pulled a stool out and sat, exhausted from the drive and the emotional roller coaster of the last couple of days.

'Nothing. Telly, and we had pizza. I want my dolls,' Evie pouted. 'It's boring here.'

Cora's eyes snapped to Fraser whose back was to her, but she saw him stiffen. Then he turned to face her.

'Yes, we haven't had time to go to the shops yet. I was going to go out and get some stuff they need, but today's been mostly about reading stories, making meals, and starting to get their room sorted out.' His mouth dipped at the edges. 'Once they knew you were coming, they didn't want to go anywhere in case you got here while we were out.' He smiled at her, but there was clearly a sadness behind it.

Cora squeezed Evie's fingers, then leaned down and kissed the top of her head. Over at the far side of the room, Ross had climbed into a white, basket chair that was suspended from the ceiling on a long chain. His chubby legs began to kick out and back, making the chair start to twist and turn, his fingers wound through the sides of the basket work.

'Can we have a chair like that at home?' Evie's eyes were bright, and Cora noticed that there was something stuck to her cheek. Cora instinctively licked her thumb and wiped at the smear, picking up the salty scent of peanut butter.

'Ouch, Mummy.' Evie tried to dodge her as Cora tutted.

'I'm not hurting you, silly goose. Keep still.'

Evie grimaced but stood still while Cora wiped the little daub of peanut from her cheek.

'There you go. Perfect.' She smiled at Evie, who grinned back at her.

'Are we going home today?'

At this, Ross stopped pumping his legs, wriggled out of the chair, trotted across the room and once again grabbed Cora's jeans.

'I want to go home.' He looked up at her, his pale eyes piercingly bright.

She glanced at Fraser, who was putting the top on a sandwich of some kind, behind him steam rising from the boiling kettle. He kept his eyes down as he worked, but Cora knew that Evie's question had struck a blow – his body language speaking volumes.

Sympathy mixed with annoyance swirled through Cora, as she tucked a twist of hair behind Evie's ear. What did he expect? Montague Road was the only home they knew now, and that was no fault of hers. She owed him nothing, but hearing his children call her mummy and ask to go home had to be hurtful, if not heartbreaking.

25

Cora bathed the children in the white, clawfoot bath on the first floor. The high-ceilinged room also had the black-and-white tiled floor, but the walls were a calming robin's egg blue that warmed the space. There was a heated rack on the wall layered with fluffy white towels, and a creamy orchid in full bloom sat on the sill of the frosted window that overlooked the back garden. The giant blossoms had inevitably brought James to mind, so Cora had texted him again to say that all was well and that she'd phone him the next day.

While Evie and Ross splashed in the bubbles, dipping two yellow ducks in and out of the water, Cora surveyed the long wooden cabinet to her left that housed two rectangular sinks. She'd looked for clues as to who lived here, perhaps a pink toothbrush, or a make-up bag, a telltale razor or lipstick, but just as she'd noticed downstairs, there was nothing particularly personal in the room.

Having dried the children and put them into the pyjamas that she'd brought with her, Cora tucked them both into the queen-size bed in the room opposite the bathroom, where Fraser had told her they were sleeping. It was a lovely room with a big sash window and long sage-green curtains that touched the ivory-coloured carpet. The duvet was a soft green and the top of it, and the pillowcases, were embroidered with twists of ivy.

The children were dwarfed by the big bed, but seemed happy to be together, their faces flushed from the bath and their eyes heavy with sleep, and Elly tucked under Ross's chin. Cora told them a story about a sister and brother who go on a big adventure to a new city, then she dimmed the overhead light and backed out of the room, leaving the door ajar.

Down in the kitchen, Fraser was making a stir fry. It had been the one dish he'd cooked when they were married, using all the leftover vegetables they had, and steaming rice in a bag that he'd toss into the pan at the end. Cora used to sit at the table and watch him, cringing at the sketchy knife skills, the dash of ketchup he'd always add, and the copious amount of soy sauce he used, but she'd keep quiet, enjoying the effort he was making. And, despite her trepidation, each time the results had been passable.

He had heard her come into the room and lowered the extractor fan one level.

'Makes a hell of a noise, but it's effective.' He gave a strained smile.

With the children safely in bed, Cora now wanted to talk about the serious stuff. What had made him make the rash decision to spirit them away, and what he thought was going to happen now, because as far as she was concerned, she was taking them home to Ballater the next morning.

He put the lid on the pan and turned the gas down low, then opened the cabinet above the stove. Taking down two glasses, he set them on the island.

'Wine? You're not driving.' He smiled again, this time more genuinely.

'Yes, OK.'

'Thanks for not ploughing into me more when you got here. I could see you wanted to.' He slid a bottle of red from the wine rack that was suspended under one of the upper cabinets and opened it.

'I was cursing you all the way down the M1, believe me.' She eyed him. 'But when I got here, I just wanted to see the kids. I couldn't exactly slaughter you in front of them, anyway.' She accepted the glass he handed her. 'Not so, now.'

'You had to know I'd never hurt them, or put them at risk though, right?' His tone was questioning; his brow deeply furrowed.

'I didn't think you'd hurt them. Of course not. But what you did, Fraser... It was hardly rational. You put them in a car with someone who, I'm sorry, but they hardly know, then drove them ten hours away from the only home they know now. Did you think that was really in their best interest?' She sipped some wine, the earthy tang pleasant on her tongue. 'What did you think would happen? I'd just say, oh fine, keep them. No big deal.' She shook her head. 'It's time you talked to me, and I mean really talk. Not half stories or asking for the benefit of the doubt when, honestly, I have no reason to trust you any more than I trust Holly, at the moment.' She pushed the glass away from her, his expression becoming pained.

Just as he was about to say something, Cora heard a metallic clunk coming from the hall. Startled, she looked over her shoulder, realising that it was likely Fraser's new partner's keys in the door. Suddenly anxious about her appearance, wishing she'd at least bothered to swipe some mascara on before leaving the house that morning, Cora got up from the stool where she'd been sitting and raked her fingers through her hair, then pulled her Arran sweater down at the back.

Noticing what she was doing, Fraser patted the air. 'It's just Chris. Home from work.' He took a third glass out of the cupboard as a tall man, approximately in his mid-fifties, walked into the room.

Confused, Cora frowned.

'Hi.' He smiled at Fraser. The wide mouth was friendly, and the even teeth as perfect as the decor, and as white as the pristine tiles behind the sink.

'You're late.' Fraser nodded at the clock above the stove that read 7.13 p.m.

'Yeah, a long debrief after a tough case.'

'Chris, this is Cora.'

Chris accepted the glass of wine Fraser held out to him, then he turned to face her. 'Good to meet you, Cora. I've heard a lot about you.' He smiled again, the deep-set turquoise eyes encircled by fine lines, and a mop of salt-and-pepper-coloured hair receding and combed straight back from a high forehead. His face was open, and there was a kindness in his eyes that was disarming.

That it was a man Fraser was living with was surprising, and unsure what the exact circumstances were, Cora took a second to reply.

'Nice to meet you, too. I'm afraid I know nothing at all about you.'

'Shit. I like you. Straight to the point.' Chris let out a sharp laugh, the noise sounding squeaky to Cora.

'Chris, try to keep it down. Remember what I told you about that?' Fraser put a hand on Chris's shoulder, and now that they were standing side by side, Cora could see that Chris was a head taller than Fraser's six feet three.

'Oh, God. Sorry, I forgot. Forgive me, Cora.' He put a giant palm to his chest, the black jacket of his suit making the gold ring on his finger jump out at her.

Her confusion growing, Cora shook her head. 'It's OK. Just certain sounds and frequencies are difficult sometimes. I'm fine, though.'

'Good.' He nodded, took a gulp of wine, then put the glass down on the counter. 'I'm going to go up and de-work myself. Back in a few.'

Fraser watched him go, then turned to Cora who was staring at him, a frown splitting her brow.

'What?' Fraser matched her frown.

'I thought you were living with...' She stopped herself, afraid to sound naïve, or offensive.

Realisation dawning, Fraser laughed softly.

'Chris is a distant cousin of mine. On my mum's side. He owns this place and rents me the room. He's Dutch by birth and works at the International Court of Justice in the Hague. He's gone almost three weeks a month, so it works out well.'

Feeling foolish, Cora's cheeks warmed. 'Oh, right. It makes sense now.'

'It's OK. Anything's possible, right?'

She took a long sip of wine, hoping her cheeks weren't on fire.

'So, I have a lot to tell you, but can we wait until after dinner? After we eat, Chris usually goes up to his office on the top floor, so we'll have some privacy.' He topped up his glass and sat across from her at the island. 'He's been a lifesaver, honestly. I'd never have got the start I did down here if it hadn't been for him.'

Cora nodded.

'I'm surprised your dad didn't think about him as someone who might know where you were. He spent months contacting everyone that had ever known you. We both did.'

Fraser swirled the wine around the glass, avoiding her gaze.

'I suppose because we weren't close as children. He grew up in Holland, so we weren't really in touch much as kids. When Mum died, his dad – Mum's stepbrother – passed away soon after. I only got in touch with Chris again a few months before I left Ballater.' He took a long swallow of wine, then met her eyes. 'I know what you think of me, Cora, and I understand that. I put you through hell, and I am truly sorry.'

Putting the pieces together, and the connection to Chris now making sense, Cora sighed.

'You were a shitty husband, Fraser. There's no denying it.' She shook her head and then let out a laugh, taking both herself, and him by surprise.

'Well, the truth hurts. There's no denying that either.' He laughed too, this time his eyes filling with relief.

Chris had been good company at dinner, talking about his wife who renovated houses in the Hague, and what it was like living with Fraser, at one point saying, 'But I don't have to tell you what he's like, Cora.'

Cora had gone along with the good-natured teasing, even agreeing with Chris on some of the annoying habits Fraser had, until Fraser had finally said, 'All right, you two. That's enough Fraser-bashing for one night.'

Chris had washed up and made a pot of decaf coffee, then he excused himself.

'I'll see you tomorrow, Cora. I hope you sleep well.' He'd given a little bow, formal and endearing, before he climbed the stairs.

Fraser now sat opposite her in the living room, the curtains drawn on the street out front and the gas fire flickering in the grate.

'It looks OK, but you can't beat the real thing.' He gestured towards the fire. 'Locharden House has the best fireplaces. I loved having one in my bedroom, when I was a kid.' His expression seemed to become veiled, as if bad memories had flooded in.

Seeing the perfect segue, Cora leaned back in the chair,

cradling her coffee cup in her lap. 'So, talk to me. Tell me everything I don't know, Fraser, and I mean *everything*.'

He eyed her, then stood up and walked to the sleek, elm sideboard opposite the door.

'I'm going to need a dram. Want one?'

Cora saw him take a bottle of twelve-year-old Macallan from the cabinet and pour a healthy measure into a heavy crystal glass.

Unaccustomed to spirits, but sensing that he would appreciate not drinking alone, she nodded. 'Just a tiny one.'

He poured her a small whisky, handed her the glass and sat back across from her in the other armchair. He looked large, almost bulky, in the low, simply designed chair. The minimalist style of the decor now made sense to Cora, knowing that Chris had grown up in the Netherlands.

She sipped her drink and the peaty burn at the back of her throat was calming, so Cora sighed. 'Right. I'm all ears.'

Fraser nodded, then began to talk.

'It's time you knew it all. I've wanted to tell you for ages, but I was ashamed. It felt hard to admit to. To face. Worse, even, than what I did to you.'

Cora frowned, unable to imagine what could be worse than leaving your wife for another woman who lived in the same village. Then bringing up your children under your ex's nose, before abandoning your new family. But determined not to say anything that might derail this long-overdue explanation, she pressed her lips together and waited.

'I'm guessing my dad shared with you what I told him, about my schooldays.' He tipped his head to the side.

Feeling a little embarrassed that he'd guessed that James had shared this confidence with her, Cora nodded. 'He did, actually. I'm sorry that happened to you, Fraser. It must have been awful.'

He nodded. 'It left me changed. My confidence was in the toilet, and then my dad... well, he never could stand weakness. In his way, he was a bit of a bully, too. Mum did what she could, and she'd often take him on about it, but it's in his DNA. That shoulders back, chin up, battle on mentality.' He mimed standing up straight, thrusting his chest out. 'So, fast-forward to meeting Holly.'

Cora took another sip and balanced the glass on the arm of the chair, unsure what the correlation was between his sad history and his second marriage, but anxious about what was coming next, she steeled herself.

26

Fraser took a deep breath, then stared into the fire.

'When I first met Holly, she was like a bolt of electricity. You and I were happy, getting on with our life, but when she started to flirt with me, tell me that you and I were mismatched, that she and I were the same kind of people, I have to admit, and I'm not proud of it, Cora, the attention was exhilarating.'

Cora kept her face impassive, though it still hurt to relive the memories.

He took another sip, his eyes glued to the flames flickering in the grate.

'Long story short, with her playing on all my insecurities, I fell for it. I started believing that you could do better, and that Holly was more my type. Someone damaged, but kind of intoxicating.' He glanced over at Cora now, his expression pained. 'Sorry.'

'No. It's OK. Go on.' She stared into the fire, hoping that she had masked her hurt. She'd asked for the truth, and he was certainly giving it to her, albeit years too late.

'It started after Evie was born. Holly had always had a

temper, but she'd only ever been verbal with me, up to then.' He paused, his jaw visibly tensing.

Cora's breath caught. He wasn't going to say what she thought he was, surely? It was too horrible to believe...

'Fraser, what do you mean?'

He leaned back and looked up at the ceiling, his jaw rippling as he clenched his teeth.

'The first time she hit me, I was in the bathroom. We'd had a stupid fight about something to do with cleaning Evie's bottles. I don't remember exactly, but I think I said that she hadn't been using the steriliser properly, and she just went ballistic.' He took a moment, lowering his chin towards his chest.

Cora was now breathing shallowly, the hairs on her arms standing to attention.

'She picked up the soap dish from the sink and smashed it into my cheek.' His palm hovered over the left side of his face. 'I was so shocked, it took me a few minutes to realise that I was bleeding. By that time, she'd stormed back downstairs.' He shook his head. 'I cleaned myself up and made sure Evie was still asleep, then, when I got downstairs, Holly had gone. Taken the car and driven off somewhere.' He let out a long breath. 'I was in shock. I couldn't believe it had happened, then I started to rerun the argument in my mind. I decided I'd pushed her too hard. Shouldn't have criticised her. That I'd asked for it, somehow.' He looked over at Cora, his eyes now glistening.

Cora was frozen to the spot, her heart clattering in her chest and tears pressing at the backs of her eyes. 'Fraser, I don't know what to say... I had no idea.'

'It's OK, Cora. No one did. I was ashamed. Believed that I deserved it.' He made a huffing sound. 'The next time it happened was a few months later, before Evie's first birthday. I saw you that day, in Mackay's. I had sunglasses on, and a baseball hat, and you made a comment about the glasses, and the fact that it was raining outside.' He halted, painful memories obviously flooding in.

'Oh, God. Wait, I remember that.' Cora's throat was tightly knotted, her hand going to her mouth. 'I often saw you with bruises, cuts on your face, and once with a black eye.' She paused, recalling the various occasions when she'd dismissed these injuries, putting them down to his clumsiness. Regret washed over her, at her dismissing what she'd seen back then. 'Harry Mackay saw the black eye, too. He asked me if you'd started playing rugby again.' She recalled the brief conversation she'd had with Harry that day, both of them rolling their eyes and saying, 'That's Fraser for you.'

'Yeah. It was hard, and part of me wanted to tell you. Especially that day, because I knew that you'd be the one person who wouldn't judge me. But after everything I'd done to you, Cora, I couldn't bring myself to. I felt I didn't deserve to be understood, let alone ask you for help. I had no right.'

Cora swallowed hard, her chest aching. 'You should have told me, Fraser. Regardless of everything that happened between us, I would have helped you.' A tear oozed over her eyelid and slid down her cheek.

Fraser got up, refilled his glass, then sat down again.

'When Ross was born, we'd been in a bit of a better place for a while, but he was colicky, and she just couldn't cope. I'd come home sometimes and find him screaming his head off in his cot while she was lying in the bath, or halfway through a bottle of wine in the kitchen. I tried to talk to her about it, but if I pushed too far, or questioned her ability to take care of him, she'd lose it...' His voice faded, his eyes haunted by images of memories that Cora could not see.

'God, Fraser. You must've been walking on eggshells the whole time. I can't imagine how hard that was.' She watched him nod, his eyes still on the fire.

'By the time Ross turned eight months, things were at an all-time low. I came home one night and saw bruises on his legs that she said had happened by mistake, that she'd grabbed him as he'd tried to roll off his changing mat, but I didn't believe her. When I challenged her about it, she burned my hand with a hot pan.' He stopped, blinking furiously as Cora gasped.

'Surely she didn't hurt him... I mean, she couldn't have, could she?'

He looked up, his face awash with pain.

'That night, I was at the end of my tether. I shouted at her, saying she was a terrible mother and that she didn't deserve to have such precious children. She took the cast-iron skillet and started hitting my shoulder, screaming at me that it was my fault. That I was always correcting her, second-guessing her.' He paused for a second. 'I just couldn't take it anymore, so I told her I was going to report her to the police, and that sent her over the edge.'

Cora could hardly breathe, images of that kind of anger, of the physical abuse he'd endured, spinning in her mind, but the most painful and hard to visualise was Holly hurting Ross. It was sickening, beyond belief, and yet for all his faults and questionable decisions, Fraser had never lied to her, so she had no reason to think he was now. What she couldn't accept though, despite her pity for him, was that he'd left the children with Holly, knowing what was happening. The night he'd run off, leaving his family behind, and causing Holly to subsequently dump the children and disappear too, now felt even more unforgivable.

Cora's head was reeling, anger rising inside her, and before she could stop herself, she blurted out, 'Knowing what was going on, or at least suspecting that she was hurting Ross, how the hell could you have run off and left the children with her? How could you be so cowardly, Fraser?' Tears were now streaming down her face, and across the room, his cheeks were glistening, too. 'It was your job to protect them.'

'I *didn't* leave them with her, Cora.'

He gulped, then drained his glass, as Cora frowned, her confusion growing.

'That night, after she beat me with the pan and I threatened her with the police, she bolted. Stuffed a few belongings in a bag and took off. It took me a while to figure out what to do, but then suddenly I knew.' He shook his head sadly. 'So, I packed up some things for the kids, wrapped them up warmly, and brought them to your house.'

Cora's mouth went slack as she stared at him in disbelief. '*You* left them there?' she gasped.

He nodded. 'Yes. I wrote the note, left them on the doorstep, then I hid across the street until you came to the door and took them inside. I knew they'd be safe with you, until I could get myself sorted out.'

Cora continued to stare at him, her long-held belief that Fraser had left first, and that Holly had dumped her children and run away from a broken marriage, shattering into thousands of pieces, along with everything else she had believed to be true, since that day.

'I knew that Ross needed to get out of that house.' He swallowed. 'Holly had never laid a finger on Evie. Her problem was obviously with men. I was scared she would hurt our son.'

Cora pictured the little boy she had cared for and loved for close to a year. The wide-set eyes, duplicates of his father's, the gentle smile, the mischievous twinkle she would catch in his expression, and her heart threatened to implode. Just a few days ago, she had sat at a table with his mother, believing that she was the better choice of parent. Now that she finally knew the whole truth, Cora was staggered at how wrong she had been. How taken in. And more than that, was it possible that Ross, even as an infant, had deeply buried memories that had caused him to shy away from Holly, when she reappeared? The chilling thought momentarily brought Cora's eyes shut.

'After my stint of living in the hostel, then on the street, I was in counselling for months. I was consumed by guilt, and gutted at leaving the kids, but I knew you'd be their rock. I also knew that you'd have Dad in your corner. You two always got on, and he adored the children, so I was certain that between you, you'd protect them.'

Cora was trembling, her throat so tightly knotted she couldn't swallow.

'But how did you know they'd stayed with me? That Holly hadn't come back and got them straight away?'

'I kept in touch with the vicar at St Giles. I swore him to secrecy, and he kept my confidence. He let me know what was happening. That Holly hadn't come back and that the children were now living with you permanently.'

Cora frowned, picturing the silver-haired vicar at the small church that Aisha attended. A gentle-natured man who, according to Aisha, often asked after Cora and the children. Little did they know that, all this time, he was in contact with Fraser, and party to what had happened.

While she had been cursing him, and picking up the pieces of his fractured family, Fraser had been watching from afar, albeit through someone else's eyes.

'He knew where you were all along?'

'No. I never told him where I was, just that I had to stay away for a while.' Fraser shook his head. 'I put him in an impossible position, but he kept his word, and also kept me informed. As soon as he told me that Holly was back in the village, well...'

'You came back too,' she cut in, the fog finally clearing around his motives.

'I wasn't going to let her back into their lives, Cora. I'd let them down so badly, the least I could do was protect them from her.'

All the missing pieces were coming together, forming a picture so sad, so hard to believe, that Cora felt numb.

'So that's why you didn't show up to the meeting? You didn't want to see her.'

He nodded. 'Being in a room with her was the ultimate challenge. I thought I was ready, but that morning, when I was getting dressed, it all came rushing back and I couldn't do it.' His face was drawn, his eyes full of shame. 'I wasn't strong enough, so once again, I let you and Dad be the kids' champion.'

Cora recalled how angry she'd been with him, assuming that he hadn't cared enough to turn up and fight for his children. If she had only known that, in his way, he had been fighting for them and doing what he could to protect them, all along.

By midnight, Cora had grown cold, so Fraser gave her a soft blanket to wrap around her shoulders. He'd made some chamomile tea, and they were sitting in the dark, the only light in the room the orange glow of the flames in the fire.

She felt bruised as Fraser talked on, telling her of more incidents of violence and his feelings of isolation.

'I was in a village where everyone knew me. Where I had friends, and family. But I was totally alone in those months. I couldn't talk to anyone or admit what was happening. I was mortified, but I also felt that I had made my bed, so to speak. Everyone in the village knew what I'd done, choosing her over you. I was already a fool, just one who'd made yet another huge mistake.' He paused. 'There was part of me that felt the children deserved better, not just than her, but better than me, too.'

She let his words sink in, the pain and self-loathing behind them palpable.

'I kept thinking this will be the last time. We'll get through this. But deep down I knew that one day I'd have to leave. Her bolting that night was the opening I needed, and I took it.'

Cora pulled the blanket tighter around her.

'And you never considered suggesting that she get counselling? Or maybe that you went together?'

He laughed softly. 'There was no way she would've agreed to that. She said that we were a normal couple just dealing with our problems, like everybody else.' He paused, the flickering light dancing on his cheek. 'There was nothing normal about that, though.'

Cora's head was full of images that she knew would haunt her for a long time, and now, knowing what she knew, her position had become a thousand times more complex. As the children's legal guardian, she was responsible for their well-being, and their safety. Holly had said all the right things, but her reaction to Cora going to London to get the truth had spoken volumes and now made sense.

'She seemed so genuine, and positive about having treatment. I should've probed more, because all she said was that she'd been in a bad place and had counselling. I assumed it was to get over your break-up. She was making progress with the children, renting a house, buying things they needed. Getting a new job. I was honestly leaning towards her, especially when you didn't follow through and come to the mediation meeting.' She looked over at him, seeing his eyes were closed. She swallowed. 'I'm sorry, Fraser. I judged you unfairly.'

He shook his head. 'No. You did what anyone would do, given you only had half the story. I should've told you right away, the first time we met up, but there was some misplaced sense of loyalty to her that held me back. But now, the thought of her alone with the kids...' He stood up and turned his back to the fire. 'I simply can't let it happen, counselling or no. We can't trust her, Cora. Particularly with Ross. They must stay with me, for their safety. That's all there is to it.'

Cora shook off the blanket and folded it over the back of the chair. It wasn't as simple as that, as him spiriting the children off to a rented house with no plan, no support or family around them, and she had to find a way to make him see it.

'I understand, Fraser, but you know I can't leave them here now. Right?'

He met her gaze, and even in the darkness, she could see the panic there.

'They have a whole life in Ballater. A family. They *adore* your dad, and he adores them. He's a huge part of their lives. Evie has started school and is loving it. Ross is going to start nursery soon, too. We eat all our meals together in the kitchen, do puzzles, go for walks along the river, and to the park, play games after dinner, read books at bedtime, spend every Sunday at Locharden House. We have built a life.' As she said it, she knew that she was talking about herself. She had built a life, one that she had grown to treasure, and the children were its foundation.

As she pictured them clinging to her earlier that day, calling her mummy and saying they wanted to go home, Cora's heart ached. If she did what she believed was best for the children, they'd have their father in their life. If she did what was best for her, for the first time in her life, then that might not be possible.

Fraser flopped back into the chair across from her. 'But the abuse, Cora. You of all people must know what that's like, as a child. You went through hell before the Campbells came into your life.' He stopped himself, as Cora flinched, her hand instinctively going to her ear.

Memories flooded in of the residential home where she had once been beaten around the head, then weeks of pain from an undetected ear infection. The resulting loss of hearing had effectively closed her off from a life that she didn't want to be in, anyway, to the point where she had felt safer behind the silence. Everything she had been through was everything she wanted to protect Evie and Ross from. In that, Fraser was right.

'There is no way I would ever let anything happen to them.

They are my number one priority, Fraser. I would protect them with my life, but they can't hide down here in a half-life. It's not fair on them.' She paused. 'And you can't hide anymore either. If you don't face her, take her on in person, it will haunt you forever.'

His eyes were full as he leaned forward, linking his fingers between his knees.

'So, what do you suggest, because we can't risk her petitioning the court for custody and possibly winning? How would we protect them then?'

Cora took a moment, then met his gaze. 'We have to report everything that happened. If you, your dad and I are united in our position, and the court knows the truth, they're not going to award custody back to her.'

'How can you be sure? She's a master at theatrics. Who's to say they won't believe her if she tries to turn it around, maybe say that *I* was the abuser?' His eyes were full of fear.

Cora let that permeate, then a tiny light went on inside her head.

'I'm not the only one who saw you, Fraser. The bruises, the cuts, the black eye. Your dad did too, as I'm sure did your friends at the pub. I know for sure that Harry Mackay noticed because he mentioned it to me. He was joking about how clumsy you were, but he saw the black eye. If we tell her that we have witnesses who will come forward, that other people in the village were aware of what was going on, she'll have no legs to stand on.'

He was staring at her, his face a mask of tension.

'So, say we do that, and she accepts that we have a stronger case, what happens then? I don't think I can come back to Ballater, Cora. My life is here now. I have finally made headway with my painting, and I can walk down the street and not feel that I'm being judged.' He dropped his eyes to the floor. 'But even with all that, there is something critical, something fundamental missing. My children.' He looked up. 'I need them in my life, and I want to be in theirs.'

Cora understood that more profoundly than he knew, the hole that Evie and Ross had left in her heart by being absent for just one night had been astounding. The bond between her and the children had become unbreakable, and there was now no doubt in her mind that she was the most stable mother figure they could have. Growing up without a birth parent was her fate, but it didn't have to be Evie and Ross's.

Cora sat in silence, letting the next thought gather momentum inside her. If there was a way to make this happen, it could be the solution that they were both seeking, and the best thing they could do for the children.

They must find a way.

27

An hour later, Cora was fading, her body aching and her eyes heavy from lack of sleep.

'Fraser, it's almost one o'clock. I have to sleep. If we're driving back tomorrow, I need rest.'

He looked at his watch. 'God, I had no idea how late it was. Of course.'

She stood up wearily, her legs feeling wobbly. 'So, we are on the same page?'

He took her in, scanned her face, then nodded.

'We are. I'll get everything sorted in the morning.'

'Good. I promise, it's the right thing to do.'

Fraser turned off the fire and followed her up the stairs. The room she was sleeping in was next to the children's room, so she popped her head in to check on them.

Ross was snoring softly, flat on his back with his arms above his head, and next to him, Evie was curled on her side, her hands cupped under her chin. The room smelled of soap and the lavender powder Cora had brought with her and dusted their little bodies with after their bath, and she took a moment to breathe it in.

The clock on the wall opposite the bed was ticking softly, the sound a rhythmic click in Cora's ear that was soothing. Blowing a kiss at each child rather than risk waking them with a real one, she tiptoed out and pulled the door almost to.

Next door, her room was a similar size, with a king-size bed, and two sleek chests of drawers with matching bedside tables. The window overlooked the street, and the carpet was soft beneath her weary feet.

Fraser had taken her bag upstairs for her earlier and now, as she took a moment to really look at the space, it struck her that there was something different about this room.

There was a fitted wardrobe along the right-hand wall, and hung above the tiled fireplace was another painting, clearly one of Fraser's. It was of the view from the back of Locharden House, the rugged slopes and outline of Lochnagar, again depicted in winter. The light that bounced off the mountain was ghostly, giving the scene a mythic feel, as if ancient spirits would walk towards you if you waited long enough. It was breathtaking in its solemnity, and yet, seeing it made her deeply happy, and less far from home.

Next to the bed, on the left-side table, was a lamp, and a framed photograph. The frame was turned towards the bed so she couldn't see what was in it, but next to it was a shallow dish with some coins in it and a short water glass, upside down on a coaster.

As she walked over and turned the photograph around, her breath caught. It was of Evie and Ross, when they'd been much younger. Ross looked around six or seven months old, wearing yellow shorts and a T-shirt with a duck on it. He sat on Fraser's knee, Ross's smile revealing a single front tooth. Evie stood next to Fraser, her small hand grabbing his forearm. She wore a polka dot smock over a white T-shirt and would have been around two, her hair in tight curls that touched her shoulders and her eyes, the green of her mother's, already startling in her heart-shaped face.

Cora held the photograph, her eyes filling as she traced the outline of Evie's face.

Startling her, Fraser spoke softly behind her. 'It's old, but I had it on my phone, so I printed it out.' He nodded at the frame in her hand.

'It's lovely.' She replaced the photograph and turned to face him. 'This is your room, isn't it?'

He nodded. 'Yep. I'm fine on the couch.'

Cora gave a half-smile. 'Thank you.'

'Of course. I'm just going to grab a blanket and I'll be out of your hair.' He opened the wardrobe and pulled a tartan rug from the top shelf. 'I hope you sleep OK. I'll take care of the children's breakfast et cetera so you can lie in a bit.' He stopped in the open doorway.

Desperate for him to leave so she could collapse into bed, Cora saw him hesitate.

'What is it? Not having second thoughts, are you?'

He turned around, a smile lifting the left side of his mouth. 'No. But you are amazing, Cora. I honestly think you are the bravest person I know.'

'You need to get out more.' She laughed softly, then she saw a need in his expression that she now knew she could fulfil. 'You are brave too, Fraser. You took your own path and stuck to it. That takes guts.'

He looked shocked, but then a grateful smile reached his eyes.

'Thank you, Cora. That means more than you know.' He walked into the hall. 'Goodnight, then.'

She waved at him as he closed the door behind him, leaving her in the quiet room, alone with her thoughts.

. . .

Cora lay under the heavy duvet, her feet in thick socks. Despite being utterly exhausted, her mind was reeling, replaying the plan she had suggested to Fraser. He had been reluctant at first, but her suggestion that they present a united front, go to the family court themselves and petition for shared custody, then inform Holly what they'd done, had won him over.

Neither Cora nor Fraser could contemplate life without the children, so the only way to give Evie and Ross everything they needed was to split their time between her and their father. What they had agreed would mean that the children would live in Ballater with Cora during the school terms, and then spend school holidays in London with Fraser. They'd also agreed that Fraser would come up for as much of the long summer break as he could, in Ballater, at Locharden House, so they could all spend time together with James, as a family.

The thought of being without the children for long stretches of time had made Cora's chest ache, but now that she knew everything, the truth about why Fraser had left, she believed that he could be the man she had always hoped he was and be the father that Evie and Ross deserved.

Their well-being was her priority, and if she had to make this sacrifice for them to have Fraser in their lives, she'd resolved to find a way to cope and fill the void they'd leave in her daily life when they were away.

'I'll come down here as often as I can, too. Now that your dad has Queenie, it'll be easier for me to get away.'

Fraser's eyebrows had jumped. 'Queenie and Dad?'

Cora had nodded, a tiny smile curling her mouth. 'Yes. It's plain to see, and honestly, I'm really happy for them.'

Fraser had taken a moment to speak. 'Yes. He deserves some happiness. It's been rough for him since Mum died, and then I went AWOL on him.'

'Well, you're AWOL no longer, and now that you and your dad are communicating again, everything is going to be different. I feel it.' She'd taken in his expression, hopeful and yet still slightly unsure. 'Trust me, Fraser. This is going to work.'

He'd smiled then, a look of calm on his face that she had not seen in years. 'For the first time in as long as I can remember, I believe it's going to be OK.'

She'd hesitated for a moment, then given him a brief hug. 'We're a good team. Let's stay on the same side from now on, eh?'

He'd nodded, swiping at his eye. 'Agreed.'

As she'd watched him hide his emotion from her, feeling closer to him than she had in years, Cora had been overcome with a sense of the rightness of this decision. The children would have a good man, and father, in their lives, and he would teach them things she couldn't. That balance being what her own mother and father had given her. The symmetry of that felt just as it should be, as long as her plan worked out.

The drive back to Ballater had taken a little over nine hours, door to door. They had decided to take just the one car and for Fraser and Cora to take shifts so that they could minimise stops and get the children home at a reasonable time.

Before they'd left London, at Fraser's request, Cora had called James to tell him everything she had learned, and to let him know the plan. Her throat had knotted while relaying the information about Holly, and the abuse that Fraser had suffered.

James's voice had shaken with disbelief. 'Oh, my God, Cora! Are you serious?'

'Yes, I'm afraid so.'

'I've been so worried about you, and the kiddos. But now everyone's fine, and you're all coming home?'

'Yes, James. Everyone's fine, and we're all coming home.'

By the time Cora pulled up in front of Locharden House, it

was nearly 7 p.m., and James was already out on the front steps, with Duchess at his side. Presumably he had been waiting for them since Fraser had phoned to say that they were ten minutes away.

James was in his kilt, and a cable-knit sweater, his dark socks, trademark brogues and wide stance making him look like a soldier standing at ease.

Ross was asleep, but Evie immediately popped open her seat belt and wriggled to get out of the back seat.

'Woah, there tiger.' Fraser laughed, as he got out and helped her. 'Grandpa's not going anywhere.'

As soon as her feet touched the ground, Evie bolted into James's outstretched arms.

'Hello, Evie-bell. I missed you.' James beamed, hugging his granddaughter. 'Where's your wee brother?'

'He's sleeping. We went on an adventure, Grandpa. We were far away.'

James patted her back, his eyes meeting Cora's as she rounded the car and stopped at the bottom of the steps.

'Hi, James.'

'Hello, m'dear. All shipshape?'

Cora nodded, as behind her Fraser took his bags out of the boot. He peered into the back of the car where Ross was still sleeping soundly.

'We should just let him sleep, as you're going straight home now. Right?'

'Yes. I'll get them home and into bed, then we'll come back tomorrow at lunchtime. Do I need to shop, James?'

'No. Queenie and I did that today. There should be plenty to choose from in the larder.'

'Wonderful.' Cora smiled at him, grateful that that was one thing she needn't worry about.

Fraser took one more look at his sleeping son, then walked slowly up the steps towards his father.

'The prodigal is back, once again.' Fraser extended a tentative hand to James, in the fashion they had always greeted each other, but as Cora watched, James stepped forward and, with Evie sandwiched between them, for the first time Cora recalled ever seeing, father and son hugged.

This transformation had perhaps been Queenie's influence, or maybe just the passing of time and James's wish to repair his family, but either way Cora was overwhelmed, and grateful, to witness it. She tried not to stare, her heart feeling as if it might burst, as Fraser's face filled with light, a look of abject gratitude that sent shivers darting through her.

They stayed still for a few moments, James saying something that Cora couldn't hear, then Fraser stepped back and gently took Evie from his father's arms.

'Right, little lady. Time you went home to bed.'

Evie wrapped her legs around him, waving to James, as Fraser walked down the steps and helped her back into her car seat.

'See you tomorrow, Cora.' James waved from the top step, Duchess's tail swooshing against his shins. 'Take care, now.'

She waved back, then turned to Fraser.

'That was unexpected. But see? I told you things would be different.'

He laughed softly, then surprised her by pulling her into a hug. She could smell the salt-and-vinegar crisps he'd eaten in the car, and stale coffee on his breath.

'Thank you. I will never be able to stop thanking you, Cora. I know we still have some hurdles ahead, but we're already so much further forward than I could have imagined, and it's all because of you.'

Cora's eyes began to sting as she stepped back from him.

'Since when were you such a mush.' She sniffed, then smiled. 'You're welcome. Now go inside. Pour yourselves a dram, and talk. Now's the time, Fraser.'

'It is. He needs to know it all.'

Cora patted his arm through the soft leather jacket.

'Good. See you tomorrow.'

Within ten minutes of getting the children fed, washed, into their pyjamas and tucked up in bed, Cora's phone chirped. As she walked down the stairs she saw a text from Aisha.

Are you home? All good?

Cora smiled as she replied.

Yep. All good.

Aisha instantly responded, *Exhausted?*

Cora typed. *Not really.*

Within a couple of seconds, Aisha texted, *Good because I'm across the street. LOL. Wine?*

Cora laughed to herself, then replied, *Never too tired for wine. Or you.*

As she walked into the kitchen and opened the fridge, suddenly starving, Cora heard the clunk of a key in the lock. By this time of night, her brain was tired of processing all the sounds of the day, and she would normally have removed the external processor from her implant for a while. Instead, she circled her shoulders, then pulled the ingredients for an omelette out of the fridge and laid them on the counter.

Aisha walked in a moment later, her face flushed as she rubbed her hands together.

'Frigging freezing out there.' She shivered. 'Hello, you.' She hugged Cora, Aisha's cheeks frigid against Cora's warm skin.

'Take your coat off. I'm making an omelette. Want some?'

'No thanks. I've eaten.' Aisha dumped her coat on a chair at the table and waggled the bottle of wine she'd brought. 'Mind if I stay over?'

'Of course not.'

Cora pointed at the cupboard where the glasses were and

went about slicing mushrooms, and shallots, a little prosciutto, and crumbling some feta into a dish. As she beat the eggs, the skillet heating on the stove, the familiarity of the space around her, and the meditative motion of the whisk, Cora sighed contentedly.

Aisha poured the wine and settled herself at the table.

'Tell me *everything*.' She took a sip and sat back as Cora cooked and talked.

Twenty minutes later, they had moved into the living room. Cora was too tired to light the fire, so they'd wrapped themselves in the soft rugs that she kept in a basket by the window and the friends sat at opposite ends of the sofa.

'So, you're taking Holly on, together? No messing around. I like it.' Aisha nodded approvingly.

'We can't take any chances, or let her move first, so we want to meet with a solicitor, as soon as we can find one who specialises in family law. Fraser's going to tell James everything tonight, the truth about his marriage, the abuse, everything, and ask him if he's on board with the plan, but I can't imagine he won't be.'

'Right, I mean why wouldn't he. I just can't believe that Fraser was dealing with that. It's shocking, and so bloody sad.' Aisha's mouth dipped. 'I feel bad, because I was always so hard on him. After what he did to you, I wrote him off. I'll speak to him about it, next time I see him.' She sipped some wine and focused on Cora, whose eyes were beginning to droop.

'He'll understand, Aisha. The way he talked to me about it, he didn't blame anyone in the village for the way they were with him. I just wish he'd felt able to talk to someone. If not me, someone else.'

'Well, he has now, and hopefully, after tonight, you'll be an awesome trifecta that Holly won't stand a chance against.'

Cora yawned widely; her empty glass cupped in her palm.

'Thanks for the wine treats, Aish, but I'm shattered. I really need to hit the sack.'

Aisha checked her watch. 'Right, it's off to bed for both of us, unless you have anything else shockingly juicy you want to reveal?' She stood up, the empty glass dangling at her thigh.

Cora laughed softly, folding the blanket that had been around her shoulders. 'I think that was quite enough for one night. Actually, for a lifetime.'

'I'll see you in the morning then.' Aisha hugged her. 'Love you, girlfriend.'

'Love you, too. Sleep tight.' Cora caught the scent of cardamom lingering in Aisha's sweater, the aromatic scent bringing Priyanka's gentle face to mind.

Aisha hesitated at the door; her eyes locked on Cora's. 'I'll be right here, if things get tough with that wench. Because they might, Cora. You know that, right?'

Determined to stay in the positive mindset she and Fraser had left things in, Cora nodded. 'I know. Sometimes the best things take more work, Aisha, but when they turn out the way they're supposed to, it's more than worth it.'

Aisha nodded. 'Without a doubt.'

As Aisha climbed the stairs, and Cora turned off the lights and checked that the front door was locked, she replayed the plan in her mind, the logic behind it feeling sound. But as Cora knew, better than most, sound logic wasn't always a guarantee of things turning out as one hoped.

PART THREE

28

JULY – SIX MONTHS LATER

James and Queenie sat at the small table in the corner of the living room at Locharden House, both smiling, intent on Ross, who was holding out a piece of the jigsaw puzzle he wanted James to place.

'Not there, Grandpa. *There.*' He pointed to a missing corner, then laughed when James pretended to put the piece in backwards.

Evie lay on her stomach on the rug at the fireplace, a book open in front of her. She was loving school, especially reading, but her favourite thing was still numbers, where she was excelling.

Fraser had been surprised when he'd first learned this, saying to James, 'Where does she get that from? It's certainly not from me.'

James had laughed. 'That's for sure. I think it's Cora's influence. She has all the brains in this family.'

That had touched Cora deeply, James always careful to acknowledge her position as the children's mother, especially since they'd recently been allowing Holly supervised visits with Evie and Ross.

The hearing in the family court had been swift, and as painless as was possible, as once all the witness statements had been presented to her solicitor, Holly had withdrawn her petition, joint custody being awarded to Fraser and Cora.

Holly had also agreed to enter a further three months of counselling, and residential therapy in Glasgow, and she'd been back for a while now. She was grateful to be able to see the children, even under supervision, a more genuine sense of calm about her that was reassuring to them all, and that boded well for the future.

The children were growing more comfortable with Holly, and both Cora and Fraser had agreed to involve her in their decision about how things would play out, long term.

Evie and Ross would continue to stay with Fraser in London during the school holidays, except for the summer when he would come up to spend time with them at Locharden House. They would be based at Cora's house, and stay with her during term time, and this arrangement would continue until they came of age, at which point Evie and Ross would make their own decisions about their relationship with their mother.

Cora missed Evie and Ross more than life itself when they were away, the house feeling so quiet it hurt, but when they came back, their reunions had been magical, filled with hugs and the children's happy squeals as they told her excitedly what they'd been up to in London. While their bond with their father strengthened, the unshakeable bond between them and Cora was no less strong because of a couple of weeks of separation.

Cora had held steady at the family court hearing, not letting sympathy for Holly sway her, and she'd been proud of the way Fraser had done the same. He'd been kind but firm, and put the children's welfare first, just as he should. He had faced his fears, exorcised his demons, and was a much happier man as a result, something that made Cora happy, too.

Across the room, he sat in his mother's old armchair, Vivaldi's Four Seasons playing softly in the background, the volume sufficiently low so as not to make Cora cringe. His legs were crossed at the ankle, his shorts revealing how tanned he'd become from two weeks of playing in the garden with the children, and also from the frequent hikes he'd joined Cora on, up Craigendarroch, as they all enjoyed the gift of a real summer.

Just as the spring concerto came to an end, Fraser heaved himself from the chair.

'OK, who's for coffee?' He patted his stomach. 'I think I might even have some room for ice cream, now.'

Evie rolled onto her back and stuck both hands in the air. 'Me too. I have room, here.' She placed her palm under her diaphragm. 'Just enough for two scoops.'

Cora laughed, surprised they could even think of dessert after the giant roast dinner they'd all eaten.

'I'll come and help you.' She closed the recipe book she was reading and followed Fraser into the kitchen.

As she spooned homemade strawberry ice cream into a row of bowls, Fraser gently bumped her shoulder, then he stuck a finger in one of the bowls and licked a daub of ice cream from it.

'Fraser, stop it,' Cora tutted, then added a little more to that bowl. 'Where were you dragged up?'

He laughed. 'Right here, in this house, which I have to say feels entirely different to when I was a child.' His eyes grew misty, and he looked away. 'Thanks to you.'

Cora felt the emotion behind his words, understanding that the sense of belonging he had now was something he'd craved for much of his life.

'Well, this is your home, and it's great that you finally feel that way. It's a wonderful home, too.' She put the lid back on the ice cream and put it in the freezer.

Fraser turned to face her, his eyes clear again.

'This is as much your home as anyone's, Cora. You know that, right?'

Cora let the statement sink in, the knowledge that both James and Fraser felt this way still something that touched her more than words could say, but unable to express that adequately without dissolving into tears, she swallowed hard and smiled at him.

When Fraser had noticed the old Rookery premises was still up for lease, three months earlier, he had talked to her about it.

'It'd be perfect. Almost karmic if you reopened it.' He'd grinned at her. 'What do you think?'

'Seriously?' Her jaw had dropped. 'I mean, I'd never given it any thought.'

Cora had been taken aback, and grateful for the new, more considerate way he was living his life now, and despite some initial anxiety, she had soon become excited about the prospect of having her own establishment. Somewhere she could get back to the more creative, experimental kind of cooking that she loved.

With the children only being with her during the school terms, and now that Queenie was practically living at Locharden House, Cora knew that she needed something new and fulfilling that she could pour her heart into. The irony was that the person who had come up with the idea was the person who, in the past, had essentially been responsible for derailing her career, not once, but twice.

When Fraser had shared his idea about the restaurant with his father, James had willingly agreed to invest in Cora's new venture and help support her until she got the business up and running.

'Are you sure, James? It could be a while before I can pay you back in full.' They'd sat in the conservatory, the spring melt making the back garden lush and dewy, and the crystal-clear sky leaving Lochnagar vivid on the horizon, the mountain keeping watch from beyond the dense tree line at the end of the garden.

'There's no rush, Cora, and I have every faith in you making a success of it.' He'd patted her hand.

'Thank you. I won't let you down.' Her throat had been thick with emotion, overcome that he would be willing to do this for her.

'You've never let me down yet, m'dear, and I've no reason to think that'll change.'

Cora had hugged him, tears blurring her vision, her mind quickly filling with everything she could do with the lovely space where she had been so happy just a few years before.

She'd been collecting menu ideas ever since, and the concept of fusing local, sustainable fish, and foraged ingredients with subtle Indian spices was exciting. To make things even better, Aisha had been more than happy to share many of Priyanka's recipes and had also agreed to come on board to manage the bar and wine cellar.

Jolting her back to the moment, Fraser's voice was soft. 'What are you thinking?'

'So many things, but all good.' Cora's eyes were prickling, her future so bright it was like staring at the sun.

'Penny for them.' He tilted his head to the side, a curious frown puckering his tanned brow.

She pulled a comical face at him and then nodded at the bowls he was holding. 'Just take those through please, nosy parker, and I'll bring the others in a minute.'

'Right-o.' He stayed still, seeming to read her expression, and body language, compassion now radiating from his eyes.

'Thanks, Fraser,' she whispered.

'No. Thank *you*, Cora.' He took a moment to make sure she'd understood him fully, then turned and walked towards the living room.

For all the times he had hurt her, in the past, she and Fraser had finally become friends, allies, and, more than that. Family. Between the two of them, and James and Queenie, Evie and

Ross would be treasured beyond measure, protected from conflict, and raised in love, something that made Cora immensely proud, and fulfilled, her wish to redress the balance of her own tumultuous early years being granted.

As she followed Fraser into the living room, Evie was now sitting on James's knee, and they were looking at the book that Holly had given Evie some months earlier.

'That's the Monarch butterfly, Grandpa. It's so pretty, isn't it?'

'It is, Evie-bell. Just like you.' He looked over at Cora and smiled, his pale eyes full of affection.

Queenie and Ross were working on the puzzle, Ross standing at her side, his heels rising from the floor each time he leaned in and placed a piece on the table.

'That's a corner. It goes here.' He pointed as Queenie mocked surprise.

'So it does, will you look at that.' She placed the piece down and drew Ross into her side.

'Help us, Mummy.' He held his hand out to Cora, his fingers tickling the air. 'We're nearly finished.'

'OK. I'm on my way.' Cora set the bowls down on the mat on the sideboard, a swell of overwhelming peace making her vision blur. 'Ice cream is here for whoever wants any.' She quickly swiped her eyes as Evie came up beside her.

'Are you sad, Mummy?' Evie leaned into Cora's side, her small hand slipping into Cora's.

'Not at all. I'm so happy that my eyes are leaking. All the happiness is filling me up and pushing some tears out.' She gave a croaky laugh, as Evie's brow creased.

'That's silly. Happy means this.' She grinned, a beatific smile that gripped Cora's heart with such profundity that she forced a swallow.

'You're right. That is what happy looks like.' She pulled Evie into her side and felt the little girl's arms go around her hips. 'Come on, let's help them finish the puzzle before these all melt.' She nodded at the row of bowls.

'OK.' Evie gave her hips a squeeze, then looked up at her. 'Love you, Mummy.'

Cora took a second, scanning Evie's mossy eyes, the shimmering hair and rosy cheeks.

'I love you, too, Evie. So much,' she whispered.

As Cora watched, Evie pushed in next to Queenie at the table, while Fraser knelt at the opposite side, next to his father, who fondly bumped him with his shoulder.

Seeing her approach, James shifted his chair to the left.

'Right. Budge up, everyone, make room for Mummy Cora, and let's get this done so we can have our pudding.'

Cora smiled at him, and as she knelt at James's other side, Ross handed her a piece of puzzle.

'Your turn, Mummy. It goes there.' He pointed to a gap in the centre of the scene, several deer running in a lush meadow, the magnificent slopes of Lochnagar dominating the background.

'Got it!' She snapped the piece into place, her eyes locking on Fraser's. 'Your daddy can do the last piece.'

Fraser grinned, picked up the final piece, popped it into place and then jumped to his feet.

'Right. Mine's the biggest bowl.' He walked to the sideboard, Ross and Evie hot on his heels.

James held Queenie's hand, and they joined the group, jostling and laughing as they all vied for the various bowls of ice cream. The hum of their banter filtered into Cora's head, a gentle, satisfying sound, a beautiful symphony, each note complementing the next.

From as early as she could remember, she had closed her heart to the idea of family, until the Campbells came into her life. Losing them had left her bereft, that sense of belonging once again feeling beyond her reach, but now that her heart had reopened, she was being given more than she could have dreamed of.

This was all she'd ever wanted, both as a child and an adult. She once again had a family that was permanent, not borrowed, but all hers. A close-knit, messy, complex, and loving family who would take on life together.

A family of her heart.

A LETTER FROM ALISON

Dear reader,

My heartfelt thanks for reading *My Husband's Child*. I hope you enjoyed it. If you would like to keep up to date with all my latest releases, just sign up at the following link. Your email address will never be shared, and you can unsubscribe at any time.

www.bookouture.com/alison-ragsdale

While Cora's story is about the challenges of experiencing neglect and an early childhood without the comfort of family, she is far from a victim of her circumstances. Her story is also about the courage it takes to re-open one's heart to love, and to change not only your own, but the fate of others, by embracing the joy a chosen family can bring.

If you or someone you love is the victim of domestic abuse, help is out there. If you, or they, can't talk to someone close, there are professional support organisations that can offer support, confidentially, like the National Domestic Abuse Helpline (UK) and the National Domestic Violence Hotline (USA).

Thanks again for choosing to read *My Husband's Child*. If you enjoyed it, I'd be so grateful if you would take a moment to write a review. They are a great way to introduce new readers to my books.

I love to hear from my readers, and you can connect with me through my Facebook author page, Instagram, Threads, X, Goodreads, or my website. I look forward to hearing from you.

All the best,

Alison Ragsdale

www.alisonragsdale.com

- facebook.com/authoralisonragsdale
- x.com/AlisonRagsdale
- instagram.com/alisonragsdalewrites

ACKNOWLEDGEMENTS

Thank you to my wonderful publisher, Bookouture. I am so fortunate to work with such a dedicated, talented, and savvy team. Special thanks to my editor, Jess, for her support and expertise, and for encouraging me to ask tough questions of the characters, and to tell their story with as much honesty and depth as possible.

Thanks also to Noelle, Imogen, Mandy, Jade, Anne, and everyone who helped this story make its way into the world. The saying teamwork makes the dream work was never so true.

As always, a special thank you to my inspiring sisters, my best friends, and most reliable beta readers. Your opinions mean the world to me.

Thank you also to all the friends, readers, reviewers, book bloggers, and my Highlanders Club members and ARC crew who support me and my books. I will never be able to express how much that means to me. Every one of you is a treasure, and you make my writing life richer by being part of it.

Finally, to my husband. Thank you for always being there, and for believing in me, even when I don't believe in myself.

PUBLISHING TEAM

Turning a manuscript into a book requires the efforts of many people. The publishing team at Bookouture would like to acknowledge everyone who contributed to this publication.

Commercial
Lauren Morrissette
Hannah Richmond
Imogen Allport

Cover design
Emma Graves

Data and analysis
Mark Alder
Mohamed Bussuri

Editorial
Jess Whitlum-Cooper
Imogen Allport

Copyeditor
Jade Craddock

Proofreader
Anne O'Brien

Marketing
Alex Crow
Melanie Price
Occy Carr
Cíara Rosney
Martyna Młynarska

Operations and distribution
Marina Valles
Stephanie Straub
Joe Morris

Production
Hannah Snetsinger
Mandy Kullar
Jen Shannon
Ria Clare

Publicity
Kim Nash
Noelle Holten
Jess Readett
Sarah Hardy

Rights and contracts
Peta Nightingale
Richard King
Saidah Graham

Printed in Dunstable, United Kingdom